the perfect rumor

(a jessie hunt psychological suspense—book 19)

blake pierce

Blake Pierce

Blake Pierce is the USA Today bestselling author of the RILEY PAGE mystery series, which includes seventeen books. Blake Pierce is also the author of the MACKENZIE WHITE mystery series, comprising fourteen books; of the AVERY BLACK mystery series, comprising six books; of the KERI LOCKE mystery series, comprising five books; of the MAKING OF RILEY PAIGE mystery series, comprising six books; of the KATE WISE mystery series, comprising seven books; of the CHLOE FINE psychological suspense mystery, comprising six books; of the JESSE HUNT psychological suspense thriller series, comprising twenty one books; of the AU PAIR psychological suspense thriller series, comprising three books; of the ZOE PRIME mystery series, comprising six books; of the ADELE SHARP mystery series, comprising fifteen books, of the EUROPEAN VOYAGE cozy mystery series, comprising four books; of the new LAURA FROST FBI suspense thriller, comprising six books (and counting); of the new ELLA DARK FBI suspense thriller, comprising eleven books (and counting); of the A YEAR IN EUROPE cozy mystery series, comprising nine books, of the AVA GOLD mystery series, comprising six books (and counting); and of the RACHEL GIFT mystery series, comprising six books (and counting).

An avid reader and lifelong fan of the mystery and thriller genres, Blake loves to hear from you, so please feel free to visit www.blakepierceauthor.com to learn more and stay in touch.

Copyright © 2022 by Blake Pierce. All rights reserved. Except as permitted under the U.S. Copyright Act of 1976, no part of this publication may be reproduced, distributed or transmitted in any form or by any means, or stored in a database or retrieval system, without the prior permission of the author. This ebook is licensed for your personal enjoyment only. This ebook may not be re-sold or given away to other people. If you would like to share this book with another person, please purchase an additional copy for each recipient. If you're reading this book and did not purchase it, or it was not purchased for your use only, then please return it and purchase your own copy. Thank you for respecting the hard work of this author. This is a work of fiction. Names, characters, businesses, organizations, places, events, and incidents either are the product of the author's imagination or are used fictionally. Any resemblance to actual persons, living or dead, is entirely coincidental. Jacket image Copyright Vladimir Gjorgiev, used under license from Shutterstock.com.
ISBN: 978-1-0943-7607-3

BOOKS BY BLAKE PIERCE

RACHEL GIFT MYSTERY SERIES
HER LAST WISH (Book #1)
HER LAST CHANCE (Book #2)
HER LAST HOPE (Book #3)
HER LAST FEAR (Book #4)
HER LAST CHOICE (Book #5)
HER LAST BREATH (Book #6)

AVA GOLD MYSTERY SERIES
CITY OF PREY (Book #1)
CITY OF FEAR (Book #2)
CITY OF BONES (Book #3)
CITY OF GHOSTS (Book #4)
CITY OF DEATH (Book #5)
CITY OF VICE (Book #6)

A YEAR IN EUROPE
A MURDER IN PARIS (Book #1)
DEATH IN FLORENCE (Book #2)
VENGEANCE IN VIENNA (Book #3)
A FATALITY IN SPAIN (Book #4)

ELLA DARK FBI SUSPENSE THRILLER
GIRL, ALONE (Book #1)
GIRL, TAKEN (Book #2)
GIRL, HUNTED (Book #3)
GIRL, SILENCED (Book #4)
GIRL, VANISHED (Book 5)
GIRL ERASED (Book #6)
GIRL, FORSAKEN (Book #7)
GIRL, TRAPPED (Book #8)
GIRL, EXPENDABLE (Book #9)
GIRL, ESCAPED (Book #10)
GIRL, HIS (Book #11)

LAURA FROST FBI SUSPENSE THRILLER
ALREADY GONE (Book #1)

ALREADY SEEN (Book #2)
ALREADY TRAPPED (Book #3)
ALREADY MISSING (Book #4)
ALREADY DEAD (Book #5)
ALREADY TAKEN (Book #6)

EUROPEAN VOYAGE COZY MYSTERY SERIES
MURDER (AND BAKLAVA) (Book #1)
DEATH (AND APPLE STRUDEL) (Book #2)
CRIME (AND LAGER) (Book #3)
MISFORTUNE (AND GOUDA) (Book #4)
CALAMITY (AND A DANISH) (Book #5)
MAYHEM (AND HERRING) (Book #6)

ADELE SHARP MYSTERY SERIES
LEFT TO DIE (Book #1)
LEFT TO RUN (Book #2)
LEFT TO HIDE (Book #3)
LEFT TO KILL (Book #4)
LEFT TO MURDER (Book #5)
LEFT TO ENVY (Book #6)
LEFT TO LAPSE (Book #7)
LEFT TO VANISH (Book #8)
LEFT TO HUNT (Book #9)
LEFT TO FEAR (Book #10)
LEFT TO PREY (Book #11)
LEFT TO LURE (Book #12)
LEFT TO CRAVE (Book #13)
LEFT TO LOATHE (Book #14)
LEFT TO HARM (Book #15)

THE AU PAIR SERIES
ALMOST GONE (Book#1)
ALMOST LOST (Book #2)
ALMOST DEAD (Book #3)

ZOE PRIME MYSTERY SERIES
FACE OF DEATH (Book#1)
FACE OF MURDER (Book #2)
FACE OF FEAR (Book #3)
FACE OF MADNESS (Book #4)

FACE OF FURY (Book #5)
FACE OF DARKNESS (Book #6)

A JESSIE HUNT PSYCHOLOGICAL SUSPENSE SERIES
THE PERFECT WIFE (Book #1)
THE PERFECT BLOCK (Book #2)
THE PERFECT HOUSE (Book #3)
THE PERFECT SMILE (Book #4)
THE PERFECT LIE (Book #5)
THE PERFECT LOOK (Book #6)
THE PERFECT AFFAIR (Book #7)
THE PERFECT ALIBI (Book #8)
THE PERFECT NEIGHBOR (Book #9)
THE PERFECT DISGUISE (Book #10)
THE PERFECT SECRET (Book #11)
THE PERFECT FAÇADE (Book #12)
THE PERFECT IMPRESSION (Book #13)
THE PERFECT DECEIT (Book #14)
THE PERFECT MISTRESS (Book #15)
THE PERFECT IMAGE (Book #16)
THE PERFECT VEIL (Book #17)
THE PERFECT INDISCRETION (Book #18)
THE PERFECT RUMOR (Book #19)
THE PERFECT COUPLE (Book #20)
THE PERFECT MURDER (Book #21)

CHLOE FINE PSYCHOLOGICAL SUSPENSE SERIES
NEXT DOOR (Book #1)
A NEIGHBOR'S LIE (Book #2)
CUL DE SAC (Book #3)
SILENT NEIGHBOR (Book #4)
HOMECOMING (Book #5)
TINTED WINDOWS (Book #6)

KATE WISE MYSTERY SERIES
IF SHE KNEW (Book #1)
IF SHE SAW (Book #2)
IF SHE RAN (Book #3)
IF SHE HID (Book #4)
IF SHE FLED (Book #5)
IF SHE FEARED (Book #6)

IF SHE HEARD (Book #7)

THE MAKING OF RILEY PAIGE SERIES
WATCHING (Book #1)
WAITING (Book #2)
LURING (Book #3)
TAKING (Book #4)
STALKING (Book #5)
KILLING (Book #6)

RILEY PAIGE MYSTERY SERIES
ONCE GONE (Book #1)
ONCE TAKEN (Book #2)
ONCE CRAVED (Book #3)
ONCE LURED (Book #4)
ONCE HUNTED (Book #5)
ONCE PINED (Book #6)
ONCE FORSAKEN (Book #7)
ONCE COLD (Book #8)
ONCE STALKED (Book #9)
ONCE LOST (Book #10)
ONCE BURIED (Book #11)
ONCE BOUND (Book #12)
ONCE TRAPPED (Book #13)
ONCE DORMANT (Book #14)
ONCE SHUNNED (Book #15)
ONCE MISSED (Book #16)
ONCE CHOSEN (Book #17)

MACKENZIE WHITE MYSTERY SERIES
BEFORE HE KILLS (Book #1)
BEFORE HE SEES (Book #2)
BEFORE HE COVETS (Book #3)
BEFORE HE TAKES (Book #4)
BEFORE HE NEEDS (Book #5)
BEFORE HE FEELS (Book #6)
BEFORE HE SINS (Book #7)
BEFORE HE HUNTS (Book #8)
BEFORE HE PREYS (Book #9)
BEFORE HE LONGS (Book #10)
BEFORE HE LAPSES (Book #11)

BEFORE HE ENVIES (Book #12)
BEFORE HE STALKS (Book #13)
BEFORE HE HARMS (Book #14)

AVERY BLACK MYSTERY SERIES
CAUSE TO KILL (Book #1)
CAUSE TO RUN (Book #2)
CAUSE TO HIDE (Book #3)
CAUSE TO FEAR (Book #4)
CAUSE TO SAVE (Book #5)
CAUSE TO DREAD (Book #6)

KERI LOCKE MYSTERY SERIES
A TRACE OF DEATH (Book #1)
A TRACE OF MURDER (Book #2)
A TRACE OF VICE (Book #3)
A TRACE OF CRIME (Book #4)
A TRACE OF HOPE (Book #5)

PROLOGUE

This was Tony Dante's least favorite part of the job.

He didn't mind picking up the towels strewn on the locker room floor. He actually enjoyed replenishing the toiletries. There was something satisfying about seeing all those colorful bottles filled to the top. Even cleaning the toilets wasn't that bad if he got into the rhythm of it.

But the steam room was something else. Of all his duties as an attendant in the men's lounge at the Spa Peninsula, maintaining it was the one he dreaded the most. Because management wouldn't let him cut off the steam during guest hours, there was no way to avoid getting sweaty if he was going to clean the area properly. Invariably, he'd have to take a shower afterward and change into a second uniform. That was why he always saved the task until near the start of his break.

It was almost that time now. So, as his routine dictated, he got out of his work shoes and slipped on a pair of flip-flops. He hadn't seen anyone in the men's lounge for a while and considered stripping down to just his shorts, but then thought better of it. Someone could walk in at any moment and if they saw "the help" shirtless, they might disapprove. So he left the shirt on, grabbed two towels along with his disinfectant bottle, opened the door, and stepped into the thick mist.

It was almost impossible to see. He started at the far right end of the room and began spraying and wiping down the white tile bench, careful to keep an eye out for anyone along the way. He hadn't seen anybody enter or leave the room in the last fifteen minutes so he was pretty sure it was empty. Staying that long in there was a Herculean undertaking, not to mention unhealthy. Still, as was his habit, he made a token effort to be sure.

"Anyone in here?" he called out, his voice sounding strangely muffled by the vapor. "Cleaning underway."

There was no response. He moved over to the longer, middle bench and sprayed it down as well. As he was wiping the tile with his towel, he noticed a dark shape in the corner, where the middle and left bench met. The fog was so thick that it was hard at first to even be sure that it was a person. But as he leaned in, he saw that it was a man, naked and slumped to the side, his head strangely suspended at an awkward angle.

"Sir, are you all right?" Tony asked loudly, hoping the man had just fallen asleep and could be woken by a booming voice. The man didn't reply. It seemed to Tony that something was off, but he was reluctant to shake or even touch the man. He didn't want to get fired for inappropriate contact. Instead, he left the room and hit the button that turned off the steam while simultaneously sucking the moisture out. It took less than a minute to complete the process.

Once that was done, he stepped back inside. What he saw made him drop the towels and the disinfectant bottle. Now that the steam had dissipated, he had a clear view of the man and he wasn't sleeping. Tony wanted to yell but was too stunned to make any sound. The reason the man's head was at an awkward angle was because it was being held up by some kind of thick band or ribbon wrapped around his neck. The other end of the material was tied to a metal handlebar a few feet above and behind the tile bench. The man's eyes were wide open. He was dead.

Tony could barely believe what he was seeing. He wanted to run. But his legs were locked up with fear and he stumbled backward, slipping on the slick, tile floor. He landed hard on his butt but shot back up and hurried out of the steam room into the sitting area, grabbed the courtesy phone, and called the spa's front desk. When the receptionist picked up, it took all his self-control not to scream into the phone.

"Call the cops," he said forcefully. "There's a dead guy in the men's steam room."

CHAPTER ONE

Jessie tried to ignore the pain.

Instead, she focused all her energy on the end goal and not the struggle to get there. Though her thighs were burning, and her breathing was heavy, she pressed ahead, her eyes fixed on her destination: her driveway.

After another thirty seconds, she was there. She dropped out of sprint mode and slowed to a walk. She pulled out her phone and hit "stop" on the time clock of her running app. It read: 42:29.

Not bad for five miles. That's just under 8 ½-minute-miles.

She allowed herself a moment of pride. She was still a long way away from getting back to the eight-minute-miles she ran in college, but she'd shown steady improvement in recent months. And considering all the injuries she'd suffered in the last few years, from stabbings, to gunshot wounds, to multiple concussions and at least two strangling attempts, she thought she was doing pretty well.

Jessie walked to the end of the block, allowing her breathing to return to normal. Her thoughts drifted to yesterday's seminar in criminal profiling at UCLA. It was one of her final ones before rejoining LAPD's Homicide Special Section full-time and the vibe was bittersweet. Students, as they had for weeks, pleaded with her to reconsider. The post-lecture Q&A session ran longer than usual, as if the kids were hoping to squeeze out every last kernel of knowledge that they could glean from her. It was gratifying and a little depressing at the same time. She didn't want it to end.

Jessie turned around and made her way back to the house, trying to shake off the gloom that came from knowing something so positive would soon be over. She had agreed to return at the request—more like pleading actually—of Captain Roy Decker, who ran LAPD's Downtown Station and oversaw Homicide Special Section, or HSS. He'd told her that she could remain as a consultant rather than an employee and continue to work with Detective Ryan Hernandez, who in addition to being her semi-regular partner, was also her fiancé. Decker also offered her a huge jump in pay.

Normally that wouldn't be the deciding factor. Even without the job, Jessie was well-off, a result of her divorce and an inheritance from her adoptive parents. But with a wedding to plan and her sister's recent "relocation," having the extra income couldn't hurt.

Jessie reached the front door and began to stretch. She knew that worrying about current and future bills wasn't conducive to loosening her muscles but she couldn't help it. Even though she didn't want some huge wedding, Ryan seemed insistent. The venues and vendors he was suggesting were all high-end, and of course, very pricey. It was increasingly a bone of contention, one that she was getting tired of relenting on.

And then there was Hannah. Jessie sighed at the thought of her. Her younger half-sister, Hannah Dorsey, now only weeks from turning eighteen, was currently a resident at the Seasons Wellness Center in Malibu. The unremarkable name made it sound like the place might be an exclusive spa. It was certainly as expensive as one. After insurance, each week there cost a minimum of $7000, and that was just for room and board.

In fact, the place was an in-patient psychiatric facility that focused on those suffering from all manner of mental illness including suicidal ideation, life-threatening eating disorders, even uncontrolled OCD. Hannah had checked in there voluntarily two weeks ago, at the insistence of the therapist she shared with Jessie, Dr. Janice Lemmon.

Officially, she was there to deal with a diagnosis of self-harm tendencies, but that didn't accurately describe her circumstance. For months, if not longer, Hannah had been deliberately putting herself in dangerous situations that could end badly. She had admitted that normal human interactions mostly left her numb and emotionless. So she courted confrontations with neighborhood bullies, creepy stalkers, drug dealers, pedophiles, and even a sexual slavery ring, all as part of a need to get a hit of adrenaline. Even if the feeling was fleeting, at least it was something.

But then an elderly serial killer called the Night Hunter trapped Jessie, Ryan, and Hannah in a remote mountain cabin. Jessie and Ryan managed to capture and subdue the man. But while he was handcuffed and unarmed, Hannah shot and killed him. She claimed it was a form of self-defense, a way to stop a man she knew would never stop searching for a way to get at them, even from behind bars.

Only later did Jessie learn that the real reason Hannah had murdered the Night Hunter was because she simply wanted to know what it felt like. As it turned out, she liked it. The act gave her a high she'd never experienced before, and she wanted to recreate it. In the weeks after she shot the Night Hunter in cold blood, she harbored fantasies of killing someone else in the hopes of recapturing the thrill of that moment.

When, over a month later, Hannah finally revealed that to Dr. Lemmon, the doctor came up with the idea of sending her to Seasons, where she'd been ever since. In her time there, she'd participated in intense therapy sessions, both group and individual, as well as a couple of sessions with Jessie. Dr. Lemmon had also ordered everything from redirection therapy to brain-mapping. All options were under consideration. Nothing was off the table. The goal was twofold: first, to help Hannah feel emotions without needing heightened situations; and second, to eliminate her addictive desire to get a high from—to put it bluntly—killing people.

As Jessie finished up her final deep stretch, she recalled her last visit, just two days ago. It wasn't a therapy session, just a casual visit, but it hadn't been particularly casual. Hannah wasn't in a very chatty mood.

"Are you just here to rub my nose in my grotesquery?" she had asked. It had gone downhill from there.

Jessie tried to shake loose of the memory as she opened the door to the mid-Wilshire house she'd inherited from her murdered profiling mentor, Garland Moses, and headed for the bedroom to undress and shower. She could hear Ryan grunting in the backyard and went that way to check on him.

Her fiancé was taking advantage of the mild, early-March Los Angeles day, doing his rehab workout session outside and shirtless. Now over eight months removed from being stabbed in the chest and spending weeks in a coma, he was about ninety-five percent recovered.

He was currently doing squats while holding forty pound dumbbells. Jessie admired him silently from behind the sliding glass door. His short black hair and dark skin gleamed in the sunlight. His normally kind brown eyes were fixed in concentration. Sweat poured down his muscled chest as he knelt down and popped back up, his calves rippling with the effort. Though Ryan wasn't vain, Jessie knew that it was important for him to regain the chiseled physique he'd had before being attacked. His six-foot, two-hundred-pound body had always been both a source of pride and a weapon he could use against the criminals he came up against. His goal was to get back to where he'd been and he was almost there.

Once he finished his set, she tapped on the glass and opened the door.

"I'm going to take a shower," she told him, "You almost done?"

"I've got about five minutes left. I'll hop in after you're done."

Jessie was tempted to suggest he finish up early and join her. But she knew he really wanted to get back to full strength and anything that interfered with that, even a mid-morning delight, was secondary right now.

So she held her tongue and headed to the bathroom. Her running top was soaked through and her black pants were starting to feel uncomfortably warm against her legs. She turned on the shower and gave herself a once-over in the mirror while the water warmed up. She was pleased to see that her five-mile runs were paying dividends.

She looked firmer than she had a few months ago. Considering she was fast approaching her thirty-first birthday, she thought she was doing pretty well. Her long legs, which contributed significantly to her five-foot-ten frame, had regained much of the muscle tone they'd lost when she was recovering from her various injuries. Her shoulder length brown hair was lustrous and her green eyes glowed with energy. Despite the ongoing stressors in her life, she thought she was holding up quite nicely. And the furtive looks she got when she walked down the street seemed to confirm it.

She showered quickly, aware that Ryan would be waiting for his turn. When she turned off the water and pulled back the curtain, he was there holding out a towel for her.

"Personalized towel service," she noted. "To what do I owe the honor?"

"I wish I could say it was just domestic kindness," he said apologetically, "but I'm here to move things along."

"Why?" she asked. "Did I take too long? I thought I was pretty quick."

"No," he assured her. "But while you were showering we got a call from Decker. He has a case for us."

"What is it?" she asked.

"He wouldn't get into particulars other than to say there was a murder at the Peninsula resort in Palos Verdes. He wants us to head there ASAP. He'll update us en route."

"Did he at least mention the victim?"

"Nope. I asked but he said he'd fill us both in when he calls back in ten minutes, when he expects that we'll be in the car. He said the police chief would be on the call too so we better hurry."

"He wants us on the road in ten minutes?" she demanded incredulously.

Ryan looked at his watch.

"Not anymore," he answered. "Now we're down to eight."

Jessie got out of the shower, still dripping wet, wrapped the towel around herself and darted out to the bedroom to find something that would look professional and appropriate for the most exclusive resort in Southern California. And now she had seven minutes to do it.

CHAPTER TWO

Jessie was annoyed.

Decker had made them run around to get ready and now he was late. By the time he called twenty minutes later, they were well on their way to Palos Verdes, a gorgeous oceanside community in the Southern California South Bay. Nestled between Long Beach and the Beach Cities, it was known for its craggy cliffs, amazing views, and eight-figure homes.

Decker texted about two minutes before the call to tell them the delay was because the chief was finishing up another meeting. He didn't give them any warning about why the head of the Los Angeles Police Department wanted in on the call.

Jessie was apprehensive. Her interactions with Chief Laird hadn't always been positive, especially when it briefly looked like he might fire both her and Ryan when they discovered police corruption in the Valley Division. Ryan was driving so when his phone rang, he handed it off to Jessie, who put it on speaker and held it out between them.

"Hello, Captain," he said.

"Hernandez," Decker said tersely, "is Hunt there with you?"

"Right here, Captain," she replied, trying to keep the nerves out of her voice.

"Good. I've conferenced us in with Chief Laird. He wanted to be a part of this conversation. Would you like to begin, Chief?"

"Why don't you give them the basics first, Decker," Chief Laird said gruffly. "Once they know what they're dealing with, I'll offer my two cents."

"All right," Decker said, then launched in. "Less than forty-five minutes ago, a forty-four-year-old man was found dead in the steam room of the men's spa at the Peninsula resort. His neck was tied to some kind of thin belt. Local police called it in to headquarters as soon as they realized who the victim was: Scott Newhouse."

Jessie recognized the name immediately and pulled up a photo of the man. Newhouse was a Los Angeles mainstay. The scion of a well-known local family, he had his hand in many pots. He was on several philanthropic boards. He had a wing named after him at the Museum of Modern Art. He was a minority owner in two local sports teams. Most importantly, for the sake of this conversation, he was good friends with Police Chief Richard Laird, at least according to the caption below one photo of the two men at a recent gala.

He was good-looking in a serious, distinguished way. His brown hair was cropped conservatively, like someone's senior yearbook photo circa 1962. Even in this picture, where he seemed to be on the verge of laughing, there was a hint of solemnity in his brown eyes. Mostly, he looked sad.

"The spa has been shut down and a team from the local sheriff's station is holding down the fort until you get there," Captain Decker continued. "I'm having our best crime scene unit deployed, along with the deputy medical examiner. They should be there by the top of the hour. Hopefully you won't arrive much later."

Jessie looked at the clock in the car. It was 10:53 a.m. Even with mid-morning traffic and using the light and sirens, it would take them close to a half hour to get there.

"Yes, Captain," Ryan said confidently as he shook his head at her from the driver's seat. "We'll do our best. What else do we need to know?"

"What you need to know, Detective," Chief Laird interjected, "is that Scott Newhouse's death is an enormous loss for this city, not to mention me personally. You will have all the resources you need at your disposal on this case."

"Thank you, Chief Laird," Ryan said.

Just as it was clear to Jessie, Ryan obviously sensed that there was something more coming.

"I would never make any improper requests," the chief said carefully, "so please don't misinterpret what I'm about to say. Our first priority as a department is without question to determine exactly what happened in that steam room. But I would ask that if the investigation hints that the nature of his death might prove to be in some way…embarrassing, that you would give me prior notice of that. To be crystal clear, I don't want you to massage your conclusions in any way. But because of Scott's high profile and his imprint on the city over the last two decades, the nature of his passing will be of enormous interest in many quarters. All I want is a little time to prepare the department's formal statement before the results of your inquiry are made public. Is that reasonable?"

Jessie was impressed. There were many reasons that Richard Laird had ascended to police chief of the second largest city in America and one of them was his ability to be diplomatic about his demands. He wanted to be looped in on this case early and often so that he could soften any unpleasant outcome. It was an unusual request, but there was nothing technically inappropriate about it. Of course, what he did after he got the results was another matter entirely.

"Of course, Chief Laird," Ryan said, well aware that he didn't have any choice but to accede to the "request." "We'll let you know as soon as we have something to share. And both Ms. Hunt and I would like to offer our condolences. We know that Mr. Newhouse was a friend of yours."

"Indeed he was," the chief acknowledged. "If it wasn't a questionable decision, I would have already called his wife, Bridget, to console her. She's all alone now, left to raise their three young ones by herself. But as you'll almost certainly need to speak to her while you're there, I didn't think it would be acceptable to reach out just yet. Assuming you clear her of any wrongdoing, please pass along my sympathies to her and let her know I'll be in touch."

"We'll do that," Ryan assured him.

"All right then," Chief Laird said, "that's all I have. I'll leave you and Captain Decker alone to coordinate your plan of attack. Good luck on this one."

He hung up before either Ryan or Decker could reply. Once he was off the phone, Decker piped up.

"I'm sorry if that was awkward," he told them. "It goes without saying that you shouldn't do anything differently than normal as you investigate, other than to update me more frequently than you otherwise might. I'll do my best to run interference with the chief."

"Thanks, Captain," Ryan said.

"What's he worried about?" Jessie asked bluntly now that she didn't have to worry about offending the big boss.

"Not sure," Decker said. "I've never heard of Newhouse being involved in anything sketchy, but you never know. I know he battled depression and was on the board of some charitable organization that dealt with the issue. Maybe Chief Laird is concerned that with the belt found around his neck, this might have been a suicide. That would send shockwaves through the city."

"I'm glad he didn't call the wife," Jessie said. "We don't need him making promises we can't keep. We all know that unless she has an iron-clad alibi, she's going to be at the top of the suspect list."

"He knows that too, Hunt," Decker said. "The man didn't get where he is by being a political idiot."

"No, Captain," she said, realizing she wasn't being especially politically adept right now herself. "Sorry."

"Just keep me apprised of developments," he said, before hanging up himself.

"What was that about?" Ryan asked, once she handed him back his phone. "You don't usually put your foot in your mouth like that."

"I guess I was just recalling our last direct interaction with Chief Laird," she said. "Don't you remember when we were investigating the case of that underage porn actress who was murdered? When one of Laird's top deputies came under scrutiny and we pursued him, the chief threatened to suspend us without pay and even wanted us arrested at one point."

"Yes," Ryan conceded, "but I seem to recall that was because Internal Affairs was already investigating the guy and Laird didn't want us mucking up their work."

"That was the official explanation he gave," Jessie countered, "but I had my doubts that he would have pushed hard on the issue without us."

"Maybe keep that to yourself for the time being," Ryan suggested. "In the meantime, we should reach out to Jamil and Beth to have them put together a rundown on everything we need to know about Scott Newhouse."

"Good idea," Jessie suggested and made the call.

Jamil Winslow was the head of research for HSS and Beth Ryerson was his newly hired researcher. They were an unconventional pair. They were both twenty-four but the similarities ended there.

Jamil, brilliant when it came to both navigating technology and legal and local government minutiae, was physically unimposing—short and skinny. But his exterior masked one of the sharpest minds Jessie had ever encountered.

Beth, on the job less than a month, was smart and eager to learn, but still learning the ropes. Still, she was infinitely more at ease with herself than her boss. Maybe that was because the former college volleyball player was six feet tall with a ripped physique. Or maybe it was because even with glasses and no makeup, she was unfussily attractive. Jessie liked to tease Jamil that he had a secret crush on his lone employee, which infuriated him and made Jessie think it might actually be true.

"Hey guys," Jessie said once Beth picked up and put them on speaker. "We're headed to the Peninsula resort in Palos Verdes to investigate the death of Scott Newhouse, the mega-rich philanthropist. We need everything you can get on him: business dealings that went awry, feuds, marital discord, lawsuits, any legal hiccups, all the way down to traffic tickets. Can you send it to us in the next hour?"

"Not a problem," Jamil assured them. "Although some of that may require more than just database searches. We'll have to make some calls."

"Just do your best," Ryan said. "Don't threaten anyone but definitely cajole."

"I may put Beth on that one," Jamil suggested.

"Wise move," Beth said. "I have advanced cajoling skills."

"Time to put them to use," Ryan said. "Let us know when you have something."

Once they hung up, he turned to Jessie and she knew he was going to change topics.

"You know," he said, "As long as we're at the premiere resort destination in Southern California, maybe we should take a look at their facilities to see if the place might work for our impending nuptials."

Jessie's jaw dropped open. Of all the things she'd predicted he was about to say, that was last on the list.

"Ryan," she said, "There are people who'd have to sell a kidney on the black market to afford a weekend at that place. How much do you think holding a wedding there would cost?"

"It's just an idea," he replied. "Besides, even if it's not the place for us, we might get some good ideas."

She was tempted to tell him exactly what she thought of the idea right then. On more than one occasion she'd hinted that, since this was the second marriage for both of them, the prospect of a big wedding just didn't feel right to her. She would be just as happy going to city hall for the ceremony, or even eloping.

But every time she broached the issue, he seemed to take offense. He said she deserved to do it up right, especially considering that her first marriage had ended because her husband was a sociopath who tried to frame her for the murder of his mistress and then attempted to kill her when she found out.

Of course, the way that relationship ended made her *less* inclined to focus on the spectacle of a wedding, not more. That ceremony and reception had been massive, and it didn't end up making the subsequent marriage any better. But Ryan didn't seem to get that she didn't feel like she was missing out if they didn't have an elaborate function the second time around.

Jessie sighed silently to herself. At some point they would need to revisit the topic, but not now. They could hash out their differences later. After all, they were headed into the lion's den, a place where wealth and decadence tended to bend everything to their will, and they needed to form a united front if they were going to get to the bottom of what happened there.

CHAPTER THREE

Jessie was white-knuckling it.

Even though the lights and siren were no longer necessary because there was so little traffic on the road that led to the resort, Ryan could only go so fast. Hawthorne Boulevard, which ran from Inglewood all the way to the ocean, was winding, with sharp, corkscrew turns and sharp drop-offs into deep canyons. After a good ten minutes of that, the coast finally came into view.

It was breathtaking. The morning marine layer had burned off to reveal rocky, tree-covered cliff sides, which gave way to the Pacific Ocean. Waves crashed against the rocks of secluded coves. In the distance, nearly twenty-five miles off the coast, Catalina Island was visible.

Eventually Hawthorne came to an end, connecting to Palos Verdes Drive just a few hundred yards from the water. Ryan went south on the new street, passing a lighthouse and a nature preserve. A few minutes later, after one final series of hills, the Peninsula Resort & Spa came into view.

As they followed Peninsula Drive downhill to the property, they got a sense of just how massive it was. There were more red rust-hued roofs and cream building exteriors than Jessie could count. A golf course seemed to weave in and out of the complex. She counted three pools, one of which looked like it stopped at the very edge of a distant cliff. As they reached a gate with an adjoining guardhouse, they were greeted by a friendly but armed guard.

"First time staying with us?" he asked warmly.

"We're actually here investigating an incident," Ryan said vaguely, holding up his ID.

"Ah, yes, Detective, we were told to expect you," the guard said. "Do you know where you're going?"

"No idea," Ryan admitted.

The guard got a paper map from the house and leaned in with it so they could see.

"We're here," he said, circling the guardhouse with his pen. "You're going to follow this road around to the right. It will take you directly to the Reception Center in the Grand Hall. There are several parking spots for resort personnel. Park in one of them and head to the reception desk. They'll have a security guard escort you to the spa area. I'll call ahead to make sure they're ready for you. Any questions?"

"No," Ryan said, shaking his head. "That was pretty comprehensive."

They followed the route the guard indicated, pausing at several stop signs and pedestrian crosswalks to make way for golf carts and guests. As they approached the Grand Hall, Jessie took in the scene. The structure, like all the others, had a Mediterranean look.

But this particular building towered over the others nearby, with a bell tower that looked to be about fifty feet high. It seemed appropriate for the place, which she'd heard would unenthusiastically accept reservations from the very rich but catered primarily to the filthy rich.

When they got to the roundabout near the main entrance, a valet darted out to help them, but Ryan waved him off and took one of the open personnel spots. The valet jogged after them and waited politely as they exited the vehicle.

"Welcome folks," he said, slightly winded. "I'm afraid that spot is for hotel staff. Can I find a spot for you or direct you to the self-parking area?"

"Thanks, but that's not necessary," Ryan said, again holding up his badge. "We're here on police business. Can you point us to the front desk please?"

"Of course, sir," the valet said. "It's right through those doors to your left."

They headed in that direction. As they did, Jessie took note of their attire as opposed to the guests around them. Despite rushing to get ready before they left, she'd tried to dress appropriately for the location, wearing a light sweater and a pair of nice slacks. Ryan had done the same, wearing slacks and a button-down shirt with a blazer. She thought they fit in pretty well, coming off as devil-may-care, vacation business-casual. The only small giveaway that they might not be in leisure mode was her still-damp hair, which she'd put in a ponytail rather than try to style in the car.

They were just walking up to the front desk when they were met by a tall, bald man in a suit and tie, with a nametag that read: Hugo, Security. He looked the part. Easily six-foot-four and 220 pounds, the man presented like he'd just switched from a football uniform into a work one.

"Detectives?" he asked, his voice low and discreet.

"I'm Detective Hernandez," Ryan confirmed. "This Jessie Hunt, a criminal profiler with the department."

"Yes," Hugo replied, nodding. "Now that you say that, I recognize you, Ms. Hunt. I saw how you took down that cult leader—very impressive. My name is Hugo Cosgrove. I'm part of our security team here at Peninsula. I've been asked to escort you to the spa. Could you please follow me?"

"Sure," Jessie said as he led them through the Reception Center. He was seemingly oblivious to Grand Hall's ornate, detailed floor tiles and the elaborate roped-off sculptures along the way. She was not and tried to steal glances as she walked past.

They passed through a massive archway and out to a huge, well-manicured lawn that was clearly the site of the larger outdoor weddings at the resort. At the far end of the lawn, only yards from the cliff side, was a gazebo for ceremonies. White, wooden chairs were being set out for one that was apparently happening today.

"When's the wedding today?" she asked.

"It starts just before sunset," he answered. "They want to exchange vows just as the sun drops below the horizon."

"That's nice," Ryan said and Jessie could see his mind racing.

"The rest of your people are already at the spa," Hugo told them, stopping at a golf cart at the edge of the lawn. "We tried to keep all the potential witnesses there as well, although we let Mrs. Newhouse return to her casita. She was very upset."

"Understood," Ryan said. "We'll catch up with her there."

Hugo got in the golf cart driver's seat.

"We're not walking?" Jessie asked.

"We could," Hugo said. "But it's a bit of a trek and I was led to believe that time is of the essence."

"It is," Ryan said, hopping in the back seat. Jessie took the front passenger seat as Hugo settled in behind the wheel.

"Hold on tight," he said as he started the cart up. "It can get a little bumpy."

Before she could object, he shot ahead, taking the resort turns the way Ryan had driven down Hawthorne Boulevard. Her wet hair slapped against the back of her neck, leaving a damp mark that gave her an uncomfortable chill when met by the ocean breeze.

They arrived outside the spa less than a minute later. Even before Jessie identified the place, she knew where she was because of the CSU truck and the medical examiner van. The entire area was cordoned off with police tape, and other members of the resort's security team were doing their best to keep onlookers at bay behind it. Hugo parked the cart and walked briskly ahead of them until they reached the entrance of the spa, where an L.A. County Sheriff's deputy based out of the Lomita station stood watch.

"I assume you're good from here?" Hugo asked once they got to the police tape.

"I think so. Thanks, Hugo," Ryan said.

"Okay," Hugo replied. "I'll be waiting out here for you when you're done."

Ryan nodded before turning to the deputy, showing his badge, and dipping under the tape. Jessie did the same. They stepped inside the building and looked around. The spa reception area was empty, apart from several other deputies milling about. The walls were all soft variations on yellow and the plush chairs were different shades of light blue. They had the desired effect. Jessie felt immediately more relaxed, if only briefly. Even though a person died here, the place had an air of serenity.

They followed the signage for the men's lounge, strolling along a hallway with frosted glass walls until they got to the massive oak entrance doors, where another deputy stood guard. They again showed their ID and the deputy stood aside. Ryan pushed open the door and Jessie stepped inside. That's when the serenity ended.

CHAPTER FOUR

The men's lounge was organized chaos.

Jessie counted at least a dozen people in the area, many of whom she recognized. Even though Peninsula was within the territory of the L.A. County Sheriff's Lomita station, it looked like Chief Laird had called in a favor because everyone working the scene was affiliated with LAPD.

The crime scene techs were all folks Jessie had worked with before and the medical examiner was one of the best in the business, Cheryl Gallagher. Jessie handled the case of a murdered social influencer with her a few months back and her work had been top notch. As always, her blonde hair was pulled back tight into a ponytail. Her expression was even tighter. Jessie and Ryan approached her first.

"What do we know?" Ryan asked her, not wasting time with pleasantries.

"He almost certainly died of strangulation," Gallagher said, "though it's too early to determine whether it was self-inflicted or done to him. Follow me."

She led them through the lounge area of the spa, past the locker room, restrooms, and showers to a large, secluded back area. At one end of the section was a giant Jacuzzi-style, whirlpool bath. To the left was a sauna with wooden interior. To the right was the steam room where Newhouse had died.

The door was propped open and several people were moving about inside. Gallagher stopped at the entrance and let Jessie and Ryan take in the scene. The man's body was lying on the floor in an open body bag. Photographs were being taken and someone was attempting to dust for prints. Attached to a metal handlebar about five feet high, built into the wall, was some kind of thin rope. It had a pattern of navy blue and white, though at one end of it, the white had turned reddish.

"Sorry," Gallagher said. "I know you like to see the crime scene as it was. But we had to cut him down. I was worried that the pressure on his neck would further damage the throat area, complicating any definitive determination on cause of death. We did take pictures, of course."

There would be official ones for them to look at later but for now Gallagher pulled up some shots on her phone. They showed Scott Newhouse, naked, slumped to the side. He was on the middle, white-tiled bench, with his torso pressed up against the right bench. The same thin material currently attached to the metal handlebar was around his neck in the photo. It was essentially holding him up. Without it, he would have likely slipped to the floor entirely.

"That handlebar seems kind of low for someone who wanted to hang himself," Ryan noted.

"I agree," Gallagher said. "But I don't want to rule it out. The material could have loosened over time after the fact. It's hard to say. One thing is for sure, it was wrapped tight around his neck. It had actually cut through the flesh in some areas."

Jessie winced at the words. Nonetheless, she looked down at Newhouse's lifeless body. There were nasty, red indentations in his neck, like a bloody choker necklace.

"We were told a belt was used," she said, "but that looks a lot thinner."

"Yes," Gallagher confirmed. "After closer inspection, the material is closer to a thick ribbon of some kind. We're not sure what it is exactly. There's nothing like it in the spa. The attendant who found him told the first deputies on the scene that he didn't recognize it."

"Any chance you'll be able to pull DNA off it?" Ryan asked.

"We'll see," Gallagher replied dubiously. "That's really our only hope for physical evidence, assuming this was a homicide and the killer didn't use gloves. Unfortunately, this room is so hot and humid that pulling prints is virtually impossible. Even determining an authoritative time of death will be hard because the heat in here messed with his body temp."

That fact alone piqued Jessie's suspicion. After all, if this was murder, what better place to commit the crime than a place where fingerprints and an accurate time of death were hard to come by?

"Maybe the attendant can help us lock that down a bit," she suggested. "Where is he?"

"He's waiting with a deputy in the locker room," Gallagher told them. "His name is Tony Dante. He's pretty shaken up."

"Thanks Cheryl," Ryan said.

They made their way back to the locker room, where a deputy was standing with his back to them, scrolling through his phone. He had apparently made no effort to comfort the young man, who looked terrified. Tony Dante was sitting forlornly on a bench in the corner, bouncing nervously and fiddling with his fingers. He had olive skin, brown hair, and appeared to be in his early twenties. When he glanced up at them, his eyes were wide with distress.

"Tony," Jessie said, pushing past the deputy, who could get an explanation of who they were from Ryan, "My name is Jessie. How are you doing?"

She sat down beside him and smiled gently. It seemed wise to ease in with the kid. There was always the possibility that Tony had killed Scott Newhouse, but for now she was operating on the assumption that he was a witness. That could always change based on his answers.

"Not great," he admitted.

She heard the deputy balk behind her before Ryan murmured something to him that she couldn't hear. She pretended not to notice.

"I can understand that," she said softly. "What you saw was pretty awful. I wish I could tell you the memory will fade soon, but that wouldn't be honest."

"Who are you?" he asked, apparently curious as to whether he could trust the word of the strange woman who had sat down beside him.

"Like I said, my name is Jessie. I'm a profiler who consults with the police. They bring me in on investigations from time to time. I'm here trying to determine what happened and I was hoping you could help me and my partner, Detective Hernandez, figure that out. Can we ask you a few questions?"

"I already told the other cops what I saw," he said, clearly dreading the idea of revisiting it all.

"We know," Jessie said quietly but firmly. "But it's often helpful for us to hear it in person from the witness. Sometimes they remember new things the second time around. When did you find the victim?"

"A little after ten," he said.

"Can you be more specific?"

"It was about 10:10," he said. "My break started at 10:15 and cleaning the steam room is always the last thing on my checklist before I clock out."

"Did you see him go in?'

"No, but I was running around the lounge a lot. I could have easily missed him. I saw on the sign-in sheet by the door that he checked in around 9:30, so I knew he was around somewhere. But he could have been anywhere—the sauna, getting a massage—and I wouldn't necessarily have known. It was pretty quiet this morning. I only came across three or four guests since I started my shift."

"Were any of them around when you found the body?"

"No," he said, shivering at the memory. "I was pretty sure I was alone because I hadn't seen anyone for a while and everyone except for Mr. Newhouse had checked out on the sign-in sheet. But I shouted out for help anyway after I called the front desk. No one answered."

"Are there cameras we can check to see comings and goings?" Ryan asked, speaking for the first time.

"Entering the spa's main reception area, yes," Tony told him, "but not in the lounges. They want guests to have privacy."

"But we could use the reception cameras to determine if guests actually left the spa after signing out in here?" Ryan checked.

"I guess so," Tony said. "You should check with security to make sure."

"We will," Ryan replied. "Is there anything else you can think of that we didn't ask about?"

"No."

"Okay, just one last question, Tony," Ryan asked as if it was the most casual thing in the world. "Did you know Mr. Newhouse?"

"I don't think so," Tony answered. "The name isn't familiar and I didn't recognize him. But, I mean, I didn't look that closely at him, you know. I actually tried not to look at him at all."

"And did you interact with anyone else during the time prior to finding the body?" Ryan pressed, asking more than his promised "one" question.

"Sure," Tony said, not totally getting that he was being asked for his alibi. "I went to get extra towels at one point and ran into Kree. She's one of the female attendants. That was about ten minutes before I found Mr. Newhouse. I also stopped by Jerald's office. He's the men's spa manager. I told him we were running low on cucumbers for the mint cucumber water. He said he'd order more from the kitchen. That was just a couple of minutes before I found the guy."

"Great," Jessie said. "We just need you to stick around a little while longer. The deputy will release you soon."

Tony nodded and they left the men's lounge and headed back to the front.

"What do you think?" Ryan asked as they approached the main exit.

"I think that Chief Laird is going to want an update soon. And since it might be a while until we get the M.E.'s take on whether this was murder or suicide, we'd be smart to talk to someone else who may be able to give us some insight on the matter."

"Who's that?" Ryan asked, though Jessie suspected he knew who she was thinking of.

"The same person who might also be our prime suspect: his wife. We need to speak to Bridget Newhouse."

CHAPTER FIVE

Hugo tore along the golf cart path like he was in a race.

As he drove them to Bridget Newhouse's bungalow across the campus, he took it upon himself to give them the quick and dirty tour.

"That's the public nightclub, Breakers," he said, pointing at a stand-alone building near a cliff edge.

"What do you mean 'public?'" Ryan shouted from the backseat.

"Anyone can get into that one, even non-guests, if they're willing to pay the cover, which is admittedly quite steep," Hugo explained. "But there's another club underneath it, carved deep into the cliff. It's VIP only—very exclusive. You have to take an elevator down. They created an artificial cove just above the water line with a massive window facing the ocean. When the waves crash, they slam into the window—it's pretty intense."

"What constitutes a VIP?" Jessie wondered.

"That information is above my pay grade," Hugo admitted. "When I've worked the place, I've seen major celebrities and people I didn't recognize that looked like they hadn't bathed in days. I have no idea what the formal criteria is for entry."

"Sounds super fun," Ryan said drily. "What's it called, The Cove?"

"Actually, yes," Hugo told him with a surprised look on his face. He recovered quickly and pointed out a large grassy area, part of which was filled with chaise lounge chairs and several all-weather loveseats. "That lawn is where we do our catered picnics. And just beyond it, in the furniture-free area, is the yoga pavilion where we do our seaside classes."

"Aren't the catered picnics a distraction for the folks doing yoga?" Jessie asked, amused and slightly appalled by the options.

"They're very careful about the timing," Hugo replied, either not getting the snark or choosing to ignore it. "Just over the next hill is where we have our falconry experience and beyond that, at the next trailhead, is the starting point for both our meditation hikes and our whale watching outings."

"Wow," Ryan said. "You guys really seem to have everything."

"Just about," Hugo said as he veered off the cliff side path and took one that led into a secluded section of the campus with large, stand-alone bungalows. "We even have a personal lovemaking coach for couples."

"I'm sorry, what?" Jessie asked before she could stop herself.

"She's very popular," Hugo explained as he brought the cart to a sudden stop. "Her name is Honey Potter."

"You can't be serious," Jessie countered, trying not to laugh and failing.

"I am," Hugo promised. "She used to be an adult film actress before she got her master's degree in human development. She's incredibly popular. There's a four month wait time for an appointment with her."

"You know, Hugo," Jessie said as she got out of the passenger seat. "In this job, I'm very rarely shocked by what I learn. But you should be proud. You somehow managed to do it."

"I'm flattered," he replied as he led them up a half-hidden, stone path that curled around to the front of a bungalow that looked modeled on a Spanish mission.

"That bungalow's nice," Jessie said.

"We call them casitas," Hugo told her proudly.

Another security guard stood in front of the casita. He was short with a thick trunk and a shaved head. He reminded Jessie of a bowling ball with feet.

"Detective Hernandez, Ms. Hunt," Hugo said, "This is Geordy. He's been assigned to make sure no one disturbed Mrs. Newhouse until you got a chance to speak with her."

"Was that a concern?" Ryan wondered.

"You just never know if information is going to leak out and to whom," Hugo said. "We decided it was better to err on the side of caution and make sure she had some support. Also, in case the enormity of the situation affected her badly, we thought it would be nice for her to have a human resource if needed."

"A security guard was assigned for emotional support?" Jessie asked, noting that Hugo had seemingly mastered a level of diplomacy rare for a security guard.

Hugo shrugged.

"We do have an on-site grief therapist but he's currently conducting a tide pool retreat. This was a stop-gap measure."

"Hugo," Jessie said. "When we first met you, you said you were merely part of the security team, but you've kept witnesses from being improperly contacted. You've ensured that the dead man's wife has personal security in case she's in harm's way. It's clear that you actually run the team—why the ruse?"

He shrugged again.

"Modesty, I suppose."

Jessie wasn't having any of it.

"Are you sure it's not because you wanted us to underestimate you and potentially reveal something about the case in your presence, allowing you to better keep tabs on things for your bosses?"

"I think you give me too much credit, Ms. Hunt," Hugo replied with a smile.

Jessie doubted it. And from the expression on Ryan's face, so did he. She let it lie for now.

"Hi Geordy," Jessie said, turning her attention to the guard, who had yet to speak. "Has she said anything?"

"No ma'am," Geordy answered. "I escorted her back from the spa at about 10:30. We've been here ever since. I've heard some crying but she hasn't spoken a word since she went inside."

"Wait," Ryan checked. "You said she was at the spa?"

"That's correct, sir."

"Was she called there after she got the news about her husband's death or was she already there?"

"I believe she was already at the spa," Geordy answered. "My understanding was that she was there for a massage at the time."

Ryan gave Jessie his best "that's intriguing" expression, though he said nothing. She was on the same page with him. If this turned out to be foul play and Bridget Newhouse was in the same building as her husband when he died, she'd have a lot of explaining to do.

"We're going to go in and have a chat with her," Jessie said. "Are you gentlemen able to stick around in case we need some assistance?"

"Of course," Hugo assured her, leading them to the front door. He was about to ring the bell when Ryan stopped him.

"I meant to mention this earlier but got distracted by the lovemaking coach stuff," he said, "but the men's lounge attendant, Tony Dante, said there are cameras that show the entrance to the spa but nothing inside. Is that right?"

"It is," Hugo said. "We don't have interior cameras for the sake of our guests' confidentiality. In fact, you'll find that we only keep cameras at the most essential locations throughout the resort. One of the perks of coming here is that our VIP guests don't generally have to worry that they're going to end up splashed all over the internet."

"Nice for them," Jessie noted, "but it's going to make our job a hell of a lot harder."

"I'd like you to send whatever camera footage there is for the spa entrance from 8 a.m. until 11 a.m. to Jamil Winslow at this e-mail address as soon as possible," Ryan told Hugo, handing over a card. "Can you do that for me?"

"Absolutely," he replied. "I'll have our people get it to your man ASAP."

With that resolved, he rang the bell. There was no answer. After a good twenty seconds he knocked on the door loudly.

"Mrs. Newhouse," he called out. "This is Hugo from the security team. I have some law enforcement investigators here who need to speak with you."

After another twenty seconds of silence, he knocked again, even louder this time.

"Mrs. Newhouse, can you please come to the door?"

After another half minute with any sound from inside, he looked over at Ryan and Jessie questioningly.

"Tell her you're going to unlock the door," Ryan instructed. "If she doesn't respond after that, open it."

Hugo gave one last knock.

"Mrs. Newhouse, considering the circumstances, I'm going to need to unlock the door if you don't respond in the next few seconds."

After ten more seconds, Ryan had enough and indicated for Hugo to do just that. He did, and then moved aside. Ryan took a step inside, his right hand resting casually on his gun holster. Jessie followed, though she kept her hands at her sides.

For a dwelling described as a casita, or cottage, the place was pretty impressive. The main living room, decked out in rustic, hacienda-style furniture, had a huge, vaulted ceiling that rose to the second floor, where Jessie counted at least five doors.

"How big is this place?" she whispered to Hugo.

"This is one of our junior casitas," he replied in a hushed voice, "2500 square feet, three bedrooms, two and a half baths."

Jessie wanted to ask what constituted a senior casita but decided this wasn't the time.

"Mrs. Newhouse," Ryan shouted, his voice echoing through the house, "This is Detective Ryan Hernandez of the Los Angeles Police Department. We're here looking into your husband's death. We'd like to speak with you. And we're concerned for your welfare. Can you please respond?"

For several additional seconds, there was no noise. Then they heard what sounded like muffled crying coming from somewhere upstairs. He looked over at Jessie and she knew what he was thinking. If some strange man charged into Bridget Newhouse's bedroom, it might exacerbate an already volatile situation.

"I'll go first," she said, taking the lead up the stairs.

She moved up quickly, undoing the cover on her gun holster as she moved but not removing it. Ryan followed close behind, motioning for Hugo to stay by the front door. Once she got to the top, Jessie followed the quiet sobbing noises to a half-closed door at the end of the hall.

"Mrs. Newhouse," she said loudly, while knocking on the door. "Are you okay in there?"

The soft crying continued but nobody responded to her words. She pushed the door open gently and cautiously stepped inside. Her hand was on her gun hip, ready to act if needed.

Bridget Newhouse was laying on her side on the king bed, with her back to the door. She wasn't moving.

CHAPTER SIX

For the briefest of moments, Jessie thought she might be injured or worse.

But then the woman shifted a little as she let out a low moan. When she moved, her long blonde hair fell to the side, revealing an ear bud in her left ear. Jessie relaxed but only slightly.

"Mrs. Newhouse," she said in a near-shout to ensure that she'd be heard. The woman let out a scream as she shot up out of the bed. She grabbed a large vase on the bedside table and whirled around violently with a terrified expression on her face.

"Who the hell are you?" she demanded in a hoarse voice.

Jessie held out her hands in front of her, palms forward.

"My name is Jessie Hunt, Mrs. Newhouse. I'm a consultant for the LAPD. I'm here with a detective named Ryan Hernandez. We're investigating your husband's death. Can you please put down the vase?"

Her words didn't seem to assuage Newhouse. Her cheeks were red with upset and her blue eyes flashed. Despite her anger and red-tinged eyes, Jessie noted that she was an extremely beautiful woman. In her mid-thirties, her blonde hair cascaded down well past her shoulders. The yoga outfit she wore revealed that she was in great shape, especially after having three kids. She had ample curves, especially up top. With the woman's petite frame, Jessie couldn't help but wonder if the woman had come by some of it artificially.

"Does that give you the right to come into my residence unannounced?" Newhouse demanded. "You scared the crap out of me."

"I'm sorry about that, ma'am," Jessie replied evenly. "But we actually did announce ourselves, multiple times. We've been ringing the bell, knocking on the door and calling out to you, trying to get a response for the last few minutes. We were actually concerned for your well-being so security let us in. They're downstairs. Now I'd *really* appreciate it if you put down that vase."

The woman glanced down and seemed to finally process that she was holding what could be perceived as a weapon. She put it back down on the table.

"Thank you," Jessie said.

Ryan stepped through the door at that point and gave a hesitant wave.

"Sorry," Newhouse said, her face softening "I was listening to some music Scott and I liked. I guess it was pretty loud. Still—," she started to say before Jessie interrupted.

"Mrs. Newhouse, I'm sorry I startled you and we're glad that you're okay. I'm also terribly sorry for your loss. That's why we're here—to try to get to the bottom of what happened to Scott. We think that you could be helpful. So how about we get you out of bed and somewhere where we can chat?"

"Okay," Newhouse said, suddenly much meeker. "We can go out on the balcony. I could use some fresh air."

"Sure," Jessie agreed, though she wasn't sure interrogating an emotionally volatile, recent widow about her husband's passing while thirty feet in the air, with just a railing to keep her in line, was a great idea.

But now that Newhouse was cooperating, she didn't want to do anything to undermine that. She ignored Ryan's glare, which suggested he also thought it was a bad idea. If he wanted to change the interview venue, he'd have to say so. But he kept silent.

They followed her out onto the balcony, which didn't seem like the right name for the spot. Sure, it was outdoors and hung over the first floor. But it was easily the size of a primary bedroom, complete with a full patio set, four lounge chairs, a fire pit, and a Jacuzzi.

Newhouse walked to the railing and leaned forward. Jessie hurried over next to her, ready to stop her if she tried to climb over. Ryan did the same on the other side of her. But the woman was just staring out at the Pacific. The tears that rolled down her cheeks were quickly dried by the strong ocean winds whipping over the cliffs.

"This was supposed to be our chance to reconnect," she said quietly, almost to herself.

"Is that why you were here?" Jessie asked gently.

"Mostly," she replied. "Part of it was just a vacation, a chance to get away from the kids for a few days. But yeah, we had all kinds of couples' activities planned."

Jessie thought of the lovemaking coach but kept any questions about that to herself.

"Had you lost the connection recently?" she asked delicately.

Newhouse looked over at her. She seemed to be choosing how much of her personal life to share with this woman she'd met less than five minutes ago. Finally her body uncoiled. She appeared to decide that there was no point in holding back.

"Sure," she sighed. "After eleven years of marriage and multiple kids, we'd lost a bit of the spark. Scott was always working. He was driven to help the city and I think he felt that any time he wasn't doing that was time wasted. Plus, he had some issues with depression, ups and downs."

"Was this a down time?" Ryan asked carefully.

"I've seen him worse," Newhouse answered. "And I know he was taking his meds."

Based on intuition alone, Jessie couldn't get a bead on whether Bridget Newhouse was better suited as a witness or a suspect. Because of the emotion of a moment like this, it was often hard to gauge credibility. But there would be time later to dig into that more. Right now, she had to ask a tough question of a woman whose husband just died.

"Do you think it's possible that he took his own life?"

"Is that what you think happened?" Newhouse wanted to know, getting visibly agitated. "They wouldn't let me see him. Does it look like a suicide?"

"It's too early to say," Jessie told her truthfully. "But I want to know if he was in the headspace where that seems like something he might have done."

Newhouse closed her eyes tightly for several seconds before opening them wide. She sighed again.

"I wouldn't have thought so," she said cautiously. "He didn't say anything unusual and he seemed like his normal self this morning when we walked over to the spa. Maybe he was a littler quieter than usual. I guess you never know what's going on in someone's head."

Jessie was about to press that issue when Newhouse continued.

"But I'd have to say no, I don't think so. He seemed like himself. He mentioned a meeting he had to call into today. Last night we talked about what kind of birthday party we were going to have for our younger son; he acted like he planned to be here."

"Okay," Ryan said, as if that settled the matter for now, though both of them knew it didn't. "Let's move on to this morning if that's okay. We're trying to establish a timeline of events."

"Okay," Newhouse said, though she still seemed to be thinking about whether her husband was capable of ending his life.

"You said you walked over to the spa together, right?" he confirmed.

"Uh-huh."

"Around what time was that?" he asked.

"We left here around 9:20-ish. I had a massage scheduled for 10 a.m. and I wanted some time to decompress beforehand. I didn't want to be rushed."

"Was Scott going to get a massage too?" he asked.

"No," she said. "He actually finds them stressful. He was always worried that he might giggle or pass gas or something embarrassing."

"So why did he go?" Jessie asked perplexed.

"Mostly just to keep me company on the walk there and back," she explained, smiling at the memory of it. "He said that he'd just relax until I was done. He mentioned going in the Jacuzzi or the steam room, then showering, and reading in the men's lounge area for a while."

The realization that he would never do any of those things again seemed to hit her and Bridget Newhouse choked back a sob.

"Are we almost done?" she asked.

"Almost," Ryan said. Jessie could tell from his tone that he was about to dive into the biggest remaining issue: Newhouse's alibi. She was right. "So you walked to the spa together. What happened once you and Scott parted ways—where did you go after that?"

Newhouse's brow crinkled as she tried to recall her activities that morning.

"I went into the women's lounge," she said. "When I got there, first I went to the locker room and changed into a robe. Then I went to the quiet room for a bit."

"The quiet room?" Ryan repeated.

"It's not as fancy as it sounds," Newhouse explained. "It's just a sound-proofed room with several easy chairs that can be extended out so that you can lie flat if you want. Each chair is separated by a black curtain attached to the ceiling, like something they'd use in a hospital room with two beds to offer some measure of privacy to each patient. It's a place to zone out for a while."

"How long were you in there?" Jessie asked.

"Not more than ten minutes," Newhouse said. "They have a steam box full of hot washcloths by each chair. I put one on my face, used the noise cancelling headphones they had on the side table, and just chilled for a bit. Then I went back to the locker room for one last bathroom break. After that, I waited in the lounge to be called in for my massage."

"Did you interact with anyone during that time?" Ryan asked.

Again, Newhouse's brow crinkled as she struggled to remember.

"Not in any meaningful way. I mean, there were other women changing in the locker room and we exchanged pleasantries. There were two other women in the first two chairs in the quiet room. I nodded at them as I passed by to get to the third chair. It was mostly just polite smiles or greetings. Why?"

"We're just trying to get a sense of things," Jessie replied nonchalantly. "So what happened after you were called in for your massage?"

"Nothing—the massage started. Everything was normal. But about twenty minutes in, we were interrupted by the assistant spa manager. She said she needed a word with me. I knew something was wrong right away. I've never had anything like that happen before. I remember pulling on my robe and shaking a little, even though I wasn't cold. She took me to her office and…"

She trailed off, unable to complete the sentence.

"Is that when she told you what happened?" Jessie asked softly.

Newhouse nodded. After taking several deep breaths, she went on.

"Yes. She said that Scott had passed away. She wouldn't say how, just that he was in the men's lounge area when it happened. They wouldn't let me see him. She had two security guards at the door of her office that physically prevented me from going to him. They said it would be too upsetting for me."

"I think that was probably a wise decision, Mrs. Newhouse," Ryan told her.

"Maybe, but then they wouldn't let me see my friends either. One of the security guys said that I should hold off on any conversations until the authorities had a chance to speak to me. So

I've been holed up here for the last hour, listening to music, waiting for word about my dead husband."

The bitterness leaked through in that last answer. Jessie couldn't blame her. If she'd been in that position—confused, traumatized, and scared—she'd be lashing out too. But she had to set aside any empathy for the time being. Until she could determine the validity of the woman's alibi, it was best not let compassion into the mix. Besides, right now she was more interested in something that Bridget Newhouse had mentioned in passing.

"Did you say that you're here with friends?"

"Yes," Newhouse replied, apparently surprised that Jessie had fixated on that, "three couples all together, including us. We came as a group. We were all going to work on building marital communication as couples through activities during the day and then decompress over long meals with friends in the evening."

"You've been friends for a while?" she probed.

"For years," Newhouse answered. "We do everything together; we know all each other's secrets. Why?"

Jessie glanced over at Ryan and saw that he was thinking the same thing as her. In Jessie's experience, if these couples were all really as close as Newhouse suggested, they were sure to have rivalries, petty jealousies, and buried resentments.

With just one statement, they suddenly had four new suspects.

CHAPTER SEVEN

Ryan looked at his watch for the third time in the last five minutes.

It was 11:58 a.m., only two minutes until the end of lovemaking coach Honey Potter's "session" with the Darcys. If he was going to catch them before they left, he needed to hurry, so he broke into a jog. It felt good to do it without worrying about whether his body would hold up.

He and Jessie had decided to split up to interview the two couples that came to Peninsula with the Newhouses: Matthew & Eleanor Darcy and Malcolm & Abigail Andrews. They checked with Hugo, who conferred with scheduling to determine where each couple was currently.

The Andrews were halfway across the property, finishing up a private yoga lesson. Jessie offered to talk to them so Hugo volunteered to drive her to meet them. That left Ryan with the Darcys.

As he made his way up the hill to Honey Potter's private coaching bungalow, he couldn't help but think that Jessie had leapt at the chance to take the other couple because she didn't want to inadvertently interrupt the end of whatever was going on there. He had the same concern but it was too late to back out now.

As he passed a garden courtyard with a dais at one end which was clearly intended for smaller weddings, his thoughts turned to the one he and Jessie were planning, or not planning as it seemed these days. All their organizational efforts had ground to a halt, largely a result of his fiancée's intransigence.

No suggestion he offered seemed to excite her. They'd visited a half dozen venues in the last month, each of which she'd rejected as too grandiose. She'd also put off appointments with a florist, a caterer, and two bakeries that specialized in wedding cakes. Even his passing reference earlier to getting ideas from this place seemed to irk her.

She kept telling him that she was happy with something small but he knew the real reason that she repeatedly said that: because she didn't want to make him feel "less than." Jessie knew that he didn't have the financial resources that her previous husband, Kyle Voss, did, and she didn't want him to feel bad if he couldn't contribute as much as Kyle had. He suspected that she worried that if she gave any hint that she wanted something bigger, he'd sink into a shame spiral. So she insisted they go small.

But Ryan wasn't having any of it. He didn't want her lasting memory of her "big" wedding to be to a sociopathic murderer. After all, Kyle hadn't just tried to kill her when she discovered he had framed her for killing his mistress. Once the guy was released from prison on a technicality, he had killed her mentor, Garland Moses. After that, he tried to do the same to her, Hannah, and Ryan. That's how Ryan ended up stabbed and in a coma—because of Jessie's ex. He simply couldn't allow the man who did all that to be the face she pictured when she recalled her big day.

So Ryan would keep at it. Eventually Jessie would realize that he wasn't afraid of the financial commitment and relent. Eventually she would let him make their wedding an event that could replace the original in her memory.

As he climbed the last hill that led to Honey Potter's bungalow, one other possibility crept into his head. What if Jessie wasn't balking at all his wedding ideas because she didn't want him to feel bad or to overspend? What if she was resisting because she was having second thoughts about getting married? The thought sent a cold chill through him.

He was just approaching Potter's door when it opened and two people who must have been the Darcys stepped out. Matthew had his arm wrapped around Eleanor's waist, though in more of a perfunctory than a romantic way.

Matthew was a big guy, well over six feet tall and around two hundred and fifteen pounds. He was wearing slacks and a yellow polo shirt that was straining just slightly against his mild paunch. Ryan, who didn't know how these kinds of sessions worked, had half-expected the man to be dressed in a smoking jacket or other similarly passion-friendly attire. His blond hair was engaged in a battle against the wind. He appeared to be about forty, still ruggedly good looking but starting to get a little saggy in the jowls and craggy on the forehead.

Eleanor was a little younger, closer to Bridget Newhouse's mid-thirties. She wore a tan sundress with an unbuttoned purple cardigan. She was much smaller than her husband, nearly a foot shorter and easily a hundred pounds less. Her black hair was cut short, pixie-style, which accentuated her sharp cheekbones and button nose. She bristled with intensity, as if she was waiting for a starting gun to go off for whatever activity she had planned next.

A moment later a third person emerged from the bungalow. Ryan was ashamed to realize he was disappointed. He wasn't sure what he was expecting. It wasn't like the woman was going to be wearing lingerie and tanning spray. But still, the modesty of her outfit was surprising. Honey Potter had on a white blouse and a red, high-waisted, pencil skirt—a term he only knew because Jessie was fond of wearing them. Both were form-fitting but not in a way that screamed "former porn actress."

She wore glasses and her brown hair was tied up in a bun, both of which gave her an academic vibe. She was attractive, but in a subdued, non-bombshell kind of way. Had he not been told of her prior profession, he never would have guessed it. Honey noticed him coming first.

"Somebody's a man on a mission," she noted drily.

"I'm sorry?" Ryan said as he got to them.

"You were walking very purposefully," she explained, "As if it was extremely important that you arrive at this place at this moment."

"You're not far off, Ms. Potter," he said, refusing to let her or anyone else take charge of the conversation. He needed this couple to recognize his authority so that they were in a compliant mood when he started asking them questions. "I wanted make sure I was able to catch the Darcys before they left. I assume I have the right folks: Matthew and Eleanor Darcy?"

"You do," Eleanor said. "I'm Ellie and this is Matt. May I ask who you are?"

"You may," he said. "But I'll need to answer privately, away from your...coach."

"My goodness," Potter replied, surprised and seemingly delighted. "This is an unexpected development."

"What's that?" Ryan asked.

"Usually men come up with excuses to get closer to me," she said, "not get away from me."

"Don't take offense," he told her. "It's nothing personal. I just need to speak with the Darcys about a time-sensitive matter."

"Of course, don't let me keep you," she said before turning her attention to the couple. "Matt and Ellie, I think that was a very productive first session. Please remember that tomorrow, you should come in less binding attire so that we can really get into the juicy stuff. But for the time being, you should head off with the detective."

Now it was Ryan's turn to be surprised.

"How did you kn—?" he started.

"I stay abreast of local news, Detective Hernandez," she said with a sly smile. "Or didn't you think someone in my position was aware of current events? Your lady friend, Ms. Hunt, is a full-on celebrity and it's hard not to take notice of the tasty side piece that's with her in half the footage I see."

"Thanks, I think?" he said, trying to avoid looking flummoxed in front of potential suspects. Not only was he slightly embarrassed, now he'd lost the element of surprise with the Darcys. Whether that was Honey Potter's intent or not, he didn't know. But if he was going to keep the advantage with them, he needed to move fast.

"You're very welcome," she replied, for the first time sounding like the cliché of the seductive temptress that he'd been expecting.

"We won't keep you any longer," Ryan said crisply, and then fixed his attention on the open-mouthed couple, "Mr. and Mrs. Darcy, why don't we head over to those garden chairs where we can speak confidentially."

It wasn't really a question and they didn't object, following him to the chairs, which were set around a small table under the shade of a large palm tree. As they walked, Ryan noticed that there seemed to be a tension between them that he couldn't quite nail down. They were close to each other but seemed somehow emotionally apart. Maybe they'd had an uncomfortable session with Honey Potter. Or maybe it was something more. Once they sat down, Matt Darcy finally spoke.

"What's this all about?" he asked, sounding both annoyed and apprehensive.

"As Ms. Potter said, my name is Ryan Hernandez. I'm a detective with the LAPD," he said, pointedly not answering the question that was asked. "I understand that you're close friends with Scott and Bridget Newhouse. Is that correct?"

"Yes," Ellie volunteered, "For a long time. Why?"

"Have you seen them today?" Ryan wondered.

Ellie shook her head and looked over at her husband who nodded that he had.

"I saw Scott this morning in the fitness center," he said. "He was wrapping up a workout on the elliptical when I got there."

"What time was that?"

"Maybe around eight?" he answered.

"Did you talk?"

"A little," he recalled. "He said he had an early call for something work-related before he and Bridget went to the spa."

"How did he seem to you?"

Darcy looked like he had some questions he wanted ask but managed to rein himself in.

"Fine, I guess," he said. "He was his normal, focused self. Even on vacation, that guy always has a plan. We talked about meeting up for a bite around lunchtime but he couldn't promise anything. He said his schedule was tight after the spa. I wasn't holding my breath. Can you please tell us what's going on now?"

Ryan had kept them at arm's length long enough. He knew that if he continued to be evasive much longer, their irritation might turn to combativeness and he didn't need that.

"I have some bad news," he said. "I'm sorry to say that Scott passed away this morning."

Both of their mouths dropped open. For several seconds neither spoke.

"Are you sure?" Ellie Darcy finally asked.

Even though it was a ridiculous question, he got it all the time. No cop would deliver news like this unless he was certain, but people rarely processed information like this quickly or coherently.

"Yes. I'm afraid so," he told her.

"But he was fine when I saw him," Matt protested. "He didn't even look tired. He's in great shape."

Jessie was the real expert at reading body language in situations like this but with his years of experience, Ryan was no slouch. And to him, neither of their reactions was dramatically out of the ordinary or suspicious. Still, he needed to press them.

"I'm afraid I can't go into many details, other than to say his death was not due to natural causes. That's why I need your help."

"Not natural causes?" Ellie repeated, dumbfounded. "What does that mean exactly?"

"There will be time to get into all that later," Ryan promised her. "But right now, you two are very important to our investigation. What can you tell me about the Newhouses' marriage?"

Ellie and Matt exchanged hesitant glances, unsure who should answer. Finally she took the lead.

"They seemed happy," she said, seeming to gather emotional strength from hearing her own voice. "I mean, no marriage is perfect, right? Hell, you met us at an appointment with a sex coach. If they had any issue, I'd say it was time. With three kids under ten and Scott's non-stop schedule, they didn't have a lot of couple's moments. Bridget told me they had to use a calendar to find some alone time. But they're hardly the only ones. Just like the rest of us, that's part of why they were here—to reconnect. They wanted to focus on each other more and then have some fun with us the rest of the time."

"Would you agree with that assessment?" Ryan asked Matt.

He shrugged noncommittally.

"I guess," he said. "It's not something we really talked about that much. Scott's a good guy but we were more 'friendly' than friends. I knew him through Bridget."

Ryan took note of the edge in the man's voice but didn't comment on it or on the fact that Matt's description of the couples' friendship was substantially different from what Bridget Newhouse had described. It didn't sound like he and Scott would be sharing heartfelt inner truths any time soon. He let that be for now so that he could keep the focus on the Newhouses.

"Did you ever hear anything about fights, infidelity, or talk of divorce?"

Both shook their heads adamantly at that. Ryan hadn't expected anything different. It was rare that someone would immediately reveal an unpleasant detail about a person, especially a friend, who just died. He'd check back on that question later on if need be.

"Okay," Ryan said, pulling out his small notebook nonchalantly, as if the important part of the interview was over and the rest was just perfunctory. "And what were you doing this morning up until your session with Ms. Potter?"

"After my workout, I went back to our casita to shower and relax," Matt answered. "Then I met Ellie for a late morning bite to eat in one of the restaurants. After that, we went back to the casita to get ready for our appointment."

"What time did you guys meet for breakfast?" Ryan asked, scribbling down the details while keeping his eyes on the Darcys.

"Ten," Ellie said.

"And what were you up to prior to that?" he asked her.

"I went for a hike down to the tide pools."

"With some friends—maybe the Andrews?" he asked, referencing the other couple that Bridget Newhouse had referenced: the one Jessie was talking to now.

"No, it was just me," she told him, her nose scrunching up in apprehension. "Are you checking my alibi for when Scott died? Am I in trouble?"

"You're not in trouble," Ryan assured her. "But part of the investigation requires that I nail down details like this. When were you on the hike?"

"I left at the same time that Matt went to the gym, about eight. I got back just before we met to eat at ten."

Ryan closed his notebook. The second he did, Matt popped up from his chair.

"Is that it? Are we done for now?" he asked. "We want to check in on Bridget. Is she in her casita?"

"She is," Ryan said. "And you can go see her. I think it would do her some good. All I ask is that you not leave the resort. We may have more questions for you."

He nodded, as did Ellie, who said nothing as they hurried off in the direction of the Newhouse casita. Ryan watched them go, trying to fit the timing of the Darcy's morning into what he and Jessie already knew.

Scott Newhouse was alive at 9:30 a.m, when he checked in to the spa men's lounge. He was found dead at 10:10 a.m. by Tony Dante. That was their window of death. And because the steam room was so hot, it would be impossible for the medical examiner to use Scott's body temperature to narrow that window.

Unfortunately for the Darcys, neither of their alibis was bulletproof. She was on a solo hike for part of the time when Scott might have died. He was showering and relaxing alone in their casita. Ryan couldn't definitively cross either of them off the suspect list. He hoped Jessie was having better luck.

CHAPTER EIGHT

Jessie feared they might topple off the cliff.

When Hugo pulled up in the golf cart at the pavilion for seaside yoga, the yoga instructor looked to be safe, but the couple appeared so close to the edge that it seemed like any loss of balance might send them over.

She was about to jump out to warn them when Hugo put his hand on her forearm.

"You're thinking they're about to fall off the cliff, right?" he whispered quietly.

She nodded urgently.

"It's an optical illusion," he assured her. "They're actually a good ten feet from the edge, and the drop-off isn't as steep as it looks. Please don't yell a warning to them. It'll ruin the lesson."

"Okay," Jessie said, settling back into the cart. "But someone should really consider relocating where they do this."

"Jude actually prefers it this way," Hugo said.

"Jude?"

"Jude Austen—he's the yoga instructor," Hugo told her, nodding toward the tall, thin man leading the Andrews through their poses. "He likes his students to have that initial fear you just felt when they arrive here. He says that it's part of the lesson—to teach them that fear doesn't have to define how you behave."

"Is he a yoga teacher or a therapist?" Jessie asked.

"He'd probably tell you both," Hugo said.

That didn't surprise her. Jude looked like a confident guy. With his height and his elegantly wiry body, he was hard not to notice. Handsome in an understated way, he looked to be in his early thirties. His longish brown hair was tied back in a ponytail and he wore yoga pants and a simple, form-fitting white t-shirt.

"Next thing you'll tell me he used to be a porn star too," she muttered.

"Not to the best of my knowledge," Hugo replied drily before adding, "the lesson's over."

The couple stood up and exchanged hugs with Jude. Jessie decided she'd been polite long enough and hopped out of the cart.

"Do you want me to stick around?" Hugo asked.

"Thanks but I've got it from here," she told him. "I'll let you know if I need anything else."

He smiled, gave a little bow from his seat, and peeled out, tearing off back toward the Grand Hall. Jude Austen and the Andrews, who had been oblivious to her presence until now, all turned around, startled. Jessie smiled broadly and headed toward them. She had them on their heels and decided to use that.

"Hey folks," she said, "Hugo didn't mean to upset the mellow vibe. At least I don't think he did."

"Can I help you?" Jude asked, stepping forward. He apparently felt a duty to protect his students from the aggressive interloper.

"I don't think so, Jude," she said casually, as if they were old pals," but I'll let you know if that changes. I'm here to talk to Malcolm and Abigail."

"It's Abby," the wife corrected pleasantly. She was grinning. Malcolm was not.

"Sorry, Abby," Jessie noted, taking in the woman. Abby was a sunny ball of energy that seemed to vibrate with enthusiasm. Her wide smile could have powered a small appliance. Her red hair flowed wildly in the wind, crackling and popping like the flames of a campfire. Her green eyes were bright and shiny. She was petite and lean in her yoga wear, but had a sturdiness that suggested she ought not to be underestimated. Jessie, who guessed that they were about the same age, had to fight the urge to instantly like her.

"Who are you?" Malcolm Andrews asked sternly, yanking her out of his wife's fairy tale positivity bubble.

"Should I call you Mal?" she asked, trying to throw him off.

The man, already looking sullen in his black t-shirt and black sweatpants, with short black hair and dark, stormy eyes, fought to control his obvious desire to ream her out. Jessie was almost amused at his irritation.

"Oh, don't do that," Abby warned playfully. "He doesn't like it when people give him nicknames."

"Apologies—Mr. Andrews," Jessie said, choosing to ease up a little. "My name is Jessie Hunt. I'm a consultant with the Los Angeles Police Department, working on a case originating here at

Peninsula. I've been informed that you and your wife might be of some assistance to me."

"Has this been authorized by the resort?" Jude interjected. He looked put out that she was interfering with his time with the guests. She wondered if maybe she'd interrupted the moment when they would have slipped him a big tip.

"Didn't you just see Hugo drop me off, Jude?" she asked mildly, before allowing an edge to creep into her voice. "He's basically been my chauffeur all morning. But if you have concerns, please feel free to take them up with him. In the meantime, the Andrews and I are going to have a little chat. I'd appreciate it if you gave us a bit of space."

Jude obviously didn't want to but kept that to himself. Instead, he turned to the Andrews.

"It was wonderful working with both of you," he said, all charm now. "If time permits during the rest of your stay, I'd be happy conduct another lesson."

"Thanks so much, Jude," Abby gushed. "We'll see if we can make it work."

Jude nodded solemnly, slipped on his sandals, and loped off on his long, muscular legs. When he was out of hearing distance, Jessie turned back to the couple.

"Is it okay if we talk here?" she asked, though it was more of an instruction. "I don't want to take up too much of your time."

"Sure," Abby said before Malcolm could respond.

"Great," she said, diving in before he changed his mind. "Some of these questions may seem random and scattershot but please bear with me. What did you guys do this morning?"

Abby looked at her husband, whose cheeks turned pink. She began to giggle.

"What did I miss?" Jessie asked.

"Nothing," Abby assured her. "It's just that I'm not sure how specific you need us to be."

"I'm looking to get a sense of your movements from about 8 a.m. until 11 a.m.," she clarified.

"Well," Abby replied, her body twisting into a pretzel like she had a secret she was trying to physically hold in. "Our movements until about nine this morning were extremely active but confined to our casita bedroom, if you get my meaning."

"Jeez, Abby," Malcolm said, covering his eyes with his hand as his cheeks went from pink to crimson.

"What?" Abby countered. "She wants a tick-tock of our morning so I'm giving her one. Right, Jessie?"

"You don't have to get quite that specific, but it's helpful to know you were in your casita until nine. What about after that?"

"After that...," Abby tried to recall. "Oh yeah, I went to do some whale watching."

"Just you?"

"I stayed in the casita to do a little work," Malcolm explained, his face starting to return to its original color.

"For how long?' Jessie pressed.

"Up until Abby came to get me to go to the yoga class, so I think it was about nine to 10:45."

"And that whole time, you were whale watching?" Jessie asked Abby.

"Part of it, right down there actually," Abby said, suddenly marching towards the cliff's edge that Jessie had thought she'd fall over earlier.

Jessie tried not to overreact and casually strolled over to the spot next to her. Hugo had been right. The drop off wasn't as dramatic as it first appeared. Instead, after a short two-foot gap, the hillside gradually sloped downward for another fifteen feet before it got steeper and eventually did become a sharp vertical wall above the water below. Abby pointed to a large rock outcropping about a half-mile down the shore that extended out to where the waves were crashing.

"That's the spot where the concierge said I'd have the most luck," Abby said.

"Did you have any?"

"Nope," she admitted disappointedly. "I was out there for about forty-five minutes and never saw one whale."

"I'm sorry to hear that," Jessie said. "What did you do after that?"

"Just strolled along the beach until it was time to come back and get Malcolm,"

"Could you come back from the edge?" her husband called out from behind them. Apparently, he'd forgotten that it wasn't as risky as it appeared.

"Did you run into anyone?" Jessie asked her, ignoring Malcolm.

"I passed a few people on the beach," Abby said. "No one I knew."

Jessie was having trouble pinning these two down. Abby Andrews was such a bundle of enthusiasm that discerning moments of deception amid her live-wire energy was proving difficult. The same was true of Malcolm. His dark sullenness, which could easily be misinterpreted as a sign of ill intent, seemed to be his default emotional position. So divining what was really going on in his head was a challenge.

"Please, Abby," Malcolm called out, this time with more intensity, "come away from the side."

"We better go back," his wife said quietly as her fiery hair whipped crazily in the wind. "He tends to get upset if he thinks I'm in danger. It's cute."

They returned to the spot where the yoga lesson had taken place earlier. Jessie could tell Malcolm was losing patience and was about to ask some questions of his own. She beat him to the punch.

"What do you two do for a living?" she asked, knowing that would almost certainly get him to open up. With guys like him, it nearly always did.

"I work in tech," he said blandly.

"That's an understatement. Don't be modest, sweetie," Abby chided before turning to Jessie. "Malcolm developed elements of the security technology used by thousands of retail apps."

"Oh wow," Jessie said, pretending to be impressed. "Would I have heard of it?"

"No," Malcolm said quickly. "It's back-end stuff."

"I'll bet you do pretty well," Jessie suggested.

"Well enough that I get to teach sixth grade math out of pleasure rather than necessity," Abby confirmed before adding in a faux whisper, "He's worth about half a billion."

"Abby," Malcolm groaned, again, turning a light shade of red. "Don't go revealing that. Someone's going to kidnap you and I'll have to pay a ransom."

"Not her—she's a cop," Abby said, before pretending to be offended, "And what are you saying—that you wouldn't pay it?"

Jessie almost chuckled. If Abby was a gold-digger, she was the most disarming one of all time. Still, the interview was starting to go off the rails and, since Abby had given her an opening to get it back on track, Jessie took it.

"I'm actually not a cop," she said seriously. "I'm a criminal profiler who consults for the department and like I mentioned earlier, I'm working a case."

"I've been waiting for you to get to that part," Malcolm said, happy to switch subjects as well. "Why do you need to know our jobs or our schedules for the day? Are we being investigated for something?"

"Not you personally," Jessie lied. "But your whereabouts may help us as we try to resolve our probe."

"What probe exactly?" Malcolm pressed. He was as relentless as his wife was chipper.

Now that she'd gotten their alibis, which both had gaps big enough to fit in a quick murder, there was no reason not to be forthright.

"I have some sad news to share with you," she told them. "My partner, who is currently talking to Matthew and Eleanor Darcy, and I are looking into the death of your friend Scott Newhouse. He passed away earlier this morning."

Both Andrews stood silently for a second before Malcolm said, almost too quietly to be heard.

"He was murdered, wasn't he?"

"Why do you say that?" Jessie asked.

For a second, he looked reluctant to reply. But then he seemed to decide he needed to.

"You wouldn't have started our conversation by getting our alibis if it was a heart attack or suicide or something like that," he replied.

Next to him, Abby, who had yet to speak, started to cry. He saw it and wrapped her in his arms.

"We're just covering all our bases," Jessie explained truthfully. "What makes you suggest suicide, Malcolm?"

"I'm not suggesting it," he said defiantly. "I just know he had some issues with depression. But I don't think they were bad enough that he would do that."

"You never know," Abby said quietly, fighting through hiccupping sobs, "I see it with kids all the time. Lots of them keep everything bottled up so tight that people, even their loved ones, don't realize how much pain they're in. By the time they do, it's too late."

"Abby," Jessie asked. "Do you think Scott might have taken his own life?"

The woman, so effervescent only moments earlier, buried her head in her husband's chest. When she answered, her voice was muffled.

"I'd just be guessing," she said. "He did get down sometimes but who doesn't? I don't want to make any assumptions. How did you find him?"

It wasn't an unreasonable question to ask under the circumstances but nonetheless, it made Jessie's antennae go up slightly. Was Abby just trying to help find answers? Was this morbid curiosity? Or was there some other reason she was asking?

"I can't really get into that at this point," she replied. "What I *can* do is make the most of what you two have to offer, which is information. Did either of you see Scott or Bridget this morning?"

Both Andrews shook their heads. There was no way to ask the next question without arousing suspicion, but she didn't have a choice.

"Would you describe them as having a happy marriage?"

"Of course," Abby said quickly, coming as close to angry as Jessie had seen her. "How can you ask that?"

"I *have* to ask that," Jessie told her. "And if you really want to help me get to the bottom of this, I need you to be honest. In situations like this, the spouse is always a suspect. I'm trying to help clear Bridget of that cloud of suspicion, but I need real answers, not Pollyanna ones."

"They were happy," Malcolm said evenly. "The worst thing I could say about them is that they may have gotten into a bit of a rut."

"What do you mean?" Jessie asked.

"Listen," he explained, "I met Scott because he invested in my company four years ago. By the time we became friends, he was already married and a father to three kids. Abby and I are a decade younger than him so we're in a different place. We don't have those kinds of responsibilities yet. But it just seemed that with the harried nature of family life and how driven he was with his work, sometimes they didn't always make time for each other. I know that was part of why they came to Peninsula in the first place—to make that time. They decided to leave the kids with the nanny and commit to a long weekend where they could really focus on reconnecting. But is that really suspicious? Haven't I just described fifty percent of marriages?"

Jessie didn't know. Her first marriage ended in attempted murder so she never had the chance to get into a rut. And the way things were going, her second one might take another few years to finally happen. She kept those thoughts to herself.

"So there's nothing unusual that you recall between them in the last few days or weeks?"

Both shook their heads.

"Okay," she concluded. "Thanks, that's all for now. But please don't leave the resort. My partner and I will likely have additional questions for you as the day progresses."

"Ms. Hunt," Malcolm said as he pulled a tissue out of his pocket and handed it to Abby, who had started to tear up again, "we're not going anywhere, other than to find our friend and see what we can do to help her."

With that, they turned and headed off in the direction of Bridget Newhouse's casita. As Jessie watched them leave, she swallowed her frustration. She didn't want them to look back and see how dejected she felt.

While the Andrews were helpful on the surface, they didn't leave her with much tangible material to work with. Other than reinforcing the possibility of suicide, they offered bland platitudes about the Newhouses. Just as bad, they'd provided alibis that would be hard to verify. Maybe Malcolm had some calls or sent some e-mails that could confirm he was at their casita but that was no guarantee. And solo whale watching and beach walking was the least provable alibi she'd heard in a long time.

She hoped that Ryan was having better luck.

CHAPTER NINE

Hannah had been expecting Nurse Ratched.

When she had "voluntarily" checked herself into the Seasons Wellness Center in Malibu two weeks ago, she'd half expected it to be a *One Flew Over the Cuckoo's Nest* situation. But to her relief (and if she was totally honest, to her slight disappointment) it was nothing like that.

Nestled into a hillside overlooking the Pacific, the place felt more like an artist colony than a psychiatric facility. If she hadn't known better, she'd have thought she'd been transported to an ocean-adjacent Santa Fe. The buildings were modern but made to look like they were from over a century ago. There were cobblestone paths and flower gardens everywhere.

The staff, medical and otherwise, was friendly and accommodating. She didn't think she'd heard a single raised voice, at least not from an employee, in her entire time here so far. Even in the "Assistance Wing," where she's stayed until today, it was mostly smiles most of the time.

Of course, she knew that things could change quickly if they had to. The Assistance Wing was described as a unit for patients who needed "a little extra observation." But that was a euphemism. It was essentially the secure wing. The security staffers there had nightsticks and tasers, though she'd never seen one used. And while not every room in the wing locked from the outside, some of the bedrooms did. The Assistance Wing was where people stayed until they were no longer deemed a potential threat to themselves or others.

Apparently, after two weeks of close observation, Hannah had passed the test. Because, in the wing that she'd just been transferred to, called Serenity Hall, there were no locks. The patients here didn't have to wear center-issued, hospital-style gowns. Instead they could wear their own clothes. There were still security officers but, other than zip ties, they didn't carry anything out of the ordinary.

The staffer leading her through the hall, a middle aged-woman with gray hair tied in a bun, stopped suddenly and opened the door to her new bedroom. It was much less antiseptic than her previous one. There were no bars on the windows and it didn't look like her bed or other furniture was bolted to the floor. There were even a few framed paintings on the walls.

"Welcome to Serenity Hall," the woman said in a pleasant but unenthusiastic tone. "The daily schedule is posted on the back of your door. You have a group therapy session at 2 p.m. Lunch starts in five minutes down the hallway to the left. If you have any questions, the help center is in the same direction. Is there anything else you need?"

"No thanks," she said and the woman left without another word.

Hannah *did* have questions but none that she wanted to ask the staff. She walked into the room and glanced at her image in the mirror on the dresser. Without the necessity to dress properly for high school, she'd gotten very casual in the last two weeks.

Her blonde hair wasn't styled but instead hung down limply at her shoulders. She had on sweatpants and a thin hoodie, and wore no makeup. Because of her more relaxed schedule these days, she'd gotten lots of sleep. As a result, her green eyes—the same shade as Jessie's—were clear and bright.

Though she was almost as tall as her sister, she doubted they'd be mistaken for twins right now. Without any of the usual stylistic adornments, she no longer looked like a twenty-something but her actual age: seventeen. Her birthday was in less than a month. She wondered if she'd be celebrating it here.

She dropped her duffel bag by the bed and sat down in the wooden chair at the small desk against the wall. The center had made a credible attempt to make the place feel homey, but in the end it was still a hospital.

She recalled when Jessie had first brought her here. They hadn't talked much on the drive up, mostly because she wouldn't answer any of her half-sister's questions. Even though she'd agreed to come to this place in order get a handle on her semi-homicidal tendencies, she couldn't help but resent Jessie for supporting the idea.

That residue of bitterness lingered, both when Jessie had said goodbye that first time, and on every subsequent visit. Even before her primary therapist told her so, she knew none of this was Jessie's fault. Jessie didn't kill her birth mother or her adoptive parents. Nor did Jessie kidnap and try to brainwash her. In fact, Jessie had taken her in when she was about to be tossed in the foster care system.

But that didn't stop Hannah from holding on to the anger. She'd made all kinds of progress in one-on-one and group therapy, but remained sullen and monosyllabic every time her sister came for "pairs" therapy sessions. There was something about watching her sister leave each visit looking wounded and guilty that gave Hannah great satisfaction, even if she felt bad about it afterward.

Her thoughts were interrupted by a loud rap on her door. She looked up to see a girl in her early twenties standing in the doorway. She had shortish black hair tied into pigtails with rainbow scrunchies. She wore a long-sleeved, tie-dyed shirt and baggy jeans. Extremely pale, with light blue eyes, she could have been mistaken for a boldly-dressed, adorable ghost.

"How ya' doin', newbie?" she asked warmly.

"Um, okay," Hannah replied, not sure what to make of this person.

"Well don't get used to it," the girl said grimly. "Your official hazing starts in two minutes out back. The Newbie Committee has pillowcases filled with potatoes and we'll be beating you with them until you pass out. But if you don't cry or rat us out, you're golden for the rest of your stay."

"What?" Hannah asked, open-mouthed.

The girl broke into a wide smile.

"I'm just screwing with you," she said. "That *was* the whole 'hazing' thing right there. I'm actually the entirety of the Newbie Committee, which is really more of a welcoming committee. Welcome. I'm Meredith Bartlett, but you can call me Merry."

"Hi Meredith," Hannah said carefully. "I'm Hannah Dorsey and I'm confused."

"Because of what I said about hazing and committees or because you're loony tunes?" Meredith wanted to know.

"Right now—the first thing."

"I just get bored easily," she replied sheepishly. "I thought messing with you might add a little entertainment to my day. I didn't mean to freak you out…too much."

"Okay," Hannah replied, not sure what to make of this Pippi Longstocking, hippie ghost girl. "Is there something I can do for you, Meredith?"

"Remember, it's Merry. And actually, it's what I can do for you that has me here."

"What's that?" Hannah asked.

"I know you came from the lockdown—er, 'assistance' wing, where they bring your meals to your room. But over here in Serenity Hall, they trust us to eat our meals together in a cafeteria setting. And considering lunch is about to start, I wanted give you a little piece of cafeteria advice. Always go for the kosher meal."

"Why?"

Merry smiled. Hannah knew it was because she'd managed to pique her interest.

"Because even though this place charges thousands of dollars a week, very little of that cash goes into food quality, as I'm sure you've noticed."

"I have," Hannah acknowledged. Her tray typically consisted of some kind of mushy meat, next to soggy vegetables, burned tater tots, and a dry piece of cake. If someone wasn't already depressed, it was enough to make them so. She hadn't cared much as her appetite had been weak lately. But it was surprising that such a posh place had such substandard food.

"They just don't seem to prioritize it for whatever reason," Merry said. "But with the kosher meals, since they're for fewer people with more specific needs, the kitchen staff is a little more creative and the selections seem a bit fresher. We're not talking restaurant quality, more like good hospital quality."

"Thanks for the tip," Hannah said. "As long as you're dispensing knowledge, can I ask you a question?"

"Of course," Merry said. "I pride myself on being the Siri of the psycho set."

"Okay," Hannah replied, uncertain that her new acquaintance was the model spokeswoman for ending the stigma around mental health issues. "Is the visitor policy here the same as in the Assistance Wing?"

"I'm not sure," Merry admitted. "What was it over there?"

"A maximum of two visits a week total from no more than two different people," Hannah told her.

"There's nothing that restrictive over here," Merry assured her.

"Can I refuse a visit?" Hannah asked. "Over there, patients are required to attend."

"I don't know," Merry said. "But why would you do that? If it were me, I wouldn't refuse a visit from anyone. No one in my family has come to see me once since I've been here."

"Sometimes that can be a good thing," Hannah countered.

"I guess," Merry shrugged, unconvinced. "But it seems like if someone is making the effort to trek all the way out here a few times a week, it wouldn't hurt to give them a little time. Of course that's just me. I don't want to judge. Maybe your visitor abused you as a little girl or something."

While abuse wasn't a concern, Hannah didn't want to get into the particulars of her dynamic with her sister and awkwardly changed subjects.

"Why hasn't your family been out here to see you?" she asked.

Merry sighed heavily.

"There are lots of reasons. But the main one is that I think they view me kind of like a broken toy. They're hoping that they can ship me off to the repair shop and get me back fixed. They're not the warmest, fuzziest folks you'll ever meet."

"How are you broken?" Hannah asked, both afraid and excited to hear the answer.

Merry stared at her and for a brief moment, it looked like her ghostly visage might actually disappear entirely. Then, without warning, she pulled up her left sleeve to the elbow. The inside of her forearm was covered in cuts and scars all the way up from her wrist.

"I have an unusual way of dealing with stress," she said softly.

Hannah knew about girls at her school that cut themselves. But she'd never seen the results of it live and in person. She did her best not to overreact, keeping her eyes from bulging and her breath steady.

"You must have a lot of stress," she finally said.

"One of my therapists says stress is what you make of it," Merry replied. "I guess I make a lot of it."

"It doesn't look like any of them are fresh," Hannah noted, "So maybe you're learning to manage it."

Merry shook her head.

"Why do you think I only showed you my left arm?" she asked. "There's a reason I don't have a glass mirror in my bedroom."

"Touché," Hannah muttered, unsure what else to say.

Merry looked like she was about to reveal something else, but then seemed to think better of it and went with a question of her own.

"What are you in here for?"

Though Hannah knew the question was inevitable, she dreaded it, primarily because this girl had been so forthright with her and she couldn't do the same.

"Anger management and self-harm issues," she said blandly, using the agreed-upon diagnosis she and Dr. Lemmon had chosen prior to her arrival. Intense homicidal fantasies about murdering people just to feel something didn't seem like an answer that would go over well.

Merry looked like she was about to pursue the matter when a loud, pleasant ringing sound, like a distant church bell, echoed over the speakers in the room.

"What's that?" she asked.

"Lunchtime," Merry said.

Hannah shot up and started out of the room.

"Why don't you show the newbie the way?" she asked.

Merry obliged, joining her in the hallway and forgetting about her question from a moment earlier. Hannah had been literally saved by the bell, at least for now

.

CHAPTER TEN

Jessie couldn't hide her disappointment.

She met Ryan by the mini-croquet court, which was currently unoccupied. After she told him about her mostly unproductive interview with Malcolm and Abby Andrews, he filled her in on his chat with Matt and Ellie Darcy. He'd come up empty too. Apparently all four of them seemed to think suicide was possible. And all of them remained credible suspects without strong alibis. None of them could absolve Bridget Newhouse either, although at least her whereabouts at the time her husband died—in a massage room at the spa—were verifiable.

"There wasn't anything suspicious about the Darcys?" she pressed.

"Sure. But nothing that had me pulling out my handcuffs," he said. "The biggest thing was that there seemed to be some unspoken tension between them, both before and after I told them about Scott Newhouse's death. They were dealing with something major. Whether that was secret knowledge about a murder or just residual resentment after an uncomfortable 'session' with Dr. Honey Potter, I have no idea."

"Is she really a doctor?" Jessie couldn't stop herself from asking.

"I was being sarcastic. To be honest, I didn't ask," he said. "Maybe you can follow up on her credentials if you run into her. What about you? No strong vibes from the Andrews?"

"Nothing definitive," she replied. "They're pretty extreme opposites. He's incredibly dour and she's a firecracker of fun. I can't help but wonder if part of her livewire energy is an act."

"You think she's secretly some Machiavellian gold-digger?"

"I don't know what to think," Jessie admitted. "The problem is that even if she is, I'm not sure that helps with the case we're trying to solve. To be honest, I still think that Bridget Newhouse is the clubhouse favorite until proven otherwise. I just don't have anything firm to base that on."

"I was going to check in with Hugo from security," Ryan said before adding, "But if you feel that strongly, maybe you should see if you can find anything firm to tie her to this."

Jessie nodded in agreement.

"That's not a bad idea. I think I'll go back to the spa and try to verify or disprove her alibi."

"While you do that, I'll see if Hugo sent that spa camera footage to Jamil by now," he said. "I'll also see if I can find any other video recordings that corroborate the other guests' statements. I know he said they intentionally avoid having cameras everywhere but maybe we'll get lucky. And maybe the medical examiner will have something for us as well. You know we're going to get a call from Chief Laird at some point soon. I want to be ready."

"Sounds good," Jessie said. "Shall we check back in a half-hour from now?"

"Sure," he answered. "And all this spa talk has me thinking—how about if one of us solves this case in that time window, the other one owes them a bedtime neck massage?"

Jessie smiled at that idea.

"Not fair," she teased. "You barely have to expend any effort if you lose. You can use one hand to get in some quality rubbing. For me, it's a whole production. Your neck's like a tree trunk."

"I don't know whether that's a compliment or not," he replied.

"Good."

*

The spa was empty.

All treatments had been postponed for the day so Jessie was able to look around without distractions. The spa manager assigned Kree, the same attendant that Tony Dante mentioned running into while re-stocking towels, to guide her around. Other than the sheriff's deputies, the two of them were the only ones left in the building.

Kree, small and quiet, with auburn skin and a shy smile, looked like she was afraid she was about to be arrested.

"Don't worry," Jessie said, trying to calm her down, "I just need you to show me a few different places."

"Okay," Kree said, "Where exactly?"

"I want to look in the women's locker room and lounge area, then massage room six, and finally the women's quiet room."

Kree nodded and led her down the darkened hallway to the oak doors leading to the women's lounge and locker room.

"Should I guide you?" Kree asked, "Or would you rather look around yourself?"

"If you turn on the lights, I think I'm good on my own," Jessie told her. "You can just wait outside. I'll let you know if I need anything."

Even with the lights on, the lounge, which mirrored the men's almost exactly, was creepily silent. Jessie walked around with her cell phone out, ready to take photos of anything that seemed unusual. But that was difficult, as she didn't really know what she was looking for.

She hadn't expected to see blood on a towel or a rag doused in chloroform—which doesn't actually work anyway— lying in a trash can. But there was nothing at all. It appeared that, despite instructions to leave everything untouched, the lounge had been cleaned. Either that or it was always this pristine.

After a fruitless five minutes, she left. Kree was standing outside, scrolling absently through her phone.

"Was the lounge cleaned after the police arrived?" she asked.

"No ma'am," Kree told her. "But it's kept tidy all the time, so it's not like there would have been anything lying around. The managers get touchy if a towel is lying on the floor for more than a minute or two."

Jessie nodded, unsurprised.

"Why don't you take me to massage room six?"

They rounded the corner and Kree pointed to a door in the middle of the next hallway.

"It's been locked since Mrs. Newhouse left, just as we were told to keep it," she said. "But I have the key. Should I open it?"

"Please," Jessie replied.

Kree unlocked the door and turned on the light. Jessie stood at the entrance and took it in. It was clear that the session had ended in a hurry. The blankets and sheets were messy and someone had forgotten to turn off the steamer for the heated washcloths. But none of that was unexpected under the circumstances.

"Where's the quiet room?" Jessie asked.

Kree led her down a third hallway to a room with a sign that read simply, "Quiet Please." She pushed the door open and saw that it was just as Bridget Newhouse had described. In the dim light of the room, she could see three easy chairs lined up against the wall. Black curtains, all currently open, could be pulled around each chair to offer some privacy. The chairs all had small tables beside them with steamers holding more heated washcloths, along with pairs of noise-canceling headphones.

Jessie walked to the last chair, where Newhouse had spent her time. She didn't know what she expected to find—maybe a pair of latex gloves in the tiny trash can by the chair—but nothing leapt out at her. The leaves of a large Ficus plant in the corner swayed slightly from the breeze coming from the air conditioner. A wall covering behind it, intended to further soothe guests, showed an ocean sunset. To her frustration, there was nothing that indicated that the quiet room was anything more than its title suggested. She turned back to Kree, who was standing in the doorway, looking perplexed.

"I think we're done here," Jessie told her.

"Did Mrs. Newhouse do something wrong?" the attendant asked.

"Not based on anything I see here," Jessie answered, unable to keep the disappointment out of her voice.

Kree led her back to the main entrance of the spa and unlocked the door for her. Just as she was stepping outside, an understatedly attractive brown-haired woman with glasses, wearing a cream blouse and a gorgeous, cherry pencil skirt walked up. She had a small, leather backpack flung over one shoulder.

"Hi Kree," the woman said amiably. "I'm here for my pedicure."

"Hello, Ms. Potter," Kree said diffidently. "I'm sorry but the spa is temporarily closed."

Jessie realized who was in front of her but did her best to pretend like she didn't recognize the name. Honey Potter was not at all what she was expecting.

"The whole spa?" Potter asked incredulously, "Why?"

"I'm afraid I'm not at liberty to say," Kree replied, doing her best to be professionally vague.

"But someone else clearly got to partake of...," Potter started to say, nodding in Jessie's direction, before her words faded off. She tilted her head as she looked closely at Jessie for the first time. "Oh, I see now—this has to do with the other thing."

"I'm sorry?" Kree said, baffled.

Jessie remained silent, watching as the other woman put the pieces together.

"Don't worry about it, sweetie," Potter said affectionately. "I won't try to force my way in. I'd much rather join Ms. Hunt wherever she's going."

Jessie was impressed. She knew that her exploits had made her something of a minor celebrity around town, but this might be the fastest that anyone had recognized her, and she hadn't even spoke a word yet.

"You have me at a disadvantage," she lied, extending her hand.

"Sorry. My name's Honey Potter. Call me Honey. I'm Peninsula's official romance coach. I ran into your partner in all things a little while ago when he was speaking to some of my clients, so I figured I might bump into you at some point. How are things going?"

Jessie debated whether to engage. She wasn't going to share anything of consequence but if she offered a crumb or two, maybe Honey would reveal whether the Darcys' session had been contentious, which might explain the coldness between them that Ryan described observing. She turned to Kree.

"Thanks so much for all your help," she said. "I think I'm good for now.

The girl seemed relieved to be done and, after offering a quick, tight smile, scurried off. Jessie returned her attention to Honey.

"I obviously can't get into specifics," she said as she started up the hill toward the Grand Hall, "but I can say that it's slow going."

"So no more progress since I spoke to Detective Hernandez earlier?" Honey asked, keeping pace with her.

"Well, we haven't solved the case yet," Jessie conceded.

"What exactly is the case?" Honey wondered. "I'm sure I'd already know if I hadn't been buried in my office for the last half hour."

Jessie knew the woman was right. Word had to have gotten around by now. If Honey started asking folks on campus, she'd probably have the basic facts, along with some wild speculation, in less than five minutes. For that reason, Jessie chose to throw her a bone.

"A guest died in the spa—in the men's lounge area, to be specific. We're trying to determine the cause of death."

Honey gave her a sly smile.

"Well, considering that you and Detective Hernandez work for a unit called Homicide Special Section, I'm assuming the guy didn't slip and fall."

"He didn't fall," Jessie conceded, "but that doesn't mean this was foul play. We've just been asked to be thorough, considering the high profile nature of the decedent."

"Okay," Honey replied, admirably not asking for a name. "So what did my clients have to do with it?"

"They're friends of the man who died," Jessie said, sensing an opening. "Detective Hernandez interviewed them to get more insight into him. But as long as we're discussing your clients, I was hoping that you could clear something up for me."

"What's that?"

"My partner said that he noticed a bit of a chill between them," Jessie told her. "Was that a result of their session with you?"

Now it was Honey's turn to play coy.

"Ms. Hunt," she said, with a grin, "while I'm not technically a medical professional and have no formal privilege, I do generally try to maintain some level of privacy for my clients. Otherwise I wouldn't have any left."

"I respect that," Jessie replied. "But anything you can offer that might help us get a fuller picture of the people who knew the decedent would be helpful."

They had reached the top of the hill where the resort staff was busily prepping the expansive lawn for the upcoming sunset wedding. Honey Potter was panting slightly. Jessie was not, which she attributed to her daily runs.

"In that case," Honey said, trying to catch her breath, "I can offer you this: the Darcys were focused on finding non-traditional ways to please each other."

"That's quite a euphemism," Jessie said, stopping in her tracks and fixing Honey with a serious stare. "What does that mean exactly? Are we talking S&M?"

Honey laughed out loud.

"Ms. Hunt, I know my reputation precedes me," she replied drily, "but just because my previous career involved some…unconventional practices, that doesn't mean I try to get my clients to employ them. Sorry if that's a disappointment."

"What then?" Jessie wondered, refusing to be distracted by Honey's teasing.

"I assure you our session didn't address anything that intense," the woman informed her. "But I think it's fair to say that some couples, perhaps including the Darcys, intermittently find that traditional lovemaking can get a bit old after a while. So we try to workshop alternatives they might be comfortable with. There are stages of experimentation. Suffice to say, the Darcys have a long way to go. But I can assure you of one thing: when our session was over, they were more connected to each other, not less. Any 'chill' that Detective Hernandez picked up on was not a result of our time together."

Jessie didn't let on, but that was actually good news. If the couple wasn't distant because of their appointment with Honey, then whatever their issue was preceded their time with her. Admittedly, it could be something as innocuous as a thoughtless comment. Or their coldness could be due something more significant, maybe some larger shared secret they were hiding. It wasn't much to go on, but it was more than she had two minutes ago.

"Thank you," she said, as they stopped at the back patio of the Grand Hall. "I appreciate your help."

"Of course," Honey said. "Now that my pedicure is off, I was going to get a bite to eat. Care to join me?"

"I'm afraid I can't; I've still got this whole investigation thing to deal with."

"Understood," Honey told her, "but I have an offer for you."

"Okay," Jessie replied nervously, sensing that it might be an unusual one.

"When I spoke with Detective Hernandez earlier, I couldn't help but admire what a tasty treat he is—all rugged, roguish intensity. And you're a long-legged, tall drink of sparkling water yourself. I'd be happy to offer you two a reduced rate for a session. Hell, I might even make it free if you wanted to make it fully participatory."

"Oh, wow," Jessie said, feeling her cheeks start to burn. "Thanks. That's very flattering. I think we're doing pretty well in that area but I'll get back to you if anything changes."

"Sure," Honey replied, handing her a business card but not pushing beyond that. "My door is always open."

"Good to know," Jessie said, well aware that her beet red face was costing her any of the professional deference Honey had given her up to that point. "Well, I should probably get back to it."

"Nice to meet you, Ms. Hunt," she said as she started to walk away. But then she turned around unexpectedly and her voice suddenly softened and became less playful, "and since I didn't say this earlier, thank you. The work you've done to save people and catch killers—it doesn't go unnoticed. Don't think I'm unaware of the justice you got for Michaela Penn. Girls in her business—in my old business—are usually just tossed away. You gave her back a little dignity."

She turned and walked off without waiting for an answer. It was the most overt nod she'd made to her porn past and she'd chosen to note it when referencing the killing of an underage porn actress whose murder had garnered little interest until Jessie and Ryan took it on. Coincidentally, it was the same case that almost led to Chief Laird firing them. Notably, Honey used the girl's real name and not her porn one, Missy Mack.

Jessie watched her go, walking straight ahead, not daring to turn around after making herself so vulnerable. As she disappeared around the corner, Jessie took a moment to bask in the knowledge that there were many people she'd never meet who were glad for the work she was doing. It gave her a renewed sense of energy. She needed to do the same thing for Scott Newhouse, wherever the truth led her.

As she stared at the empty space that Honey had previously filled, she was shocked by the sight of a new, unexpected figure. For a moment she thought it was a human mirage. But no, she was real.

CHAPTER ELEVEN

Walking toward Jessie with a huge grin on her face was none other than her best friend, Kat Gentry.

"What the—?" she began before Kat interrupted her.

"Are you tailing me?" she demanded jokingly, "because if you are, you're terrible at it."

If not for the snarky remark, Jessie might not have believed it was Kat. Her friend still had the well-toned body of a former Army Ranger, which she'd been for a decade, as well as the long vertical scar under her left eye, a result of an IED explosion.

But otherwise she was transformed. Instead of her standard attire—blue jeans with a bland shirt and a brown leather jacket, she was wearing a long, sky-blue dress under an unbuttoned yellow sweater. Her dirty blonde hair, almost always tied back in a workmanlike ponytail, was loose, with the styled tresses licking at her shoulders when she moved. A woman who rarely wore jewelry, she was currently decked out in earrings, a necklace, and a bracelet. She even wore heels, something Jessie had never seen her in. Admittedly, they were only two inches high, but still.

"Who are you and what did you do to Katherine Gentry?" Jessie demanded.

"It's me," Kat whispered jokingly as she pulled her in for a hug. "Want me to burp to prove it?"

"That's okay," Jessie said, pretending to push her away. "I know we haven't seen each other in a few weeks, but I'm good without the Gentry belch."

"What are you doing here?" Kat asked. "Is this where you've decided to have the wedding? Because I thought you were looking to keep it small."

"That is definitely *not* why I'm here," Jessie assured her. "Ryan and I are on a case."

"Oh, is it the Newhouse death that everyone is talking about?" Kat asked. "I didn't realize that was a murder."

"We're not sure that it is," Jessie said. "We haven't ruled out suicide. But apparently Chief Laird was tight with the guy so he asked us to check it out."

"If it *is* murder, do you have any good suspects?"

"At least five and we've only been here a couple of hours," Jessie said, happy to reveal the truth to one of the few people she knew wouldn't spill any details. "But enough about me—what are you doing here dressed like you're pledging this resort? You're on a case too, aren't you?"

Kat, who was a private investigator, pretended to be offended.

"How do you know I'm not just here for a weekend getaway?"

"First of all, I don't see Mitch around," Jessie noted, referencing Kat's long-distance Sheriff's deputy boyfriend. "And secondly, I have eyes. If you were really here to kick back and relax, that's not how you'd dress. You be in sweats and sneakers, with a baseball cap on. And there's no way you'd be wearing jewelry and heels. Plus you can't afford this place. You're on a job, undercover, I'm guessing."

"That's why they pay you the big bucks, Hunt," Kat sighed, before quietly admitting. "I'm working a case for the resort. There have been a lot of thefts in the last month and management thinks it might be a member of the staff."

"So why didn't you have them 'hire' you as a new employee?" Jessie wondered.

"See, that's why you're the profiler and I'm the private eye," Kat teased. "If I come in as a staffer, it'd take forever to ingratiate myself and gain trust with the others. Plus, I'd be expected to do real work that would interfere with my ability to investigate. I'd probably have guests demanding stuff from me all the time. This way, my only job is to go where I want and do what I want. It's a free pass to watch what's going on. And with all the shiny crap I'm wearing, maybe I'll catch the thief's eye. Even if I don't catch the person red-handed, I've tagged all the jewelry, so I can track it."

"That's not bad, Kat," Jessie said admiringly. "I just have one question: where did you get all those baubles? I know you didn't bring them from home."

"The resort loaned them to me from their jewelry store. This joint has everything," she marveled. Suddenly her eyes widened. Clearly she had an idea. "Hey, do you think it's possible that we're looking for the same person? If your guy was killed, maybe my thief did it. Could Newhouse have caught the culprit in the act and paid the price for it?"

"That's interesting," Jessie mused. "I guess it's possible that Newhouse discovered the thief, who then had to shut him up. But it might have been hard to do logistically."

"Why?"

"Because Scott Newhouse's body was found naked in the men's steam room, with some kind of ribbon tied around his neck."

"That's why you think he might have killed himself?" Kat asked.

"That and because he supposedly had a history of depression," Jessie revealed. "But I have my doubts. We're waiting to hear from the medical examiner, but the angle he was found at makes it hard to imagine he could have hung himself. I don't think the ribbon he used was tied high enough."

"But wouldn't that support the theory that the thief was the killer?" Kat countered. "If Newhouse walked in on the thief stealing stuff from the locker room, maybe he killed him, stripped him, and then dragged him into the steam room, where he tied up his neck to make it look like suicide. But if the killer was in a hurry, it might be done sloppily, which would explain why the angle isn't right."

Jessie thought about it.

"It's not impossible," she allowed. "We'll know a lot more when we find out if he really died from strangulation or if that was a cover. But I'm not sure about your theory. The men's lounge attendant was in and out of the area all morning. It's hard to imagine that all that could have been done in one of the brief stretches where he wasn't around."

"Could he be your guy?"

"We haven't officially eliminated him as a suspect," Jessie said. "But he has witness alibis for the likely time of death. And while this isn't very scientific, I just didn't get the killer vibe from him."

"You're staking his innocence on a vibe?"

"God, no," Jessie swore. "I like to think I have pretty good instincts but they've been wrong before. That's why Ryan and I will have Jamil and Beth do a background check on him."

"As long as you're at it, maybe you could have them run checks on all Peninsula staff to see if any of them have a criminal record," Kat suggested with a sheepish smile. "I'd do it myself, but as I don't have the same resources as LAPD, it'd probably take a week."

Kat had helped her too many times not to return the favor.

"I'll see what I can do," she offered.

"Thanks," Kat said. "I better get going for now. It might look weird if a fancy person like myself was seen spending too much time with a worker bee like you."

"You do I know I'm worth millions, right?" Jessie pointed out.

"I do. But these folks don't and that's all that matters," she said, grinning, before loudly and dramatically adding, "Now stop bothering me, you law enforcement serf!"

Then, with a flourish, she whipped her hair and turned away, storming off across the lawn to points unknown. Jessie tried not to laugh as she watched her go. After all, it wouldn't look good for her to be enjoying herself too much while investigating a possible murder, which she had to get back to.

*

Jessie considered it quite a comedown.

While resort guests were less than fifty feet away, gorging on a lunch buffet that included crab legs, tri-tip, and strawberry cheesecake, she and Ryan were holed up on the other side of the wall, in an empty office, eating grilled cheese sandwiches, as they reviewed resort staff files over the office speakerphone with Jamil and Beth.

"Remind me again," Jamil said. "Do we really think that Kat Gentry's thief is our steam room killer?"

"It's a long shot," Jessie conceded. "But as long as we're reviewing all the staff to see if they have a record of violence, it can't hurt to determine if they have any history of theft."

"So basically it's a favor," Jamil said bluntly.

"Yes, Jamil," Jessie replied slowly and deliberately. "It's a favor. Is that okay with you?"

"Of course," Jamil said quickly. "I love Kat. I just wanted to make sure I understood the situation."

"The situation," Ryan piped in, "is that this resort employs over six hundred people. And until we get news from the M.E. or a break on our guest suspects, this is the best use of our time. Speaking of, were you guys able to glean anything from the camera footage Hugo sent you?"

"Nothing super useful," Beth volunteered. "The spa cameras show all the other male guests at the spa leaving when their signouts claim they did. None of them were around during the time of death."

"But that doesn't preclude someone sneaking in without signing in," Jessie noted. "Is there any footage of people entering or exiting the spa with their head or faces covered?"

"Yes, lots," Beth said. "A bunch of people arrived in their Peninsula-issued, blue, hooded, robes. And since it was brisk this morning, many of them had the hoods up, so it's impossible to tell them apart. And because there are no interior cameras at the spa, there's no way to tell where they went once they got inside."

"What about other cameras around the campus?" Ryan prompted. "Anything to confirm that Abby Andrews was whale watching, Ellie Darcy was at the tide pools, or either Matt Darcy or Malcolm Andrews were in their casitas?"

"Nothing definitive," Jamil told them. "Like that security guy told you, there's not a ton of footage to work with. There aren't any cameras near where the ladies were allegedly doing their activities and the cameras near the casitas don't show the entrances to either couple's. I do have a record of Malcolm Andrews briefly on a business call originating from his casita, but it ended well before the window of death, so that's not dispositive."

"What about cell phone geo-location?" Jessie asked.

"Spotty at best," Beth explained. "Because you're so isolated down there, and you're right near the cliffs and ocean, the signal doesn't get super specific. It shows all of them at the resort but doesn't get granular about where they are on the campus."

"This just keeps getting better and better," Ryan grumbled as he took a bite of his sandwich.

"I do have some news for you," Jamil said, "though I don't know whether it's good or bad."

"What's that?" Ryan asked.

"The spa attendant that found the body, Tony Dante, comes back clean. He has no record, not even a traffic ticket. And as far as being the thief, that looks unlikely. He's been at Peninsula for eight months and the thefts only started up in the last five weeks."

"Good to know," Jessie said, "though not that surprising."

"Should we limit the search to just folks hired in the last couple of months?" Jamil asked.

"No," Jessie instructed. "That might be useful for Kat's investigation. But for us, it would leave off too many potential suspects."

She took a bite of her sandwich too. After all that time talking, it had gotten cold.

"I may have found something that will surprise you," Beth said. "As I go through these staff files, I'm finding quite a few sealed juvenile records."

"What do you mean?" Ryan asked.

"Statistically, it's a small number," Beth explained, "But so far, I find seven employees who spent some time in the juvenile system. Because those records are sealed, I don't know what they were in for."

"She's right," Jessie added, "Technically that's barely over one percent of the staff. But for a place like this, it seems high. I wonder what that's about. Are you able to prioritize all the workers with juvenile records and check to see if anything comes back once they became adults?"

"Working on it now," Beth told her.

While they waited for a response, Jessie and Ryan both scarfed down the last of their sandwiches. Jessie followed hers up with a glug of bottled iced tea. Before they got any answers, Ryan's phone rang.

"It's Chief Laird," he said. "Jamil, Beth, we're going to put you guys on hold while we take this call. We'll be back on after."

"Not a probl—," Jamil started to say before Ryan cut him off.

He grimaced in momentary embarrassment before answering the call.

"Hello, Chief," he said, putting the call on speaker. "I'm here with Jessie Hunt. How can we help you?"

"I thought you were going to keep me in the loop, Hernandez?" Laird launched in sternly. "But I haven't gotten a call. It's been a few hours now and I'm in a holding pattern. Do we know if this was foul play or suicide? Am I able to call Bridget Newhouse yet? I had Decker put you two on this thing because you're supposed to be the best and here I am in the dark."

"Sorry, Chief," Ryan said, though Jessie noted that he didn't look especially apologetic. "We've been grinding hard on this and figured you'd rather we be working to solve the case than wasting your time with inconclusive updates."

"Are they inconclusive?" Laird demanded. "You don't know *anything* yet?"

"Nothing definitive," Ryan said. "We're waiting on the medical examiner's preliminary report as to whether the death was a result of strangulation. Until then, we don't even know for sure if he died some other way and was placed in the steam room afterward."

"Does that mean you're leaning away from suicide?" Laird asked.

"We can't be sure, Chief," Jessie said. "The angle of his body in relation to the ribbon around his neck seemed odd if he did it himself, but 'odd' isn't enough to rule it out. And everyone we've spoken to who knows him acknowledged his struggles with depression."

Laird was quiet for a moment. Jessie wondered how much the chief knew about those struggles and whether he was feeling any guilt about not doing more to help.

"Assuming this wasn't his doing," Laird asked, "do you have any credible suspects?"

"We're still looking at Mrs. Newhouse," Ryan told him, "as well as two other couples that joined them here for the weekend. None of them have iron-clad alibis and we're exploring potential motives for each of them. We're also looking into staff at the resort. Our research team is checking for criminal histories among them. There's been a rash of thefts in recent weeks and while they may not be connected, we're checking on that as well."

"How realistic do you think that possibility is?"Laird asked skeptically.

"We don't want to rule anything out, Chief," Ryan said noncommittally.

"So to be clear," Laird pressed, "you're telling me that it's still not advisable for me to reach out to Bridget?"

Ryan looked over at Jessie to get her thoughts. She responded carefully.

"I don't think there's any harm in offering your condolences," she said. "But maybe don't do it directly. You could have your assistant call on your behalf and tell her that you've personally assigned us to the case, or maybe you could send flowers through the resort. I would just avoid any direct communication where she could ask you about the case or request any special treatment. If she *is* somehow involved, you don't want it to look like you compromised the case or your credibility."

"Do you think my credibility is in question, Hunt?" he demanded haughtily.

"Of course not, Chief," she answered immediately, "But you never how the press will spin it. Once we've cleared her, we'll let you know right away and you can smooth things over. But until then, I'd avoid any personal contact."

"Fine," Laird said, sounding more like a petulant child than a police chief. "But if I wait too much longer and she's not a part of this, the damage will be done. I don't want her telling the media that the police chief was insensitive to her loss. So move fast. Maybe put a little pressure on that M.E."

"Yes, Chief," Ryan promised.

Jessie observed that he chose not to mention that he'd called the medical examiner's office not fifteen minutes earlier and been told they didn't have anything yet. It also occurred to her that there might be another way to show Laird that they were pursuing all angles.

"One more thing, Chief," she said quickly. "Peninsula hired a private detective named Katherine Gentry to investigate those thefts that Detective Hernandez mentioned. We know her well. If you authorize it, we could make her a temporary consultant and she could assist on our case. It would give us an additional resource without drawing unwanted attention."

"I suppose that's alright," Laird said reluctantly. "Captain Decker can make it happen. Just have her keep a low profile."

It was several seconds before they realized that they been unceremoniously hung up on. Neither of them commented on that as Ryan took Jamil and Beth off hold.

"We're back," he told them.

"Good, Jamil said excitedly, "because I think I may have a lead for you."

"Shoot," Ryan told him.

"It's one of the employees with a sealed juvie record," Jamil explained. "But he's also got two adult convictions."

"What for?" Jessie asked, trying to control her anticipation.

"One was for assault. The other was for theft."

CHAPTER TWELVE

As they hurried down the hall to the main laundry room, Jessie noticed Ryan adjust the holster on his gun. She did the same.

Jamil had given them a name—Ronnie Nance--as well as a mug shot. When they passed Ronnie's name along to Hugo, the head of security checked with staff services and found the guy was on laundry duty today. When they got to the door of the laundry room, they found Hugo waiting for them.

"Resort management wants me present for your interview," he explained apologetically. "I'll try not to get in the way. Do you want me to make the introduction?"

"Sure," Ryan said. Jessie agreed that it was good move. Maybe if Ronnie saw a familiar face first, he he'd be more likely to talk.

Hugo opened the door and they entered the massive laundry room. Jessie knew she shouldn't have been surprised that a resort as big as this had what amounted to a gym-sized facility to launder thousands of guest towels, not to mention clothes. She saw one large machine that she couldn't identify with steam coming out of the top. It looked like something from the nineteenth century.

As Hugo led the way, she scanned the employees' faces, looking for any that matched the mug shot they'd seen. Ronnie had pockmarked skin and a shaved head, with brown eyes and a nose that looked like it had been broken more than once. His file said he was twenty-two and that he'd been convicted twice and served two separate stints in prison totaling fourteen months. He'd also been arrested twice more, once for burglary and another time for vandalism, though he wasn't convicted on those charges. Jessie wondered how someone with that record had managed to get a job here in the first place.

She was about to ask Hugo that very question when Ronnie came into view. He was folding blue towels at a large table stacked high with them. Even though his back was to her, she knew it was him because of the tattoo of a cross that took up his entire left forearm, just as described in his file. Like everyone else working in the laundry, he wore a white t-shirt and white slacks. He wasn't a big guy, maybe five foot seven and 140 pounds, but he had a coiled, wiry build that suggested he ought not to be taken lightly.

"Hi Ronnie," Hugo said as he stepped into the man's sight line.

Ronnie looked briefly startled before replying.

"Hi, Mr. Cosgrove," he said hesitantly, "what's up?"

His eyes were bouncing around and he had a twitchy, unsettled manner that likely explained why he had a job in the laundry rather than something more guest-facing. Jessie wondered if that was his natural state or if he might be high right now.

"Ronnie," Hugo said casually, nodding at Jessie and Ryan, "I have a couple of folks here who wanted to ask you a few questions."

Ronnie took one look at them and his eyes narrowed.

"I'm pretty busy here," he said. "Can it wait?"

"I appreciate your work ethic," Hugo told him, "but this takes priority. Don't worry. I'll clear it with your supervisor."

Ronnie still didn't look enthusiastic but without any more reason to balk, he shrugged and put down the towel he was folding. Then he leaned in close to them so he didn't have to yell over the noise from the machines.

"Could we at least talk somewhere more private?" he pleaded. "It's really loud in here. Plus I don't want the other guys to think I'm in trouble or something."

Hugo glanced over at Jessie and Ryan, who both nodded.

"Let's go to the laundry manager's office," Hugo suggested, pointing at a door at the far corner of the room. They started that way, weaving in and out of several other tables piled several feet high with freshly folded blue towels, all monogrammed with a large cursive "$\mathcal{P}$."

They were just reaching the end of the maze when, without warning, Ronnie turned and hopped onto the table behind him, sending towels flying everywhere. Before Jessie totally processed what was happening, he had leapt from that table to another one, and then a third, heading back in the direction they'd just come from.

She was about to shout to Ryan when she saw that he had already started moving, running back the way they'd come, in and out of the tables. Jessie took the long way around, sprinting around the edge of the section of towel tables, hoping to make up for the extra distance with an unobstructed path. Hugo followed the same route as Ryan.

As she ran, she kept an eye on Ronnie, who continued to jump from one table to another with impressive skill. When he got to the second to last table before reaching a clear path to the exit, he glanced back to see where his pursuers were. It was a mistake, as he lost his balance and tumbled to the floor.

For a moment, Jessie thought they had him, but he popped right back up, darted around the final table, and made a break for the door. Ryan, still weaving in and out of the tables, was a good thirty feet back and Hugo was well behind him.

She was about the same distance away from Ronnie as Ryan, but with no obstacles in her way, she could go all out. She focused all her attention on the back of Ronnie's shaved head as her legs pumped hard, closing the space between them. By the time Ronnie reached the exit, she was less than fifteen feet away from him.

He must have sensed her presence without looking back because as soon as he passed through the door, he grabbed it and slammed it shut. Jessie had to pull up hard in order to avoid crashing into it. She glanced back to see that Ryan, laboring slightly, was just now clearing the labyrinth of tables. She couldn't wait for him.

She yanked the door open with her left hand while she undid the snap on her gun holster with her right, ready in case he was hovering on the other side, ready to pounce. Instead, she saw him bounding up the stairs, two at a time, to the main level. She did the same. Only with her long legs, she was able to take three steps at once.

When she reached the top, she caught sight of him rounding a corner out of the staff only hallway, through a pair of swinging doors, into what she knew was a large courtyard that was popular with guests. The last thing she needed was a desperate Ronnie Nance plowing through innocent bystanders. She forced herself to run even faster.

When she pushed through the doors, she saw him at the far end of the courtyard, about to pass under an archway that led out to the expansive lawn used for weddings. In fact, in the distance a large group was out there now, rehearsing the procedure for their ceremony later that evening.

People nearby in the courtyard stared open-mouthed at the action. Jessie dodged an older woman with a glass of champagne and a waiter carrying a cheese tray, before picking up speed again.

Ronnie had just made it onto the lawn when someone appeared from off to the right, blindsiding him with a tackle before rolling over him and popping upright. Jessie slowed to a jog as she processed who the attacker was: Kat.

Her friend brushed grass off her blue dress as Ronnie lay on the ground, moaning and hugging his ribs. A few of the people from the wedding party glanced back at the sound of the commotion but Kat quickly stepped in front of Ronnie, blocking any clear line of sight to him. When they turned away again, Jessie bent down, pulled out her cuffs, and snapped them on Ronnie's wrists. As she stood up and tried to catch her breath, Ryan arrived, followed closely by Hugo.

"Hi folks," Kat said amiably, as if they'd she just bumped into each other on a relaxing stroll.

"How the hell did you—?" Jessie panted before Kat waved her off.

"Take a second, ma'am," she said, apparently still pretending not to know her.

"Really?" Jessie asked once she'd taken a few big gulps of air. "You think after that display, anyone's still going to think you're just a lady who lunches *and* plays middle linebacker?"

"Probably not," Kat conceded. "But I like to commit to the role."

"You just happened to be in the perfect spot to nail this guy?" Ryan asked though gasps for air.

"First of all," Kat said. "Hello, Ryan. It's nice to see you again, and looking so spry."

"You too, Katherine," he parried. "It's been too long. And I've never seen anyone in a party dress make a tackle like that. But still—."

"I know," Kat interrupted. "You're dubious about my ability to be in the right place at the right time. It's possible that when I hugged Jessie earlier, I might have put a tracker on her. And it could be that when I saw her moving so fast just now on my phone screen, I suspected something was up and headed to where she was. Good thing too. If I wasn't around, that guy would have plowed through that wedding party and be halfway to Long Beach by now."

"You put a tracker on me?" Jessie demanded incredulously.

"Out of love," Kat tried to claim. "I was worried about my friend's well-being, what with investigating a possible murder and all."

"Wait," Hugo interjected. "How well do you know these people?"

"Keep up, Hugo," Kat teased.

"We go way back," Jessie told him. "And I appreciate my dear friend's concern for me. But she's leaving out a crucial detail: we hugged *before* I told her about the Newhouse case, which means she put the tracker on me prior to having any reason to worry about me. Isn't that right, Kat?"

The private eye shrugged meekly.

"I might have also thought that keeping tabs on you would get me closer to solving my case," she said, looking down at Ronnie. "Did it, by the way? Did I tackle a thief or a killer? Maybe both?"

Ronnie, who had finally regained the ability to speak, protested.

"I didn't do any of that stuff!"

"We'll see about that," Ryan said, hoisting him up. "But I have to say, making a run for it before we could ask you any questions doesn't reflect super well on you."

"I was just scared," Ronnie insisted. "I thought that you might be serving me papers from my ex."

"That's sounds believable," Ryan said rolling his eyes as he turned to Hugo. "Do you have a conference room where we can speak to Ronnie privately?"

"I'll do you one better," the security officer replied. "We have an interview room in the security office. It has recording equipment and everything."

Ryan, though he was still struggling to catch his breath, couldn't help but smile.

"Lead the way," he said.

*

"I'm telling you, you got the wrong guy," Ronnie said again, this time more combatively than the first time.

Jessie didn't find him any more convincing this time around.

They were in the security office interview room, where, after having his rights read and waiving them, Ronnie Nance had continued to expound on the elaborate tale of how he was just trying to avoid getting served by his ex, who claimed he was the father of her newborn baby and was trying to force him to take a paternity test.

"I don't know anything about no stolen crap or any dead people," he maintained. "What I *do* know is that I'm going to sue that chick who cheap-shotted me. Why don't you invite her in here so we can go at it a fair fight?"

"First of all," Jessie replied in reference to Kat, who had been specifically prohibited from entering the room and was sitting in the security office waiting area, "that 'chick' is a former Army Ranger who could kill you with just her thumb and forefinger. So I wouldn't go making any challenges. You got off easy. Second, you're still not winning me over here, Ronnie."

"What are you talking about?"

"You started working here six weeks ago," she reminded him. "The thefts began two weeks later. You have a record of theft. A man died today under questionable circumstances. You have a record of assault. Doesn't that all seem a little too coincidental to you?"

Ronnie opened his mouth but before he could reply, the door opened.

A well-groomed man in an immaculate suit stepped in.

"This interview is over," he announced.

CHAPTER THIRTEEN

Jessie and Ryan exchanged shocked looks.

She could tell he was pissed even before he turned to the guy in the suit.

"Excuse me?" he said, struggling to keep his irritation from being apparent. He did a pretty good job, despite the tightness in his voice and his clenched jaw. "Who are you?"

The man, tall and thin, was completely bald. His suit, which looked like it had just been pressed, came complete with matching yellow tie and handkerchief. He appeared to be about forty.

"Care to tell them, Hugo?" the man said officiously, looking at the embarrassed security officer.

"Detective Hernandez, Ms. Hunt," he said quietly, "this is Peter Lane, Peninsula's senior resort manager."

"That's correct," Lane said. "And I insist that this harassment of our employee end immediately."

Jessie saw that Ryan was about to blow up and tried to short circuit it.

"Why don't we continue this discussion outside," she said quickly. "While we do, Ronnie can stay in here and try to refresh his recollection."

"I'm gonna be recollecting all this harassment, like Mr. Lane here said," Ronnie declared as they left the room.

They passed through the waiting area, where Kat sat, silently watching the group traipse into Hugo's office. Once the door closed, Ryan spoke up.

"I'm a little confused here," he said slowly. "Didn't the resort hire Katherine Gentry to look into the recent string of thefts here?"

"Yes," Lane said. "In fact, I hired her personally on Mr. Cosgrove's recommendation."

"Okay," Ryan replied. "And aren't Ms. Hunt and I here to get to the bottom of what happened to Scott Newhouse?"

"That was my understanding," Lane confirmed superciliously.

"Then where is this harassment crap coming from?" Ryan demanded. "We were in the middle of determining if the guy in that room is responsible for one or both of those crimes. Isn't that what you want?"

"Yes, but I want it done quietly," Lane hissed. "That's why we had Ms. Gentry pose as a guest. We wanted her to present her findings to us so we could resolve the situation without fanfare. Instead, you initiate a wild chase through our laundry facility, nearly knock over a septuagenarian guest in the courtyard, and almost ruin the wedding rehearsal of a family that is spending a quarter of a million dollars to be here this weekend. That is *not* the Peninsula way."

Jessie found herself losing patience with this stuffed shirt too. Not even the dollar figure he'd just mentioned, still ringing in her ears, was enough to give her pause.

"Is the Peninsula way to interfere with a potential murder investigation, Mr. Lane?" she asked, "Because by storming into that room and asserting 'harassment,' you may have irrevocably destroyed out ability to get honest answers from Ronnie Nance."

Peter Lane's nose went even higher in the air if that was possible, and when he spoke, he sounded more like a corporate lawyer than a fancy hotel manager.

"It is the opinion of the Peninsula that Mr. Newhouse died as a result of a suicide or at the hands of someone he knew. We have no reason to believe that an employee was involved."

"It's the *opinion* of the resort?" Jessie asked incredulously. "Where did the Peninsula get its degree in criminology, I wonder? I've got to tell you, Mr. Lane that it sounds suspiciously to me like the Peninsula is concerned that a staffer being charged with murder might hurt business. And if you're not careful, you may find yourself dangerously close to being charged with obstructing an investigation—you personally, Mr. Lane, not *the Peninsula*."

"There's no need for threats," Lane said huffily. "I'm just conveying the position of my superiors."

"Maybe your superiors should have thought twice before selecting a resort manager who hires guys with lengthy criminal records," Ryan pointed out.

"That wasn't my doing," Lane objected.

"Are you trying to pin the blame on Hugo's team?" Ryan asked.

"No," Lane said, glancing over at the security officer uncomfortably. "Mr. Nance, along with several others, was hired over the objections of our security staff."

"Why?" Jessie demanded.

Lane sighed, as if deeply pained that he had to answer the question.

"Peninsula underwent a change in ownership about six months ago," he said. "The new owners established a revised hiring doctrine intended to increase the diversity of the staff. It's been a smashing success. We're very proud of it."

"Sounds great," Ryan said. "So what's the problem?"

"We may have been a victim of our own success," Lane answered. "Three months ago, the owners, one of whom has a brother who was once incarcerated, decided to up the ante and open the resort to hiring people who had served time. They started slowly, with young people who had been convicted of a crime while a juvenile. We have a committee that vets prospective candidates and makes recommendations. As of now, we have seven employees hired through what we call the 'Second Chance' program."

"That's admirable," Jessie said. "And in general I think it's a great idea. But Ronnie Nance doesn't just have a juvenile record. He's been convicted of two crimes as an adult and served hard time."

"Yes," Lane conceded, "There seems to have been a hiccup somewhere in the vetting process. We're trying to determine where. Nonetheless, there is no evidence suggesting that Mr. Nance stole anything, much less killed someone. To make those kinds of accusations is reckless and unfair."

"He ran when we tried to talk to him," Ryan pointed out. "That's evidence that he has *something* to hide. We were trying to find out exactly what when you interrupted."

There was a long, awkward pause in which Lane seemed to be struggling to think of justification for his actions. Jessie jumped in to give him a lifeline.

"Despite that," she said, "I have an idea that may solve both our problems."

"What do you propose?" Lane asked, his eagerness trumping his attempt to maintain a stately bearing.

"My understanding is that you have on-site staff quarters," she said. "Since they are resort property, you can allow us to search Nance's living space without a warrant. Let us do that and collect any evidence we find. Maybe there are 'missing' items in there. Maybe there's a picture of Scott Newhouse with a big red "x" through his face. Maybe there's nothing at all. It won't necessarily answer all our questions, but getting a look at Nance's stuff could get us part of the way there. What do you say?"

Even before Lane responded, Jessie knew he would say yes. It was an eminently reasonable suggestion, one he couldn't oppose without seeming obstructionist. Even his body language seemed to soften a bit before he spoke.

"I suppose we could allow that."

*

They all marched down a long basement hallway to the staff quarters in a single file line.

Hugo led the way. Next was the resort manager, Peter Lane, followed by Ryan. Then came Ronnie Nance, hand-cuffed and fidgety. After him was a giant security guard, appropriately named Spike. Jessie walked right behind him with Kat bringing up the rear.

Jessie kept her eyes on Ronnie, looking for any signs of anxiety or fear beyond what he'd already displayed. He was definitely nervous, constantly licking his lips and tugging at his handcuffs. But she couldn't say with certainty that his behavior suggested he knew that some major secret was about to be uncovered.

"You really think we're going to find anything?" Kat whispered in her ear as they walked. "Unless he's an idiot, it's hard to believe he would have stashed anything in his room."

"We don't have firm evidence that he's not an idiot," Jessie said. "Besides, if he's been stuck at the resort until his next extended time off, where else could he put something incriminating without worrying that it might be found? Until a half hour ago, he had no reason to think anyone was looking at him for murder *or* theft."

"What if we don't find anything?" Kat asked.

"That's not our only play," Jessie reminded her. "According to Hugo, all staff nametags are geo-tagged. That might not help solve your thefts, but if he was near the spa when Newhouse was killed, it should show up in the resort's system. Hugo has his tech people checking now."

"Let's hope they're as good as Jamil," Kat said.

"That's not possible," Jessie noted. "But for something like this, they don't have to be."

They walked on quietly for a few seconds before Kat spoke up again.

"By the way, I'm sorry about the whole tracking thing."

"Don't worry about it," Jessie muttered back. "You can make it up to me with a nice bottle of red or paying for a pedicure."

"You're really not pissed?"

"Sure, I'm a little pissed," Jessie admitted. "But you've saved my ass often enough that I'll let it slide this time. And truth be told, if I was in a tough spot, I might have done the same thing. Oh, by the way, we got LAPD to authorize you as a temporary consultant so that you can help out on our case if we need it."

"Are you serious?" Kat asked, sounding as giddy as was possible for her.

"I am," Jessie said. "You'll even get a check when it's all over."

Kat squeezed her shoulder appreciatively.

"You didn't just put another tracker on me?" Jessie asked wryly.

Before Kat could reply, they arrived at the appropriate door. Hugo knocked politely.

"Who is it?' came a startled male voice.

"It's Hugo Cosgrove from security, Marlo. Please open up."

They heard a string of muttered profanities on the other side of the door, followed by what sounded like some kind of aerosol being sprayed.

"Now, Marlo!" Hugo repeated, banging on the door louder. "Don't make me open it myself."

The door popped open a second later to reveal a scrawny-looking teen with bed head in shorts and a t-shirt.

"Sorry," he said. "I was taking a nap and needed a second to get dressed."

His red-tinged eyes, along with the combined scent of Lysol, a vanilla candle, and the unmistakable smell of pot, suggested he'd been doing more than napping.

"Can you step outside for a moment please, Marlo?" Hugo requested, not commenting on either the scent or the excuse.

"Yes, sir," Marlo said, trudging out with his head slumped, as if he was headed for the guillotine. Jessie didn't care what he was smoking and she doubted anyone else here did either, with the possible exception of Peter Lane.

"That's Ronnie's area," Hugo said, pointing to the right side of the small room, which barely seemed like enough space for one person, much less two.

Ryan stepped into the room, snapping on his evidence gloves. Jessie did the same and pulled out a plastic evidence bag. They moved over to Ronnie's bed, where Ryan lifted up the mattress. There was nothing under it.

"I told you!" Ronnie shouted triumphantly.

Ryan didn't even look back at him as he moved over to the small dresser, opened every drawer, and carefully searched each one. Still nothing.

"I'm gonna sue you so bad," Ronnie chirped.

"Good luck with that," Kat mumbled under her breath.

Jessie and Ryan stepped over a pile of dirty clothes to the locker against the far wall. It had a combination lock. Ryan turned back to Ronnie.

"Care to share, Hurricane Carter?" he asked, unable to keep the sarcasm out of his voice.

"I got a right to privacy, man!" Ronnie proclaimed.

"Not really," Jessie pointed out. "You're on resort property. They own the locker."

"Get a warrant, lady," Ronnie shot back. "Or a blow torch."

"Actually," Hugo volunteered, "I have a key that overrides any combination and opens all the lockers, so we can probably skip the blow torch."

"Please do the honors," Ryan said, stepping aside.

Hugo unlocked and opened the locker, before stepping back. Ryan carefully searched its contents, but again came up empty.

"See," Ronnie announced victoriously. "This is a civil rights violation."

Ryan, though he was clearly frustrated, turned back to the kid and offered a sad smile.

"You're a white, twice-convicted criminal who ran away when you were about to be questioned. I'm a Hispanic police officer who at no point touched or threatened you. How do you figure I violated your civil rights, Ronnie?"

"Don't try to get out of this with cop talk," Ronnie said belligerently. "You are going down."

He laughed in glee, raising his eyes to the ceiling like he was in cahoots with the gods. Jessie saw his eyes gleam as they landed on one particular spot above him. She looked up too, following his gaze. He saw her do it and quickly lowered his eyes to floor, getting suddenly quiet.

"Are we done here?" Peter Lane asked, sounding relieved.

"Not quite," Jessie said, staring up at the place Ronnie was aggressively looking away from now. It was the air vent. "Can someone open that vent up there?"

"Sure," the extremely tall Hugo offered, standing on the edge of Ronnie's bed. He peered closely at it. "It's loose."

"Take these," Ryan said, handing him some gloves.

After he put them on, Hugo grabbed the metal slats of the vent and tugged. The whole thing came free without needing to be unscrewed. He dropped the vent on the bed and felt around. Jessie didn't need to wait for any word from him to know what would happen next.

Ronnie had gone completely silent and was slouching forward, staring a hole in the floor.

"I've got something," Hugo said, pulling out a canvas shopping bag.

He handed it down to Ryan, who untied and opened it, letting everyone see what was inside. There weren't any photos of Scott Newhouse or ribbons that could be used to strangle someone. But there were over a dozen pieces of jewelry, including several rings, watches, and bracelets. Jessie looked over at Kat.

"Looks like your case just got solved," she noted.

"Yeah," Kat replied excitedly before quickly turning sympathetic, "but apparently not yours."

It was true. They'd have the crime scene team come back and thoroughly go over the room. But nothing they'd found so far linked Ronnie to Scott Newhouse's death.

As Hugo got off the bed, his cell phone rang. He answered it and Jessie watched him closely, hoping for news from his tech folks. His face betrayed nothing as he listened.

"Okay, thanks," he said. After hanging up, he looked over at her and Ryan. "Can I have a private word with you two?"

The three of them stepped out into the hall. When Hugo spoke, his voice was low so no one else could hear.

"My people just got back to me on the geo-tagging. They say that Ronnie Nance was in the main building during the entire window of death for Scott Newhouse. He never went anywhere near the spa."

"Could he have just removed his nametag and left it somewhere while he went to the spa," Ryan asked hopefully.

"I don't think so, Detective," Hugo told him. "The tag moved constantly and my people say all those movements are consistent with where he was supposed to be and what he was supposed to be doing. He may be a thief, but from 8 a.m. to 11 a.m., it looks like he was doing his job."

Jessie sighed and turned to Ryan. She could tell that he was thinking the same thing as her: they were back to square one.

CHAPTER FOURTEEN

Jessie suspected Hugo felt bad for them.

Otherwise why would he have secured a casita for them to use as their working home base, rather than a bland conference room? That's where they were now—herself, Ryan, and Kat—as they pondered next moves.

It was mid-afternoon now and they hadn't made any major progress since the Ronnie Nance disappointment. Jessie could feel the pressure from Chief Laird, somewhere out there, on the verge of calling them again and reaming them out.

Kat, who had been given a complimentary casita for the night as a "thank you" from Peninsula management, was flipping through the list of remaining employees with criminal juvenile pasts.

"Well, it's official," she said closing the file. "Of the seven 'Second Chance' hires made by the resort, Ronnie was the only one that slipped through that had an adult conviction. Of the remaining six, four were working on campus today. None of them was near the spa area during the time in question."

"Wonderful," Ryan muttered.

"I think it's time we check in with the medical examiner again," Jessie suggested. "It's been a few hours."

"Don't you think Gallagher would have reached out if she had news?" he objected.

"Actually, I think she knows how important this case is to Laird and is worried that offering even preliminary analysis could come back to bite her. We need to push a little harder."

"Okay," Ryan said with a resigned shrug as he called. Once she answered, he put her on speaker. "Hey Cheryl, Jessie and I were hoping you might have an update."

"I still don't have anything official for you," she said, slightly annoyed.

"We get that," Jessie piped in, "but it might be days before you do. We've got Laird breathing down our necks."

"I know," Gallagher said. "That's why I don't want to jump the gun."

"Listen," Jessie said cajolingly, "we don't expect what you tell us now to go in any final report. Right now, we just need your best guess so we can determine where to put our energy. We've got some extremely wealthy, very powerful people—all potential suspects—that we may have to start getting aggressive with. If you think this thing was likely a suicide, we can avoid that unpleasantness. If not, we need to rip the Band-Aid off and get that process started."

There was silence on the other end of the line. Finally Gallagher answered.

"Okay, fine," she said reluctantly. "I won't sign my name to this conclusion, but if my life depended on it, I'd say this was probably *not* a suicide. First of all, preliminary blood work shows no sign that he stopped taking his anti-depressant medication, which might have indicated that he was heading down a bad road. And the spot where the ribbon was tied off to the handlebar doesn't make sense in relation to where his body ended up. It's hard—just spatially—to envision how he could have done this to himself. I'm not saying it's impossible. That steam room was all slick surfaces. Maybe he started to hang himself and slipped somehow, so his body ended up how it did."

"What percentage would you assign to that scenario?" Jessie pressed.

"Ten percent, maybe fifteen," Gallagher ventured. "Far more likely is that this was done *to* him. I'm not the expert on how that would have worked logistically. But assuming someone could get in that room, it makes much more sense that they wrapped that ribbon around his neck, choked him to death, and then tied the other end of the ribbon to the handlebar to make it look like suicide."

"There is another possibility," Kat volunteered.

"Who is that?" Gallagher asked nervously.

"Oh, sorry," Ryan said. "We have Katherine Gentry here with us. She's a private investigator who was working another case here. She's also a friend. You can trust her."

"Okay," Gallagher offered hesitantly. "So what is this other possibility?"

"Could it have been a case of auto-erotic asphyxiation gone wrong?" Kat asked. "Maybe once the other participant realized what had happened, they just bailed."

Jessie was embarrassed that the idea hadn't occurred to her.

"That's certainly as credible as the suicide theory," Gallagher acknowledged. "The one thing that has me skeptical is that the ribbon that choked him cut really deep, breaking well through the skin of the neck. It was bloody. That doesn't seem to comport with a consensual sex game."

"That reminds me," Ryan said, "were you able to pull any DNA off the ribbon? If someone was squeezing so tight as to cut through his skin, wouldn't that leave all of kinds of skin cells from the killer's hands on it?"

"That is one area where I can offer you some new information: we didn't pull any DNA off the ribbon other than Newhouse's, at least not in our preliminary analysis."

"I'm confused," Ryan said. "Doesn't that suggest suicide then?"

"Not necessarily," Gallagher warned. "Other than the throat area, we only found small samples from him. If he had tied this ribbon off on the handle and his neck, I would have expected more than we found from all the grabbing and tightening."

"But," Jessie volunteered, suddenly exercised. "If someone wearing gloves wrapped the ribbon around his neck and he made a futile effort to grab at it, would that match the amount of DNA you found?"

"That fits better," Gallagher conceded.

"So," Ryan concluded. "There's a very small chance this was a sex game gone awry. There's a higher percentage possibility, though still not great, that he killed himself and ended up in a strange, hard-to-explain position. And there is a pretty reasonable chance that someone wearing gloves killed him. Is that a fair assessment?"

Gallagher again paused before committing to an answer.

"Unofficially, yes," she allowed.

"Okay, thanks Cheryl," he said. "We won't shout this from the rooftops but it's helpful to know. Please do let us know as soon as you're ready to make it official."

"Will do," she said, hanging up before they could ask any more questions.

"So what now?" Kat asked.

"I better call Chief Laird to break the bad news," Ryan said. "I know he'd be upset either way: if his friend killed himself, and even more so if he was murdered. But still not being able to say anything publicly one way or another is going to really eat at him. He's not the kind of guy who likes to let the facts come patiently to him. And not being able to contact the widow to offer personal condolences, even hours later, is going to rile him up even more. I don't relish this."

"I can get on the call with you," Jessie offered, though the idea didn't enthuse her.

"No," Ryan said. "There's no reason for you to get berated too. Hell, you're not even officially back full-time yet. That ought to justify a free pass on this."

"Okay then," Jessie replied, happy not to argue the point. "Then I think I'll go to Bridget Newhouse's casita. I'm assuming the other couples will be there too. That way I can break the bad news to all of them at once."

"What news?" Kat asked.

"That we can't rule out murder, they're all potential suspects, and we don't want them leaving Peninsula until we know more. That means they're staying the night."

"Weren't they all planning to do that anyway?" Kat asked.

"Yes," Jessie said. "But now that this is a likely murder scene, it might not be all that appealing to stick around. And pretty soon, Bridget Newhouse is going to start making noise about wanting to see her kids and plan her husband's funeral. I'm going to pitch this as a chance for her to work through this privately before having to tell her children. But even if she goes for that, I'd guess we have until midday tomorrow, tops, before the pressure to let them leave gets too strong."

"Then you better get over there," Kat said, trying to buck her up. "In the meantime, I'll be tackling a very important task of my own."

"What?" Ryan asked.

"Getting some snacks," she answered. "We're going to need fuel to get through the rest of this day."

Jessie was happy for any quip that could get her to crack a smile and headed out with Kat, leaving Ryan to his unpleasant conversation. Once outside, they split up. Kat headed up to the Grand Hall and Jessie made the short walk to the Newhouse casita. When she arrived, Geordy was gone, but another security guard, equally thick through the torso, stood at the door. This one, according to his nametag, was named Lewis.

"Hi," Jessie started to say. I'm—,"

"I know who you are, Ms. Hunt," he said quickly. "I'm Lewis and Hugo Cosgrove has you on the list of people authorized to enter. Mrs. Newhouse is inside with several other guests."

"Thanks, Lewis," Jessie said, relieved that at least the start of this mission was going smoothly.

She knocked on the door, which unlike the last time she was here, opened quickly. She was greeted by Abby Andrews, still looking as sunny as ever, though she was doing her best to mute it.

"Hi, Ms. Hunt," she said.

Behind her, there were voices in the kitchen. The tone suggested that people were trying to console Bridget Newhouse.

"Hi Abby, is Bridget here?" she asked, even though she knew the answer.

"Yes, come on in." Abby opened the door wide and Jessie stepped inside but waited to be led into the kitchen.

"Hey everyone," Abby said, when they entered. "Ms. Hunt from LAPD is here."

The room went silent. Everyone she expected to see was there: Bridget Newhouse, Malcolm Andrews, as well as Matt and Ellie Darcy. There were open bottles of wine on the counter and from their flushed faces and bleary eyes, it was clear that at least a couple of the folks had already had their fair share.

"Hi everyone," she said somberly. "I just wanted to give you all an update on our investigation."

"It's about time," Malcolm Andrews said, showing all the charm he exhibited at the cliff side yoga spot.

"Please, Malcolm," Bridget pleaded, her voice rough and trembly, "let her talk."

The woman looked exhausted and her eyes were red, though whether that was due to crying or drinking, Jessie couldn't be sure. She imagined it might be both.

Unsure how best to break the news diplomatically, she decided to just be honest. There were so many people in the room that it would be hard to observe all of their reactions, but she didn't have much choice.

Maybe I should have brought Kat with me for this.

But it was too late for that.

"I'm afraid we don't yet have a definitive cause of death—," she began before Matt Darcy interrupted her.

"We all know it was strangulation," he said much more loudly than was appropriate. It was clear that much of the wine had been consumed by him.

"That's correct," she replied calmly. "But we are still waiting for results from the medical examiner that will tell us whether he did this to himself or if someone killed him."

She scanned as many faces as she could. Bridget, Malcolm, and Abby all looked surprised at the revelation. And although she had never spoken to them before, it appeared that neither of the Darcys seemed shocked at the news.

"So you think he might have been murdered?" Ellie asked flatly, as if confirming a suspicion she'd already had. Jessie recalled how Ryan said that during his interview with them, the Darcys seemed to be cold to one another, for reasons he couldn't determine. She sounded equally chilly now.

"It's certainly a possibility that we're looking into," she acknowledged.

Bridget Newhouse stifled a sob, regrouped, and spoke very slowly, as if taking her time would keep her emotions in check.

"What am I supposed to do with that?" she asked.

"I'm sorry," Jessie consoled, "but we don't have much more than that now. We're hoping that will change by tomorrow," she said to Bridget specifically before speaking to the whole group. "That's why we need everyone to remain here at Peninsula overnight. We'll want immediate access to all of you should we have additional questions."

"Are you saying that we're suspects?" Malcolm Andrews demanded indignantly.

"In a situation like this, everyone's a suspect until they're not," she said plainly. "Don't take it personally. It's better to view this as an opportunity to help get justice for Scott."

"None of us is going anywhere anyway," Matt Darcy said, with less volume but the same belligerence as before. "We're Bridget's friends and we're here to support her."

"That's right," Ellie agreed. "We already called their nanny and had her take the children over to our place to be with our kids and my mom. The press is sure to get a hold of this story, if they haven't already, and we don't want them staking out Bridget's place with their TV trucks while the little ones are there."

"That's very considerate of you," Jessie said, not mentioning that Ellie Darcy seemed super on the ball for someone dealing with such a shocking tragedy. She couldn't determine if the woman was just built that way or if there was something else going on.

"Thanks so much," Bridget said, walking over and giving Ellie a hug. Neither woman let go and Jessie began to feel awkward.

"I'm going to get back to it," she said. "We'll try to let you know when we have more information. You should expect that we'll have additional questions for all of you so please stay by your phones. And I would recommend that no one talk to the press. We don't need this to turn into a circus. That will just make it harder to get to the truth."

"I'll walk you out," Abby said. When they got to the door, she took Jessie's hand and gave it a tight squeeze. "Thanks for everything you're doing."

"It's my job," Jessie told her.

"We appreciate that. And if there's anything I can do to help, let me know."

"I will," Jessie said. She was about to leave when she added, "Actually, if you or anyone else thinks of anything that might feel relevant, no matter how small, please don't hesitate to reach out."

"I won't," Abby said. "But I'm not sure how much good any of us will be to you tonight. We're planning to take Bridget to that bar, The Cove, and help her drown her sorrows."

Jessie wasn't sure it was such a great idea for these folks, all of them close to Scott Newhouse but any of whom might be responsible for his death, to go to a bar while raw with emotion. But she kept her mouth shut. If they were at the bar, that meant they were at the resort. And that's what she'd come here to ensure.

With that mission accomplished, she had to get back to her partner and fiancé. She hoped that in the time she was gone, he'd had some kind of epiphany about the case. But she wasn't holding her breath.

CHAPTER FIFTEEN

It was actually Kat who had the unexpected insight.

As soon as Jessie returned to their bungalow, she was physically accosted by her friend, who pulled her over to the living room couch. Ryan was already sitting there, noshing on a finger sandwich, one of the many snacks that Kat had collected from the buffet.

"What is it?" Jessie asked, not sure if her friend was excited about the food or something more significant. She turned to Ryan. "Do you know what this is about?"

"She wouldn't say anything until you got here," he said, finishing up his sandwich and grabbing a piece of cornbread.

"Okay, let me start at the beginning," Kat said excitedly.

"Always a good plan," Jessie said.

"Don't get smart, Hunt," Kat said. "I may be saving your bacon here."

"That reminds me, have some bacon," Ryan said, handing her a piece.

Jessie took it and began nibbling as Kat filled them in on her adventure.

"When I went to the restroom up at the Grand Hall, a couple of employees came in. I was in a stall so they thought they were alone. One of them is apparently a maid who cleans all the offices in what's called 'the therapeutic wing.'"

"What's that?" Ryan asked.

"I checked to find out," she said. "It's off in a secluded corner of the Grand Hall, sort of an annex. It houses the resort's on-site chiropractor, physical therapist, and marriage and family counselor. They even have a financial advisor there."

"I'm surprised that Honey Potter didn't set up shop there too," Jessie said.

"I'm not," Ryan said. "There's probably a good reason she conducts her sessions in a stand-alone bungalow away from all the others. I bet they get noisy."

"Anyway," Kat said, steering them back to her point, "this maid was talking about seeing a story about Scott Newhouse's death on the news and realizing she recognized him and his wife."

"How?" Jessie asked, sensing that Kat was coming to her big reveal.

"She said that late yesterday afternoon, when she was cleaning the physical therapist's office, she saw them coming out of another office, where they'd just had an appointment."

"Which office?" Ryan pressed.

"The marriage and family counselor," Kat announced proudly.

Jessie and Ryan were quiet for a second, and she knew they were both thinking the same thing: if the Newhouses were meeting with a marriage counselor in the middle of their couple's retreat, they were likely dealing with a significant issue. It sure would be nice to find out what it was.

"Did she say which marriage counselor they met with?" Jessie asked.

"She didn't have to," Kat replied. "I checked. There's only one. His name is Cedric Cleaver."

Jessie turned to Ryan.

"Maybe we should see if the man is in right now," she suggested.

"He is," Kat assured her.

"How do you know?" Ryan asked.

Kat smiled devilishly.

"Because I scheduled a session today for you guys today."

"You did what?" Jessie demanded, feeling her face start to flush. Was this Kat's sneaky way of getting them into therapy to discuss their wedding disagreement?

"I made you an appointment," Kat repeated. "I figured that if you started out telling him you wanted to question him about other clients, he'd shut down. But if you go in under the guise of a couple who needs advice, he'll be less suspicious. Then you can hit him with the questions. I know it's not completely kosher, but you've both done worse."

"That's okay," Ryan said. "Normally, I don't like to start an interview under false pretenses. But with Laird breathing down our necks, I don't mind a little trickery if it guarantees we get in the door."

"Did your conversation with him go that badly?" Jessie asked.

"About as expected," Ryan told her. "He fumed for a while, mostly because the press is hammering him with questions and he has to be so cryptic in his answers. To be honest, I think that's much more of a concern for him than the inability to console Bridget Newhouse. But in the end, he understood. We've probably got another 18 hours before his ego overwhelms his good sense."

"Then I guess we better go to see this Cleaver guy soon," Jessie said. "Frankly, I feel a little bad for the guy. Honey Potter is booked months in advance but we can walk in the same day? When did you make the appointment for, Kat?"

"3 p.m."

Jessie looked at her watch.

"It's 2:49 right now," she objected.

"I know," Kat said, seemingly enjoying her friend's distress, "so that doesn't give you much time to finish those lamb skewers I got. They're really good, by the way. Maybe you should take them to go."

*

Jessie almost felt bad for him.

Cedric Cleaver welcomed her and Ryan into his office warmly, clearly oblivious to whom he was dealing with or what their real intentions were. The man was in his mid-fifties, with a soft face, thick glasses, and a thick mop of conservatively parted brown hair. He was short, with a little belly. He wore a beige sweater over a collared shirt, along with casual black slacks. He reminded Jessie of Mr. Rogers if he had been melted down slightly.

Cleaver motioned for them to sit on the loveseat across from him before settling into a high-backed chair and pulling out a legal pad and pen, which he left in his lap.

"So Jessie and Ryan—my understanding is that you're recently engaged," he said in a tone so soothing that Jessie considered secretly recording him so she could use it later to help get to sleep. "Is that correct?"

"It is," Ryan said. He left it there, holding off on dropping the interrogation hammer.

"Well, I think that it's great that you're coming in so early on," Cleaver told them. "So often, couples wait until they're officially married to address their concerns. It's sometimes helpful to nip them in the bud before they become something larger. So what can I do for you?"

Jessie glanced over at Ryan hesitantly, wondering if he might take Cleaver's comments to heart and let the session play out before revealing their true intent. But her fiancé, who seemed oblivious to the opportunity, went a different way completely.

"Well, before we get into that, do you mind if I ask you a question?"

"Of course not," Cleaver told him with an open smile.

"How often does this work?" Ryan began. "I mean, most of the couples who come to see you aren't regulars, right? They're here on vacation, so it's a 'one time' or 'one weekend' type of thing. Is that really effective?"

"That's a totally reasonable question," Cleaver said. "And not the first time it's been asked. The truth is that, generally speaking, I recommend that couples see one counselor on a regular basis, for the sake of continuity and because it allows you to go deeper. However, I've found that there are times when couples actually prefer to see someone they know they won't be interacting with again."

"Who would want that?" Jessie asked, genuinely curious.

"Often it's couples like yourself, who haven't been in counseling before and want to try it out with no strings attached. You meet with me and can then determine whether longer-term counseling is right for you. If it is, and you're local, I can even make recommendations for counselors or therapists in your area. I've also found that this setup appeals to couples who may not want to address a specific issue with their regular counselor. Maybe it's so sensitive that they want to discuss it with a stranger before bringing to their regular therapist. Or maybe they only want to talk about it one time, and then put it in a box and lock it away. Does that answer your question?"

"It does, thanks," Ryan said, looking over at Jessie.

She knew what he was thinking: it was time to end the charade and let Cleaver know why they were really there. She could also tell that he wanted her to be the one to do it. She knew why. He was hoping that if she revealed the truth, using her more delicate touch, Cleaver might not react as badly. But she doubted it would make much difference, whoever it came from. She was willing to do it, but not the way Ryan wanted.

"What should we call you?" she asked.

"Cedric is fine," he said.

"Cedric," she said with a sweet smile she knew wouldn't soften what came next. "What was it for the Newhouses? Were they here to discuss an issue with you first before going back to their regular therapist or were they planning to put it in a box?"

Cleaver's face fell and his back immediately stiffened.

"What's the meaning of—?" he started to say before she cut him off.

"I'm sorry to blindside you," she said sympathetically, hoping to keep him off balance by constantly changing his perception of what she was after. "But as you surely know, Scott Newhouse died this morning. We're here investigating that for the LAPD. Ryan is a detective and I'm a criminal profiler. Our probe so far indicates that his death wasn't due to natural causes. And since we know you met with them late yesterday afternoon, it's important that we determine if anything in your session with them could be helpful in learning what happened to him."

She stopped and waited, watching as the man's head swam with everything he'd just been told. He went from anger to bewilderment to fear and then back to something close to anger.

"May I please see your identification?" he asked tersely.

They both showed it. Jessie noted that he barely looked. It seemed that his request was more of a stalling technique intended to give him extra time to decide how to reply. Ryan obviously picked up on that too because he immediately jumped in, not giving Cleaver time to think.

"Time is a priority here, Cedric," he said. "A man you saw just yesterday, who came to you for help, died today, either from suicide or more likely, murder. We need to know what was said in that session yesterday that could have bearing on this case. This isn't the time for caution. We need answers."

That seemed to get Cleaver's back up.

"Surely you know that I can't violate a client's privacy like that. Even if they only visited me once, I have a professional obligation, if not to Mr. Newhouse anymore, then to his wife."

"His wife is a potential suspect," Ryan informed him. "You could be protecting a murderer."

Jessie knew that he was skeptical of that theory, but she didn't blame him for using it to his advantage. Cleaver sighed heavily, silently weighing his options. After a long pause, he finally spoke.

"I can't tell you about the specific content of our discussion without a court order," he said with more steel than Jessie had expected. "No client would ever trust me again. It would ruin my career."

Jessie was about to reply but stopped herself. He wasn't done.

"What I *can* tell you is that nothing in our conversation was of earth-shattering consequence. There was no 'black box' level revelation. They were just trying to work through standard marital issues. However—and I hesitate to even say this—I think it would be worth your while to have a frank conversation with someone else in the Newhouses' orbit. I obviously can't tell you why. In good conscience, all I can say is who. Even that feels mildly inappropriate, so much so that I would greatly appreciate you not sharing with this person how you came to him."

"We'll do our best," Jessie said, doubting she could live up to that. "So who is it? Who should we be talking to?"

"He's a friend of the Newhouses," Cleaver said softly. "I believe he's here on campus right now. I don't recall his last name, but his first name is Matt."

Jessie looked over at Ryan, who had the ravenous, wolf-like expression he always got when he was closing in on prey.

"Thanks, Cedric," he said standing up quickly and fixing his eyes on her. "We should go."

CHAPTER SIXTEEN

Eden Roth was giddy.

She'd waited so long—weeks now—that she had started to doubt her time would ever arrive.

When she'd been activated, her instructions from Andy Robinson, passed in coded language through an intermediary, had been clear. She was to wait until Jessie Hunt was in the news again before putting her plan into action.

Only then could she begin her task, the one she promised Andy that she would complete way back when she dedicated herself to Principles, when they were both inmate patients at the Female Forensic In-Patient Psychiatric Unit at the Twin Towers Correctional Facility. She had been preparing all this time, so that everything went off without a hitch. Sometimes at night, she'd dream about it, picturing the blood of her victims, as it left their bodies, along with their life force.

She had other dreams too, ones that she felt both ashamed of and exhilarated by. They often involved her in more than a friendly embrace with Andy, sharing the same prison cell bed, spooning, with the other woman's breath on the back of her neck, her blonde hair falling slightly into Eden's face.

She wasn't ashamed about how she felt toward Andrea Robinson. Rather, she was ashamed that occasionally those feelings interfered with her ability to focus on the task at hand. Sometimes she'd be sharpening a weapon or studying a map when Andy's visage would suddenly fill her mind. She saw her so clearly: her bright blue eyes, so intense that it was hard to look at them for too long, her blonde hair tied back in a devil-may-care ponytail, her mischievous grin, her proper curves.

Eden knew that she was the antithesis of Andy: short, skinny, curveless, with wilted brown hair, pale skin, and dull, gray eyes. Despite how she saw herself, Andy thought she was beautiful. She'd told her so.

Eden knew that she was unlikely to ever see Andy in person again, much less touch her. Her mission made that a virtual impossibility. But she'd made her peace with it, consoling herself with the knowledge that they'd finally embrace again in the next world, the one Andy promised they'd share together.

The time when she would enter that next world was infinitely closer than it had been just hours ago. That was because of a story on the evening news. She was watching and taking notes, as she did every night, when the anchor mentioned the death of a prominent Los Angeles resident at a fancy Palos Verdes resort. The police were investigating it and there were unconfirmed reports that the death might be a murder, because LAPD's HHS unit, and specifically famed criminal profiler Jessie Hunt, had been spotted at the scene.

That was all she needed to leap into action. She went to her closet and pulled out the small chest in the corner. After placing it on her bed she removed all the essential items one by one, making sure that everything was in working order. She checked the map again, and then the calendar to make sure her chosen date would still work.

Because of her preparation, she realized that there was nothing else to do but wait. Once the designated day arrived, she would take up the mantle from Livia Bucco. Livia was to be respected for being first. But Eden knew she could do better. Livia had slaughtered one young woman with a machete before they caught her and she had to sacrifice herself for the cause. That was small potatoes compared to the carnage Eden had in store for this city.

Secure in the knowledge that she was primed for what had to be done, Eden returned everything to the chest, and then to the closet. Afterward she rewarded herself with another viewing of her favorite movie, *Clueless*, which she watched every night. This was to be screening number 833. It never got old.

*

Andrea Robinson watched the evening news and smiled.

The second she heard Jessie's name mentioned, she knew the rest was inevitable. She could picture Eden's plain, gullible face lighting up as she processed that her time had come, that she could finally fulfill her mission.

She could imagine the bland young thing's body shaking with excitement, much as it had when Andy would offer a furtive, delicate stroke on her forearm or whisper something in her ear, allowing her warm breath to make the hair on the girl's neck stand up. Eden had been so easy to manipulate that it almost wasn't fun. But the girl was marginally smarter than that cow Livia had been, and smelled better too, which was why she'd been assigned the more ambitious task.

Andy stood up and stretched, then walked around the lounge to loosen up, pretending for a moment that she wasn't incarcerated in a psychiatric lockdown facility. Sure the Western Regional Women's Psychiatric Detention Center, or PDC, was much nicer than the Twin Towers. The furniture wasn't falling apart. Patients were rarely stun-gunned into submission. Nobody painted feces on the walls. The medical staff actually seemed to want to help the patients get better. But there were still bars on the windows, armed guards everywhere, and barbed wire fencing around the facility.

But that too would all change eventually. At some point, she anticipated relocation, or possibly even freedom, for her part in stopping a killer. After all, once Eden began her butchery, Jessie would investigate and discover that she'd spent time at Twin Towers with Andy. Her boss, Captain Decker, would insist that Jessie take advantage of her willing human resource.

As part of the arrangement that got Andy in this more palatable facility, Jessie would come to her demanding insights into the girl's mindset, anything that might help catch her before she did more damage. If she resisted and didn't ask for Andy's help, then any future murders committed by Eden would be her fault. And if she did ask for help and got it, she would be in Andy's debt. Of course, Andy had no intention of calling in that debt. That wasn't the plan.

Instead, Andy simply wanted to rebuild the trust she'd lost. Admittedly, when one goes from being friends with a person to trying to poison them, it can be hard to mend the relationship. But Andy was sure that over time, her repeated, altruistic efforts to help Jessie catch disturbed people doing terrible things would win over her once and future friend. Admittedly, she was creating the very violence that she would later help stop. But that was a pesky detail.

Eventually, inevitably, Jessie would start to soften. She would acknowledge that Andy's assistance was helpful, even vital. She would hear from the doctors at PDC that Andy was making real progress in therapy, showing genuine remorse. She would begin to consider the possibility that Andy was capable of change.

From there, it was short trip back to friendship and whatever lay beyond. Andy knew that Jessie had a best friend already, a brutish thing named Kat. She knew Jessie had a half-sister, a basket case named Hannah. And she knew Ryan Hernandez, Jessie's partner and now fiancé. He was an attractive but unworthy man. Soon, all of them would recede in Jessie's estimation, surpassed by Andrea Robinson. And if by some chance, they didn't fade from her heart, Andy would ensure that they left her life in more dramatic ways.

"Andy," a voice called out, snapping her out of her reverie, "Are you okay?"

She turned around to see one of the facility attendants, a dolt named Dewey, staring at her.

"Of course," she said with a sweet smile, "why?"

"It's just that you've been staring out that window, not moving, for a few minutes," he said with real concern. "I just wanted to make sure nothing was wrong."

Dewey had the twin gifts of being both somewhat dim-witted and easily manipulated. All it had taken was some perfunctory flirting and feigned interest in his life to make him her bitch boy. He wasn't going to help her escape or anything crazy like that. But if she needed to make a phone call after hours or have an unapproved visitor stop by, he'd happily bend the rules a little.

At some point, she'd take greater advantage of that, but right now it was enough to keep him on simmer. Being in this place was boring and playing Dewey like a yo-yo offered some measure of amusement. But very soon, if Eden did her job well, things would get much more entertaining. It was all coming together.

CHAPTER SEVENTEEN

Jessie convinced Ryan to wait.

As much as he had wanted to storm over to Bridget's casita right after talking to Cedric Cleaver, Jessie had persuaded him not to.

"They're all going to The Cove bar tonight," she had reminded him. "Let's hold off until then. Matt Darcy will have had a few more drinks by that time. He was already getting lubricated when I saw him earlier. By the time we go to the bar, his defenses should be down. We'll find a moment to get him alone and then see what we can squeeze out of him."

Ryan had acquiesced, which was why they, along with Kat, had spent the last few hours eating dinner while on the phone with Jamil and Beth, all of them reviewing resort video and financial documents from the Newhouses, Darcys and Andrews. It proved mostly fruitless.

"This could all be for nothing," Ryan had eventually blurted out in frustration. "Assuming that Scott Newhouse was killed, there's no certainty that it was any of these people. It could have been some random guest in the men's area of the spa who killed him for thrills. If the killer was wearing a hooded robe and didn't sign in or out, we'd never know. We're fixating on these five people because we have no choice, but it could be a wild goose chase."

After several seconds without anyone talking, Kat finally spoke up.

"Talk about a negative Nellie," she teased. "You're bumming me out, Hernandez."

Even though he made good points, Jessie agreed. Maybe it was falling behind earlier when they were chasing Ronnie Nance through the laundry, which might have bruised his confidence. Maybe it was all that talk about pre-marital counseling from Cedric Cleaver. But Ryan just wasn't as relentlessly confident as she was used to seeing him. She decided it was time to shake things up.

"It's almost 8 p.m.," she said, standing up and stretching dramatically. "I think it's time we let our brilliant research team clock out for the day. Besides, it's getting late enough that we can head over to The Cove to see if Darcy is feeling chatty. What do you say?"

"I say let's go," Ryan replied immediately, standing up as well.

Kat waved her arm in opposition

"And *I* say, since I'm absolutely coming with you guys, I need ten minutes."

"Why?" Ryan protested.

"You two may be stuck wearing the clothes you arrived in," she noted. "But I've got a whole wardrobe of fancy clothes on loan from this place, one of which is a cocktail dress I'll never have another chance to wear. I'm not wasting the opportunity."

While she went off to change, Jessie entertained herself by watching her fiancé fidget and pace nonstop, completely unaware that he was doing it.

*

Getting into The Cove was an undertaking and Jessie was losing patience with it.

There was no easy way into the VIP-only bar. It was built into the side of a cliff, just feet above where waves crashed against the rocks that formed its outside. But it was only accessible via Breakers, the less restrictive club high above it, which sat atop the cliff.

To get in, they first had to navigate the massive throng outside Breakers. Because the nightclub was set apart from the rest of the resort at the edge of that cliff, there was no protection from the whipping winds or the raucous crowd outside.

Rather than continue to battle through people inside the ropes to the bouncer, they changed tactics and went to a side entrance, where Ryan banged on the door. Eventually a dishwasher opened it, looking put out.

"LAPD," Ryan said, flashing his badge. "Official police business—let us in please."

The dishwasher seemed a little skeptical when he caught sight of Kat in her cocktail dress, but said nothing and held the door open for them. They passed through the kitchen, wending their way past the staff and glass racks, until they reached the swinging doors that led to the club proper. The heavy bass from the music was making Jessie's chest vibrate.

"Ready?" Ryan shouted so as to be heard over the noise. "Everyone put in your ear buds and we'll start a group call to stay in touch. Let's find The Cove entrance as fast as we can. The longer we're up here, the more people are likely to recognize Jessie, and the harder it will be to do our job."

Jessie knew he wasn't blaming her but it felt a little that way. She said nothing. When Ryan was focused on a mission, in this case finding and questioning Matt Darcy, he got a bit single-minded and social graces took a backseat. It was part of what made him such a great detective, but it was occasionally off-putting in a romantic partner. Of course, she could often be the same way so she was in no position to complain.

Once the call connected and they could all hear each other, they stepped through the kitchen doors and into the kaleidoscopic "Willy Wonka on psychedelics" world that was Breakers. The music, EDM from about a decade ago, was like a heavy aural blanket thrown over Jessie's head. The place looked like it had been designed by a toddler version of Jackson Pollock, with paint splashes all over the walls and the floor, occasionally interspersed with what looked to be a child's drawings of imaginary sea creatures. Disco balls shot rays of light everywhere and images of crashing waves were projected on the already busy walls, making it seem like the waves themselves were vomiting up entire boxes of crayons. It was incredibly disorienting and Jessie felt mildly nauseated.

The three of them split up. Jessie immediately hurried away from the lights of the dance floor. The decision was two-fold. First, she feared she was on the verge of a migraine. Secondly, she doubted the entrance to The Cove would be in such a visible, highly populated area. As she moved, she could hear Ryan talking through her ear buds but it was hard to make out everything he was saying—something about going to the bar.

She finally steered through the revelers, reaching the edge of the dance floor, where she had a better view. The club seemed to have all kinds of hallways, leading to side rooms and alcoves. She started down the hallway closest to her, hoping to get lucky.

But as she peeked into different nooks, all she found were people sitting or standing at tables, drinking and shouting to be heard over the music. She circled the entire club without seeing any room that screamed "entrance to secret, exclusive club here."

"I'm not having any luck," she heard Ryan bellow through her earpiece.

"Me either," Kat added.

"I'm coming up empty so far too," Jessie informed them.

"I think we should reach out to Hugo Cosgrove," Ryan suggested. "Maybe he can just have someone help us."

"That's not a bad idea," she shouted back. "We'll probably need his help to get in anyway. I'd rather not use our LAPD bona fides as a cudgel to get in. That might draw more attention than we want."

"Hold on," Ryan said. "I'll try to loop him into the call and then bring you guys back on. Putting you on hold briefly."

While she waited, Jessie decided it was good time for a bathroom break, where it might be quieter and she could give her unsettled nervous system a little reprieve from the visual and aural assault it was facing. She found the restrooms and her heart immediately sank.

As usual, while the line for the men's room was non-existent, the one for the ladies' room extended out the door and well down the hallway.

"Do you know if there's another restroom?" she asked the last woman in line, a blonde who was swaying slightly.

"There's one on the other side of the club," the blonde slurred," but that line is even longer than this one."

Jessie sighed and resigned herself to a long wait. She leaned against the wall, willing herself not to feel ill. But after a few seconds with nothing to focus on but her upset stomach, she gave up and started moving again.

Just down the hall, in a darkened recess set back a little, she notice a black curtain, and had a resurgence of hope. Maybe she'd found the secret entrance to The Cove. But once she pulled it back, she saw that it was just a gender neutral restroom.

Though she was disappointed, she still would have been all over if it didn't have an "out of order" sign on it. Then again, as unsettled as she felt, she considered taking advantage of it anyway. After all, if the toilet was already broken, what harm was there in throwing up in the bowl?

As she debated the social ethics of that choice, another question entered her head. Why was there a curtain hiding a gender neutral restroom? There was no need for that kind of discretion these days now that bathrooms like this were ubiquitous.

Maybe there's another reason for the curtain.

It occurred to her that an out-of-order restroom was something folks would want to steer well clear of. It was also exactly the kind of place no one would think might be the entrance to a secret club. But if party-goers saw multiple people entering the restroom despite the sign, they might get curious. That would explain the curtain.

Jessie glanced around to see if anyone was looking her way. Nobody was paying any attention to the ashen-skinned, thirty-year-old in non-club attire, so she ducked behind the curtain. She tugged on the door handle but it was locked, which made perfect sense if it was actually out of order.

Of course it also made sense if management didn't want just anyone traipsing into a place intended for VIPs. She knocked on the door and waited. Nothing happened, which wasn't a shock if it really was out of order. Still, she knocked again, louder this time.

"Find another bathroom," a gruff male voice said, "maintenance is working on this one."

Though the reply was reasonable, she couldn't shake the feeling that she'd stumbled onto something.

"Please," she pleaded, "I feel like I'm going to throw up. I just need someplace quiet to regroup. The ladies' room line is so long."

Though she still didn't feel great, her curiosity was temporarily pushing her physical discomfort to the backseat.

"Go outside," the man instructed.

Jessie was almost certain the guy was covering.

"Hey guys, are you hearing this?" she whispered into her ear bud.

"I think Ryan's still trying to reach Hugo," Kat answered. "But I am. You're using your 'I think I found something' voice. What's up?"

"I think I found something," Jessie replied. "Why don't you come on over? I'm on the west side of the club, just beyond the ladies' room. There's an out-of-order gender neutral bathroom hidden behind a curtain that's making my Spidey-sense tingle big time."

"I'm on my way," Kat said.

Jessie didn't wait. She banged on the door even harder.

"You better let me in or I'm going to make a real fuss," she said, bordering on a shout. "My girlfriends are just down the hall and I may have to have them come over and really get nasty with you. I may even get a manager. You've got three seconds before I start shouting for my friends to come over. One, two—."

The door opened to reveal a tall, well-built man in a maintenance uniform. He had an earpiece in his ear, which seemed odd for a guy fixing a toilet, and wore a scowl.

"Listen, ma'am," he said in an annoyed hush, "you don't want to use the bathroom in here if you're not feeling well. Trust me—it'll only make things worse. If the ladies' room is unavailable, I really suggest you go outside or back to your room."

"I know this isn't really a restroom," Jessie said. "Let me in now or I'll share that info with everyone."

The guy stared at her, unsure how to respond. She internally debated whether, despite her reluctance, to make use of her LAPD ID. Before she had to decide, Ryan's voice came back on.

"Everyone still there?" he asked.

"Yup," Jessie replied.

"Right here," Kat said. Jessie heard here voice on the call and in person and turned around to see that her friend was now right behind her.

"I've got Hugo on the line," Ryan said. "I've explained the situation to him."

"Lady," the maintenance man said urgently, "you and your friend there really need to go. I'm not allowed to let people in here. It's unsafe.

"Hold on," Jessie said to him. "I'm on the phone with your boss."

The man looked skeptical.

"You there, Hugo?" she asked.

Suddenly the guy's eyes widened in surprise.

"I am, Ms. Hunt," he said. "Detective Hernandez has filled me in on the situation. I've agreed to let you two, along with Ms. Gentry, into The Cove under one condition."

"What's that?" she wondered.

"While Peninsula doesn't endorse or facilitate any illegal behavior on its premises, we cannot be held responsible for what consenting adults choose to do. I would ask that unless you find that they directly relate to your investigation, that any…unconventional behaviors you might encounter not be prioritized."

"Did you already agree to this, Ryan?" she asked.

"Only if you're cool with it," he replied.

"I am," she said, "as long as no one is in immediate danger, that is."

"Then we have an agreement," Hugo said.

"Good," Jessie said, feeling better as each second passed. "Then can you please convey that to your bouncer dressed up as a maintenance guy in the gender neutral restroom that's really an entrance to the club—because he's giving me a hard time."

She couldn't help but smile as the bouncer's shocked face perfectly matched the dejected groan over the phone from Hugo. Clearly, he wasn't happy that his clever ruse had been uncovered.

"Give me a second," he said, "I'll call him now."

CHAPTER EIGHTEEN

The ruse was actually pretty damn cool.

Once everything was squared away and Ryan had joined them, the bouncer opened the door to the one stall in the bathroom. He pushed the button to flush the toilet. Jessie waited apprehensively. For a second, nothing happened. Then, silently and without warning, the entire back wall retracted, along with the toilet, and slid to the left.

"Welcome to The Cove experience," the bouncer said with considerably less enthusiasm than she suspected he usually mustered. "Please enter. The elevator and stairs are on your right. I recommend the elevator unless you want to go down seven very steep flights."

Jessie looked at the other two, who both indicated that she should step in first, perhaps as some reward for uncovering the place. She carefully made her way into the dark expanse where the wall used to be. Once there, she saw a dim overhead light, which shined weakly on an elevator to the right. Just beyond that, she saw a door with the words "stairs" on it. After the others arrived, she pushed the button and they waited.

When the doors opened, they saw that it was small, almost claustrophobic—barely big enough for four adults to fit in. Once the doors shut behind them, Ryan started prepping.

"I think we should use our phones like we did upstairs. The less we're all together as a group, the less attention we'll attract. Sound good?"

"Sure," Jessie said. "And let's remember, we don't know why Cedric Cleaver thinks we should be talking to Matt Darcy. We shouldn't make any assumptions about his guilt. No need to be aggressive until we have a reason."

"So I can't put him in a headlock to start off?" Kat asked facetiously.

"Not to start, Kat," Jessie quipped. "But it's good to know you have that in your back pocket."

The elevator came to a gentle stop and the doors opened. Jessie girded herself for more migraine-inducing noise and color. But as she stepped out, she felt a huge sigh of relief. There was music, but it had more of an ambient electronica vibe and it wasn't overwhelmingly loud. Even better, the place was dark with no flashing lights anywhere. With the sensory attack on her over, Jessie's nausea had faded away completely. Unfortunately, it was so dark that she almost bumped into a couple standing right in front of her before spying them at the last second.

The Cove's décor was best described as "chic grotto." In certain sections, the walls were the actual rocks that had been carved out to create the space. Dim lights had been drilled into them at various spots. The ground was carpeted but had been designed to look like the floor of a cave, with gradations of gray that made her think she should watch her step despite it being flat. Much of the furniture, including tables and chairs, had glowing strips on them so that patrons wouldn't inadvertently stumble into them.

The farther she edged into the bar, the more amazed she was. It was quite literally cavernous, to the point that she worried the place had been hollowed out too much and that it might cave in. She noted that instead of one big bar, there were three, placed at strategic points throughout the cavern.

Off to the right was The Cove's essential element. The entire cavern wall along the ocean-facing side of the club had been replaced with a gigantic window that was only a basketball hoop above the water line. Easily thirty feet across and fifteen feet high, it was the size of a small movie theater screen. Spotlights placed somewhere on the cliff outside the club shined out on the waves as if they were stars on a Broadway stage.

As Jessie stared in awe, she noticed a particularly large wave forming off the coast. It got bigger as it approached, rising high in the air so that it appeared to be equal in height to the top of the window. She clenched her teeth and squeezed her fists as it barreled toward them, appearing that it would hit the window while at its apex.

But then, with only seconds to spare, the wave broke, collapsing in on itself. Even so, the water slammed into the entire bottom third of the window before slinking back down into the depths. Amazingly, she heard nothing and wondered just how thick the window was.

"Should we split up?" Ryan asked quietly, before she could bring it up. "Whoever finds Matt Darcy first can give the others a heads up."

Jessie and Kat nodded and they all headed off in different directions. Jessie made her way to a section of the club that had piqued her interest. It was the only area, as far as she could see, that had a man-made wall instead of rock. When she got closer, she noticed something odd.

There seemed to be a space between the human-built wall and the cave wall, as if there might be space in between the two. She looked for an opening, walking the entire length of the thing, which was a good forty feet. She ran her finger along the wall and noticed something else: it looked like wood but was actually made of some thicker composite. Finally, she found a spot at the far end of the wall where there was a narrow, easy-to-miss door. She grabbed the recessed handle and turned.

It opened without a struggle. She peered into almost total darkness. Quickly, she stepped in and closed the door behind her. She was about to use the flashlight on her phone when she got an odd sensation. First of all, this area was much warmer than the rest of the club. In fact, the air was heavy, almost to the point of being sticky.

But there was more. The room was clearly soundproofed, as all the vocal noise from outside had dampened as soon as she'd closed the door. But that wasn't what had her blood pumping faster. Although she couldn't hear anyone speaking over the music, she got the distinct feeling that she wasn't alone in here.

The room felt thick with people, though she hadn't heard a word. Then, as she strained to listen, she noticed something: a heavy sigh, then another one, followed by a soft moan and a barely audible whimper.

Her mind flashed to some of the past horrors she'd encountered—kids being enslaved and kept in darkened rooms, used for the grotesque pleasure of sick adults. The only thing that stopped her from immediately turning on her light was what Hugo had said before allowing them in. Surely, if there was some secret child sex ring being run out of The Cove, he would know, and if he was involved, he would never have let them down here.

Then the door opened as someone else came in. A thin stream of light snuck in, silhouetting what was happening before her. Jessie tried not to gasp.

As far as the eye could see, there were intertwined naked bodies lying on pillows, writhing about like a scene out of Caligula. Suddenly the humidity and moaning made sense. As best she could tell, these seemed to be consenting adults—a lot of them. She guessed that there were at least two dozen people in the room. She didn't see anyone tied up and no one appeared to be in distress.

The door closed and everything was once again thrown into darkness. Satisfied that there was no crime taking place in here, she moved toward the exit as quickly as she could without risking tripping and drawing attention to herself. She brushed past the person who had just entered but said nothing. Once she found the door, she opened it and left without looking back.

The second she was out, the air became lighter and fresher. She gulped it down as she wiped a dribble of sweat from her brow. Now that she was safely out and confident that no one was being harmed inside, she let out a half-laugh at her reaction. She wasn't a prude, but that had been well out of her comfort zone.

"Everything okay?" Ryan asked through her ear buds.

"Yeah," she said. "Let's just hope one of you finds Darcy, because if he's in the room I just left, someone else is going to have locate him."

"Why?" Kat asked.

"Because I stumbled into an orgy and I'm not going to be the one to break it up to look for him in there. That's cop stuff."

"Coward," he teased, chuckling in her ear.

"Luckily you won't have to," Kat told her. "I think I spotted him. He's on the second level."

"There's a second level?" Jessie asked looking up and seeing a small, overhanging balcony section she hadn't noticed before. It was a good two stories above them and blended into the cavern so well that she didn't feel too guilty for missing it.

"Yup," Kat said, "and it looks like there's another bar up there. From what I can tell, he's alone."

"Sounds like perfect timing," Ryan asked. "Shall we go say 'hi,' Ms. Hunt?"

CHAPTER NINETEEN

Getting to the upper level balcony was an adventure.

It was only accessible by a narrow metal staircase built into the wall of the cave. Jessie let Ryan take the lead. When she followed, she gripped the thin rail tightly.

Kat stayed below. She wasn't official law enforcement and her presence wouldn't be appropriate. Besides, this way she could warn them if someone else from the group started upstairs. They were almost to the top when they heard Kat's voice in their ears.

"I've located the rest of the gang," she said. "Malcolm and Abby Andrews are on the dance floor. They're all over each other. It's either adorable or disgusting, depending on your perspective."

Jessie was tempted to try to find them but thought better of it. She wasn't looking down unless she had to.

"You see the others?" Ryan asked.

"I do," Kat confirmed. "Bridget Newhouse just came out of the restroom. She looks pretty rough. Her eyes are puffy and she's not dressed in fancy club attire. I think she's wearing yoga clothes. She just sat down at a table with Ellie Darcy, who doesn't seem anywhere near as broken up. She's got a drink with an umbrella in it and she's laughing at something. Apparently she's not bothered by her husband being nowhere near her or by her friend crying over the loss of her husband."

"Okay," Ryan said. "Let us know if anything dramatic happens. Otherwise we're about to talk to Matt Darcy."

As they walked across metal floor of the second level, each step echoed. Jessie wasn't confident that the thing was strong enough to support the weight of everyone up there. In addition to the two of them and Darcy, there was the bartender and a couple sitting at a small table in the corner.

Darcy was seated alone at a cocktail table with four seats, staring down at the giant, wave-deflecting window. He had taken off his sports jacket and his dress shirt was halfway untucked. His blond hair was plastered against his forehead. He was slumped over, his eyes were glassy, and his breathing was labored. He was very drunk.

This was just what Jessie had been hoping for. If things went well, the guy's inebriation would act like a truth serum.

"Hi, Matt," Ryan said, plopping down beside the man. Jessie quietly took the other seat. After taking a moment to focus on the man suddenly sitting across from him, Darcy managed to find his words.

"Who the hell are you?" he demanded in a sloppy garble.

"Don't you remember me?" Ryan asked. "I'm Detective Hernandez. I spoke to you and your wife after your visit with Honey Potter earlier today."

"Oh yeah," he said, vaguely registering the memory. "You're looking into whether Scott was murdered, along with that hot profiler chick."

Only then did he glance over and see Jessie. He looked mildly embarrassed.

"Hi, Matt," she said sweetly.

"Hi," he said loudly, his shame quickly gone. "I didn't know they let regular people like you two into clubs like this. I thought you had to be special."

"Are you special, Matt?" Jessie asked, her pleasant tone hiding her distaste for him.

"I run one of the most successful west coast-based mutual funds in the country," he informed them. "So yeah, I'm kind of a big deal."

"That's why we want to talk to you," Jessie told him. "A guy as important as you could really be a help to us. At least that's what a source told us."

"What source?" he wanted to know.

Jessie looked over at Ryan, who indicated that she should continue.

"I can't get into particulars other than to say it was a counseling professional that Scott and Bridget were seeing," she said as vaguely as possible. "And that counselor seemed to think you know more than you told Detective Hernandez when you spoke before. Care to fill us in?"

Darcy's bloodshot eyes narrowed.

"I don't know anything about that," he grumbled, "Sounds like this 'counselor' got some bad intel."

"And yet you were specifically mentioned," Jessie pointed out.

Darcy stared at her lazily, then turned his attention to Ryan. After a few seconds of apparent indecision, he wheezed a response.

"I might have something to say, but not in front of her," he said, pointing at Jessie. "This is guy talk—only for guys."

"Hold on a sec—," Ryan started to say, sounding irritated.

"That's fine," Jessie cut him off, standing up. "You boys have a nice chat. I'll just head back down."

As she turned around and headed for the stairs, she whispered to him through her ear buds.

"However we can get him to talk, let's do it. I'll be downstairs. Maybe I'll check in on his lovely wife Ellie. It sounds like she's a little tipsy too."

With that settled, she focused her attention on surviving the walk back down the narrow metal staircase.

*

Ellie was still laughing as Jessie walked over. As she approached, she muted Ryan so that she could concentrate on her own conversation.

"Where's Bridget?" Jessie asked Kat over the shared phone line.

"She went back to the restroom," Kat said in her ear. "I don't think she appreciated how festive her friend was being."

"I see she's at least removed the umbrella from her drink," Jessie noted.

"Yep," Kat said. "It was making it too hard to take big gulps."

"Okay. I'm going to try to make this quick. Let me know if Bridget comes out of the restroom again."

Jessie took a chair next to the loveseat where Ellie was loudly sharing a story with another woman, who didn't look like she was enjoying it anywhere near as much Ellie enjoyed telling it. When Ellie took a breath, Jessie jumped in.

"I think you have a phone call," she told the other woman, giving her a "this is your chance to get out of here" look. The woman understood immediately and stood up quickly.

"Sorry. I've got to go but it was nice talking with you," she said to Ellie before mouthing a silent "thank you" to Jessie and darting off.

"Hey, I know you," Ellie said, gripping the arm of the loveseat for balance. "You're the famous profiler lady who came to Bridget's place earlier. Solve the thing yet?"

"I'm sure you've been on pins and needles waiting for an update," Jessie said, careful to keep her tone from betraying her disdain, "but unfortunately we're still gathering information. Maybe you can help with that."

"I doubt it," Ellie said with an overly dramatic hand flourish, almost hitting a drink on the table and sending it flying, "but go for it."

"Thanks," Jessie said, glancing anxiously in the direction of the ladies' room. She wanted to move this along so that they were done before Bridget got back, but if she pressed too much, Ellie might pick up on it, even in her state. "So this was kind of a couples' retreat, right?"

"Yup," Ellie confirmed between glugs, running her hand through her short, black hair. "We were all here to make our marriages the best they could be."

"I think that's great," Jessie said, taking note of the insincerity in the woman's voice. "So did you and Matt meet with any counselors yet like the Newhouses did?"

Ellie scrunched up her nose in confusion.

"I didn't know they'd done that," she replied.

"Oh, yes. Apparently they saw someone just yesterday," Jessie said. "My understanding is that your husband's name may have come up during their session—any idea why that might be?"

Ellie actually snorted at the question. She was so loud that Jessie heard Kat mutter "jeez" over the open phone line.

"I assume that's a 'yes?'" she asked leadingly.

"I can guess," Ellie said bitterly. "It probably has something to do with the fact that Matt and Bridget used to date. She broke up with him when she met Scott but they 'stayed friends.' Of course, that means different things to different people."

"What did it mean to each of them?" Jessie wondered.

Ellie finished the last of her drink and waved at a nearby server for another, then returned her attention to Jessie.

"To Bridget, it meant they stayed friends," she said. "To Matt, it meant that even after she married Scott, even after he started dating me and we tied the knot, he mooned over her. He was like a puppy dog tripping over his own paws any time she called for him. I know that after all these years, Scott had gotten pretty tired of it. I bet it came up in their session."

"And what about you?" Jessie asked. "You don't seem as pissed off as I would expect from someone whose husband carried a torch for another woman."

Ellie shrugged.

"I made my peace with it a long time ago," she said resignedly. "I knew what I was getting into when I married Matt. It's not like he was great at hiding it. He's actually a pretty decent husband. He just has this one blind spot. Besides, I found ways to keep myself entertained."

Ellie's tone was provocative and Jessie was tempted to pursue more about the exact nature of how she kept herself entertained. But time was short and she had other, more pertinent questions. Again, she glanced at the ladies' room. The door was closed.

Kat must have noticed and read her mind because she whispered over the line, "She's been in there a while. I'll go check on her status."

Jessie wanted to acknowledge her words but couldn't without giving herself away so she just pressed on.

"Do you think Bridget got tired of Matt's mooning too?" she wondered. "Or was she maybe still interested in him?"

"I think she got the best of both worlds," Ellie said, the resentment clear in her voice and her tightly drawn face. "For her, it was long over with Matt. But that didn't mean she was above using him to make Scott jealous, or using Matt when she needed something. He's gotten her opera tickets, backstage at concerts, invites to private parties, all things Scott could have gotten also but was often too busy to be bothered with. I'd say she considered him 'useful.'"

"Do you think the animosity could have reached the point of violence?" she asked, well aware that even in Ellie's drunken state, this question wouldn't seem innocent to the woman. She was right. Ellie blinked several times and when she fixed her gaze on Jessie, her eyes were considerably more focused than before.

"Do you mean 'did my husband kill Scott so he could be with Bridget?'" she asked archly. "Or do you mean 'did Scott confront Matt about his endless crush, making Matt panic and kill him?' Because my answer to all of those would be 'no.' Matt's a lot of things, but he's not a killer. Besides, he wasn't in the spa when Scott died, right? I thought he was in our casita."

"That's what he said," Jessie confirmed, "just like you were hiking down to some tide pools, right?"

Ellie seemed to get that the question wasn't just curiosity and looked about to respond defensively when the server brought over a new drink. She paused long enough to take a sip. As she did Kat's voice came over the phone.

"Bridget Newhouse is on her way out," she said urgently. "She was being comforted by some random women who found her crying in one of the stalls. They're all leaving together, taking their time, but I'd say you've got about thirty seconds. Better wrap up."

Jessie would have liked to but Ellie had put her drink down and appeared to be warming up for some sort of cutting comment. But before she could get a word out, they both heard a screech from up above.

Jessie looked up to see the couple on the second level rushing down the metal staircase. The woman was screaming bloody murder. She scanned the area where Ryan and Matt Darcy had been sitting. It was empty. Then her attention was pulled toward movement to the right. She saw Darcy's large body lunge forward clumsily. In a moment of frozen horror, she realized that he was taking a swing at Ryan.

Her fiancé dodged the punch easily, sidestepping it with grace. But the force of Darcy's effort sent the bigger man careening forward. He slammed into the balcony railing before his considerable weight sent him toppling over it and down toward the first level, at least thirty feet below.

CHAPTER TWENTY

Ryan grabbed Matt Darcy's left wrist with both hands and braced.

As he did, he could feel his whole body tense up at what was about to happen. The bigger man's weight pulled him down and for a second he thought he was going to tumble over the railing too, but he managed to hook his feet between the floor and the bottom rail. His arms strained and his knees buckled. He pressed his waist hard against the railing to get traction.

Darcy's wrist was slick with sweat and Ryan felt his grip starting to slip. He knew he only had a short time before he lost it entirely. He looked down into the man's face and saw the fear in his red eyes.

"Grab the bottom rail with your other hand," he grunted through gritted teeth. "I can't hold on much longer."

Matt Darcy stared up at him as if he was speaking another language. Ryan's hands were no longer holding his wrist but his palm and the back of his hand. In less than five seconds, he wouldn't be holding anything.

"Matthew," he ordered. "Wrap your right arm around the rail right now!"

Maybe it was hearing his full first name spoken like a parent would say it that snapped the guy out of it, but whatever the reason, Darcy did as he was told. Just as he hooked his right elbow around the bottom rung of the railing his fingers slipped through Ryan's grasp.

He dropped but didn't fall, though he did howl in pain as his arm torqued at an awkward angle. Ryan ignored that, quickly wiped his palms on his pants, jammed his feet even more firmly under the railing and reached down, bending as far as he could go. This time he hooked his arms under Darcy's armpits and clenched the back of his dress shirt.

"Matthew," he said calmly, "I know it hurts but I need you to pay attention. When I tell you to, let go of the railing. I'm going to pull you up. But we need to do this fast while I still have the strength for it. Do you understand?"

Matt was half screaming and half crying but he managed to nod weakly.

"Okay," Ryan said, "here we go. Let go now!"

Darcy unhooked his right arm and Ryan yanked him upward in one propulsive burst, like he was a sack of potatoes with arms. The man cleared the railing and Ryan wrapped him in a bear hug, pulling him back toward him. Ryan fell backward to the floor and Darcy—all 215 pounds of him—landed hard on top of his chest, knocking the wind out of him.

He gasped for breath, which was made that much harder by the heavy lump lying on him. When he was finally able to suck in enough air, he shoved Darcy off and rolled over onto his stomach. Every part of him, especially his arms, legs and back, was throbbing with a mix of pain and intense tingling.

He was just pushing himself onto all fours when he saw Jessie leap up from the metal stairwell onto the balcony, with Kat right behind her.

"Watch him," she instructed Kat, pointing at the other man as she darted over to him with a worry etched into her face. "Don't try to get up yet. Give yourself a minute."

"Everything hurts," Ryan whispered, still trying to catch his breath.

"I'll bet," Jessie said quietly. "Do you think anything's broken?"

"Too soon to tell," he grunted, "but I don't think so. I'll know better once I'm standing."

After waiting a minute, she helped him gingerly to his feet. Darcy was still lying on the ground, groaning and hugging his right arm with his left. Ryan moved his arms around and took a couple of hesitant steps. It all ached but there was no sharp pain.

"I think I'm okay, or will be," he said.

"What are we doing with this guy?" Kat asked. "Do we want to call a squad car to take him to the station?"

Ryan thought about it for a second, trying not to let his anger at the man cloud his judgment.

"I think I've got a better idea."

*

They stepped out of The Cove manager's office, leaving Matt Darcy inside, cuffed to a file cabinet. Ryan glanced back at the guy before shutting the door, just to make sure he was totally secure. Even if Darcy wasn't attached to a big metal rectangle, Ryan didn't think he looked in any shape to put up a fight at this point.

A security guard, one specifically assigned to the task by Hugo, stayed inside with him just in case. Darcy's arm rested in his lap. A doctor who'd been partying at the club had agreed to look at it.

"Nothing is broken," he had assured them. "It's a mild sprain. He can wait until tomorrow to get it checked out."

After he left, Ryan, Jessie, and Kat stood in the hallway just outside the room with the club manager, a small, balding twenty-something guy in a tuxedo, who still looked shell-shocked.

"Thanks for your help," he said. "You'll have your office back soon, I promise. We just need a moment to confer privately. Please tell Mrs. Darcy that we'll let her see her husband momentarily. But make sure the security guard with her keeps her at that table until we say otherwise."

The manager nodded and scurried off, happy to be assigned a task within his skill set. Only once Ryan, Jessie, and Kat were alone did he feel comfortable talking freely. Before he could say anything, Kat did.

"Are you planning to interrogate him in there?" she asked.

"I'm not planning to interrogate him at all," he said, clearly surprising both her and Jessie. "In his condition, he's pretty useless at this point. Besides, he already told me everything worthwhile."

"Like what?" Jessie wanted to know.

"He said that he and Bridget used to date about a decade ago and that they were still close. He said that made Scott jealous."

"I got a slightly different version of that story from Eleanor Darcy," Jessie noted. "According to her, Matt wanted them to be tighter than they really were."

"That doesn't shock me," Ryan replied. "In fact, it was when I suggested that the feelings might be a one-way street that got his dander up. He smashed his glass on the table. When I told him to calm down, he got chesty and stood up, threatening to kick my ass. I warned him that he was making a bad choice. That's when he made a worse one and threw that swing that sent him flying over the railing."

"Well, you've got dozens of witnesses to that part, so it shouldn't be hard to charge him," Kat said.

"I'm not inclined to that," he replied, "at least not yet. I'm not sure it will help much."

"Why not?" Jessie asked.

Ryan shook out his arms before responding. They were getting stiff and he knew he was going to have to pop a few pills for the pain soon.

"First of all," he said. "I haven't seen any evidence that makes me think he's our guy. It sounds like he came up in that counseling session as more of an annoyance than a threat. And I'm not sure how killing Scott Newhouse helps him."

"Maybe he thought that with her husband dead, Bridget would turn to him for comfort," Kat suggested.

Ryan had considered that possibility.

"I think he'd be more likely to believe he could win her over if he could show her that Scott had wronged her in some way: maybe that he was cheating on her or something. But it's hard for me to buy that Matt Darcy thought he could kill Scott Newhouse and then romance the man's grieving widow. Despite his protestations, it was clear to me that Darcy knew Bridget didn't reciprocate his feelings. He had to know that killing her husband would only make her more devoted to Scott's memory."

"I think that's an open question," Jessie countered.

"Fair," he replied. "But regardless of that, his key card swipes verify his entry into his casita this morning at the time he said he was there and nothing we've found yet indicates he was anywhere near the spa. I'm not saying he's innocent. But I am saying we don't have anything that suggests he's guilty."

"We've arrested people for less," Jessie pointed out.

"Yes, but unless we have him dead to rights, I think it's counterproductive. He'll lawyer up. All of the others in the group will probably do the same. Even if they don't, they're sure to stop cooperating. And considering that they're the only real suspects we have, I'd rather keep them open to talking. But if we don't arrest him, it might garner some good will from him and the others. We'll tell them we're more interested in getting to the bottom of what happened to Scott than arresting people for drunken mistakes. Add that to the fact that I saved the man's life *after* he tried to knock me out. I'm hoping that anyone in the group who's not a murderer will take all that to heart and be *more* inclined to help."

"So what do you propose?" Jessie asked.

"I think that we let Eleanor Darcy take him back to his casita with instructions not to leave, maybe have a security guard posted outside to make sure he doesn't. Then we start fresh tomorrow. Anyone who makes things difficult for us after that act of big-hearted forgiveness will look churlish, and worse, suspicious."

"So we let him off the hook, appeal to their better natures, and come back in the morning?" Jessie asked.

"Actually," Kat volunteered. "I think you can do better than that. Let's call Hugo back. You just saved a guest's life and prevented dozens of other from seeing him turned into a bloody pancake. I think that at least merits a room for the night."

Jessie was about to protest that they needed to get back home to Hannah. But then she remembered it wasn't an issue right now.

CHAPTER TWENTY ONE

Kat was right.

Jessie wasn't surprised. One thing about being a private detective constantly scrapping for cases was that it made her friend unafraid to make bold requests. Jessie was still trying to incorporate that attitude into her personal life.

As it turned out, Hugo made no mention of the fact that it was Ryan's questioning of Matt Darcy that instigated the near-pancaking. Instead, the security chief offered them the very casita they'd been using as their home base all afternoon. He even sent someone to provide them with clothes from the resort shop, all monogrammed with the same "𝒫" found on the towels and take their current ones to be laundered.

"It's a lovely gesture," Jessie said to Ryan once Kat had left and they were changed and settling in for bed. "And I don't want to sound ungrateful. But I think Hugo's generosity is as much about pressuring us to wrap up this case fast as it is intended to make our lives easier."

"Either way," Ryan replied. "This robe is super soft. Between that and the meds I took, my body is finally starting to throb a little less."

"Good," Jessie said, relieved. "I was really worried about you. I was sure that by the time I got to that balcony you'd have gone over the side."

"Me too," Ryan admitted. "But I guess all that rehab I've been doing paid off. There's no way I could have pulled Darcy up like that even six weeks ago."

Jessie gave his forearm a gentle pat.

"Well, hopefully the rest of this investigation will be less physically eventful," she said. "Although, I'm not sure we're going to resolve this thing in time to satisfy Hugo and resort management. Our suspects include a widow without a bulletproof alibi who admittedly seems to be taking this very hard, her ex-boyfriend, who is still into her, and his wife, who clearly resented the whole situation. That doesn't even account for the surly tech genius or his aggressively sunny schoolteacher wife."

"Nor does it account for the less likely, but still viable possibility that Scott Newhouse killed himself," Ryan reminded her.

"Maybe we take another run at that couple's counselor, Cedric Cleaver," she suggested. "We didn't really get into whether he saw signs of depression in Newhouse during their session."

Ryan shook his head.

"I don't think we're getting anything else out of that guy without a court order, certainly nothing as sensitive as his client's mental state. And we don't have time for that. I'm pretty sure that Chief Laird is going to bring the hammer down on us tomorrow."

Jessie knew he was right on both fronts. As she sat on the bed, leaning back against the headboard, with him doing the same thing beside her, she found herself wondering how her fiancé could be so clear-headed when analyzing other people's intentions and motives and so dense when it came to understanding his own.

She still couldn't get him to appreciate that she didn't want a big wedding at a place like this or to explain why he was so insistent on pressing ahead with an event like that. Maybe it was the talk of the couple's counselor or of mental states, but she was tempted to bring the issue up now. She knew that if she didn't, it would eat at her, making sleep impossible.

She decided to broach it lightly, and not make mention of any issue other than this one. Her simmering discontent about how fellow HSS Detective Susannah Valentine flirted with him was a discussion for another time, especially considering that wasn't his fault.

"Maybe we should pay Cleaver a visit ourselves when this is all over," she said quietly, shocking herself for suggesting the very thing she'd been worried Ryan might mention just hours earlier, "or someone else like him."

"Why?" he asked, clearly as stunned at hearing the words as she was at saying them. "Is something wrong?"

"Not wrong," she said quickly. "But I think our communication could be clearer sometimes."

"About what?" he asked apprehensively.

She couldn't stall any longer. This was the moment of truth.

"I've said this before, but I don't think you've really taken it to heart," she said in a tender voice. "I don't want a big wedding,

Ryan. I think you suspect I'm just saying that to take pressure off you or something. But I genuinely, actively do not want that. Yet you keep pushing for it. It's like you can't hear me or you just dismiss it as if I'm saying it so I don't seem grasping or spoiled. I feel like you think that I'm one of those people who says they don't like surprise parties but secretly, desperately hopes she'll get one. But I'm not. You should get that by now. And if you don't, we've got a bigger problem than between a band or DJ."

He stared at her with his eyes wide. She could tell that he was hurt but she didn't know what to do about that. She'd been as tactful as she could while still making her point plain. He needed to hear it. She waited for him to say something but he seemed at a loss for words. Finally, he stood up, adjusted his robe, and slid his feet into his slippers.

"I'm going for a walk," he said and left the bedroom.

A few moments later, she heard the front door open and then, without another word being spoken, it closed.

*

Ryan walked slowly.

After a couple of minutes, he had to remove the slippers, which kept sliding off his feet on the path, and walked barefoot.

He tried to keep his head clear, but it was a jumble of conflicting thoughts. Part of him hoped that this was just the pressure of planning everything getting to her. But her comment about potentially having bigger problems was ominous.

She sounded like she meant it. And Ryan didn't doubt that in that moment, she did. But he worried that the second he agreed to a smaller wedding, it would change her perception of him. She'd no longer view him as an enthusiastic partner in making preparations for their future, but something less. He feared she'd view him as not trying hard enough, being willing to settle, maybe even being relieved that he didn't have to shell out so much money while on a cop's salary. Just because she was independently wealthy and could probably pay for a lavish affair all by herself wouldn't matter. She'd see him as diminished in some way.

It wasn't an idle concern. In fact, though he'd never told Jessie, that was exactly what had happened in his first marriage. Shelly had repeatedly insisted they go small. He fought it up until the moment that he didn't and he saw the look of disappointment in her eyes when he seemed willing to foreclose on her childhood dream.

That was far from the cause of their marriage's demise but it didn't help. And Jessie was nothing like Shelly. But he couldn't help but worry that in this one way, they might not be so different. He feared that she was just protecting his feelings, that she didn't want him to feel like a kept man. He worried that despite her protestations to the contrary right now, she would regret going small later and look back sadly, wishing they'd done something more memorable.

He listened to her compare this to someone claiming not to want a surprise party but really hoping for one. She said that wasn't her. But sometimes it was. After her debacle of a marriage to Kyle, she'd expressed distaste for the idea of ever getting re-married. But then they got engaged and she was happy about that. She'd talked about how the trauma of her own childhood made her wary of being a parent. But she'd embraced the role with Hannah, even if that wasn't going so great right now. What if this was like those times? What if she changed her mind? He wanted to accede to her wishes but he didn't want her to resent him once he did.

He glanced at his watch and was startled to realize that he'd been walking around for almost forty-five minutes, repeatedly turning over the same concerns in his head. He had to set that aside for now. There was a case to solve and he needed some sleep if he was going to do it. He and Jessie could deal with their personal issues once all of this was over. Right now they had a job to do.

When he returned to the casita, Jessie was asleep.

CHAPTER TWENTY TWO

Hannah didn't love this doctor.

Even before she met him, she resented that he was making her come to an 8 a.m. therapy session. It only got worse once she entered his office. Dr. Ken Tam, a short, plump man in his thirties with wispy brown hair and a droopy mustache, had an attitude.

Unlike Dr. Janice Lemmon, the therapist she shared with Jessie, who had convinced her to voluntarily check in to this facility, this guy was brusque and condescending. As tough and frank as Dr. Lemmon was, Hannah always felt that the woman respected her and truly heard what she was saying. Dr. Tam, on the other hand, seemed more interested in his own voice than hers.

She tried not to judge him too harshly. After all, he was the substitute's substitute. Dr. Lemmon couldn't make it out to Malibu today, for reasons no one would explain to her. And her preferred fill-in, Dr. Rose Perry, was currently dealing with an "unexpected patient issue" over in the secure Assistance Wing. Hannah had heard through the grapevine that someone had a psychotic break and Perry, as the on-call psychiatrist, was dealing with it.

It didn't help that Hannah couldn't tell Dr. Tam the real reason she was here. Dr. Lemmon had expressly warned her that if she had therapy sessions with doctors other than her, she shouldn't mention her semi-regular, intense desire to see the light die in someone's eyes as a result of something she did or the thrill she felt the one time it happened. Once that got out, there could be consequences outside her control.

Instead she was to stick to issues that were legitimate but more generic. She could discuss her anger management issues, specifically her inclination to want to respond aggressively when wronged. She could also talk about her need to put herself in risky situations as a way to cut through the emotional numbness that she felt most of the time. Those topics were fine, just no mention of wanting to kill someone for the high.

So she talked around her issues—that is, when Dr. Tam let her talk. She used safe psychological euphemisms. She played the game.

"It's difficult for me to find joy in small moments," she acknowledged.

"Maybe you're looking in the wrong places," he offered unhelpfully.

"I hate to see bad people get away with bad acts," she said later, "and I often want to punish them when the system won't."

"But then you'll be the one who gets punished," Tam pointed out blandly, not even looking up from his notepad.

That was fine with Hannah. She didn't want him taking too keen an interest in her case. But it would have been nice if her time with him wasn't completely useless. She was tempted to be combative just to get the guy back on his heels and out of his comfortable arrogance. But that would only make her life more unpleasant, so she fought the urge.

As the session drew to a close, and without offering an explanation, he indicated that he would likely recommend that Dr. Lemmon add a tranquilizer prescription to her medication regimen. Hannah nodded compliantly. She might have been worried if she didn't know Lemmon would countermand that prescription immediately.

When the session ended, she thanked him for his time, managing not to mention to him how disappointed she was that Jessie's money was just spent on what she considered to be a wasted fifty-five minutes. Instead, she headed over to the cafeteria for a late breakfast.

Seasons Wellness Center was a good facility in many respects, but there were definitely some gaps. She resolved to make a list and give it to Dr. Lemmon at their next meeting. After all, there were patients here who weren't in a position to speak up for themselves. She could and she had access to one of the most respected behavioral therapists on the west coast. She ought to take advantage of that for the benefit of others.

When she arrived, the place was mostly empty. She ordered the kosher meal, as Merry Bartlett had recommended, and was happy to be rewarded with a yogurt parfait and a veggie scramble to go with her coffee. Once through the line, she picked an unoccupied table in the corner of the room, with a clear view of the ocean. She was just taking her first bite of yogurt when she felt someone's eyes on her.

She looked up to see a skinny guy in his twenties with a buzz cut and a scowl staring daggers at her from across the room. He was holding a tray with two muffins, a croissant, Danish, and a huge glass of milk. He marched straight towards her.

Pretending not to notice, Hannah turned her attention back to the window as she took a long, slow deep breath. She could see the guy's reflection in the window getting closer. As casually as she could, she picked up her coffee and took a sip. She didn't know what his problem was, but she wasn't going to be intimidated by a guy with crazy eyes and a bunch of pastries. She kept the coffee in her hand, ready to toss the hot liquid in his face if he made a sudden move.

He stopped two feet from her table and hovered there, waiting for her to acknowledge him. When she was good and ready, she glanced over and gave him a sweet smile. He glared down at her.

"You are in my spot," he growled. His voice was raspy, as if he'd yelled himself hoarse.

Now that Hannah knew what she was dealing with—a guy with some kind of mental health issue who felt possessive of an arbitrary table in a cafeteria—she felt slightly more comfortable. It was always easier to navigate the crazy you understood more than the crazy you didn't.

"What's that?" she asked, not because she didn't understand but so she could stall a little and determine how best to handle this.

Under normal circumstances, she'd stand her ground and simply decline to move, actually relishing the potential conflict to come. She could sense other people watching and knew that as long as she appeared to keep her cool, she could probably bait this guy into a poor choice. He already appeared to be operating on a knife's edge. When he acted inappropriately, she could reluctantly "defend" herself, getting him thrown in the Assistance Wing and leaving her with this table for the remainder of her stay.

But that was exactly the pattern she was trying to break. She was mainly at this place to control the craving to kill someone for the adrenaline rush. But that was just an exponential extension of the buzz she got when she had a brush with danger, a conflict with someone menacing. How was she supposed to manage the former if she couldn't stop the latter?

"You are in my spot," he repeated through gritted teeth. "This is where I sit. Everybody knows it. Move."

Hannah closed her eyes for a second, trying to keep her cool. She reminded herself that just because this skinny carb-hound deserved to be put in his place didn't mean she had to be the one to do it. Besides, she didn't know what his damage was. Maybe this spot was special to him; maybe it was a safe haven where he'd shared a meal with a loved one or a cherished friend. She decided to cut him some slack.

"Okay," she said, putting the coffee on her tray and standing up. "Enjoy the view."

She picked up the tray and was about to move when he stepped forward and blocked her path.

"You gotta say 'sorry' too," he hissed. His breath reeked and it was all she could do not to gag. His hands were shaking with rage, making the plate full of pastries rattle on his tray.

"What?" she asked slowly, feeling her sense of restraint fading away fast. Out of the corner of her eye, she saw another patient waving to get the attention of a security guard who was too far away to intervene in time to stop whatever was about to happen.

"You tried to take my spot," he repeated. "That is not allowed. You have to say 'sorry.' Do it now."

Hannah put the tray back down on the table and let her hand rest near the still-steaming cup of coffee. She opened her mouth, about to share the words "make me" with him, when a voice called out from nearby.

"Hey Silvio, what kind of muffins do they have today?"

Hannah looked over to see Merry Bartlett, complete with her pigtails and rainbow scrunchies, walking over. Instead of jeans and a tie-dyed shirt, today she was wearing a completely tie-dyed, long-sleeved dress that looked like she made it herself.

"Blueberry and banana nut," he said without hesitation. "And this girl has to apologize for taking my spot."

"Hey buddy," Merry said playfully, "Hannah didn't know about your spot. She only got here yesterday. You can't expect her to learn everything all at once."

"Maybe not," Silvio replied, his hands and the tray still shaking slightly, "but she still has to apologize to make it right."

Merry glanced over at Hannah, who shook her head 'no' ever so slightly. Silvio missed it but Merry seemed to get it. There was only so far Hannah could go. She wouldn't poke the guy. She'd even move. But she wasn't going to apologize to this sewer-breath obsessive.

"I apologize on her behalf," Merry said cheerily. "That should be good enough, Silvio. After all, you love me."

That seemed to break the tension. The tray stopped shaking just as the security guard arrived. He stood directly in front of Silvio and put his hand on his shoulder.

"We're going to have our meal in our room, today, Silvio," he said firmly.

At that instruction, all the agitation seemed to evaporate from his body. It was as if, freed of having to make the choice for himself, all his stress disappeared. He walked off meekly, with the guard's arm still on his shoulder.

"Thanks," Hannah said to Merry once Silvio had left.

"No problem," she replied, "but I would still sit somewhere else. There are lots of tattlers around here and if it gets back to him that you took the seat anyway, he might hold it against you."

"What would he do then?" Hannah asked, placing her tray one table over and sitting down.

"Hard to say," Merry said, sitting down opposite her. "He might pee in your bed. That wouldn't be a first. He might smash a chair through the window, which also wouldn't be the first time. Best not find out if you don't have to."

"It sounds like maybe Silvio should be in the Assistance Wing."

"He bounces back and forth," Merry explained. "But he's had a good last month on this side. It would be a shame if he couldn't stick around."

"Any idea why he's so fixated on that table?"

"That's where he was last year when he learned his mom had died of cancer," Merry said. "His dad told him that she'd gone to heaven and every time a wave crashed on the beach, it was her sending a kiss down to him. So he likes to sit there and watch them crash."

"I see," Hannah said, proud of her self-control earlier, "In that case I'm glad I didn't throw my coffee in his face."

"You'd do that?" Merry asked, her eyes wide with shock.

"Only if I felt threatened," she said, picking up the cup to take sip and noticing Merry flinch. "Don't worry, you're safe. You don't seem like the threatening type."

Merry beamed with happiness at the comment and much to her surprise, Hannah felt an odd, warm stirring in her gut that she imagined others might call affection. Was she actually making a friend?

Who would have guessed that all it would take was two weeks of self-imposed commitment to a psychiatric facility?

CHAPTER TWENTY THREE

Neither of them said a word about last night.

Jessie thought about it in the shower, at breakfast, and on the walk to Bridget Newhouse's casita. She would have liked to have confided in Kat but her friend was on a well-deserved break, going on a coastal morning hike, and was unreachable.

Besides, as much as Kat's presence might have eased tensions a bit, what Jessie really wanted was to talk to her fiancé about all this. But if Ryan wasn't going to say anything, neither was she. Maybe he didn't know what to say yet. Or maybe he just didn't want to get into it when they were in the middle of the case. That was fine with her. She needed to keep her focus on finding out if Scott Newhouse was murdered and by whom. Her personal issues could wait.

As they approached the Newhouse casita, they reviewed the plan.

"We need to get Bridget to retrace Scott's steps from the start of the trip," Ryan said. "We don't know much about what happened on the day they checked in, other than their appointment with Cedric Cleaver. Maybe they went somewhere or did something that could shed new light on what happened."

"You think we might have missed something?" Jessie asked, glad to get into the rhythms of the case and away from anything personal.

"I think we don't even know enough to determine if we might have," he replied, following suit. "I want to at least have a new avenue to pursue when Chief Laird calls."

"When do you expect that to happen?"

Ryan looked at his watch.

"It's just after nine now," he said. "I'd say we have until about noon if we're lucky."

"Maybe we should ask Captain Decker to run interference for us," Jessie suggested.

"I would," Ryan said as they arrived at the Newhouse casita, "but now that Laird has a direct pipeline to us, he's not going to be put off by Decker."

Spike, the security guard outside the casita this morning, stepped aside and Ryan knocked on the door. It didn't take long for Bridget to open it. She was dressed in jeans and an oversized sweatshirt and didn't have on any makeup. Her eyes were puffy and red and her skin looked pasty. There didn't seem to be anyone else there.

"Come on in," she said, opening the door wide.

"Where are your friends?" Jessie asked.

"Ellie and Matt are at their casita, per Detective Hernandez's orders," she said, her voice sob-strained and weak. "Malcolm and Abby said they wanted to give me some private time, but the way they were going at it in the club last night, I think *they* wanted the private time."

"So you were here alone all night?" Jessie wondered, surprised at the callousness of her friends.

"Yes, but it was okay," Bridget insisted. "I actually needed some time by myself to process all this. Getting drunk or relentlessly bucked up by people isn't going to solve anything. Having said that, I was hoping you'd have some information for me. My sister's flying in from New Jersey today to help me but she won't get here until early evening. The nanny's been holding down the fort but I can't ask her to keep this secret from my kids much longer. It's not fair. I need to tell them before they hear it on the news or someone lets it slip out. Plus, I have to start making plans for Scott's funeral. It's so weird to hear those words come out of my mouth."

"We get how difficult a time this is, Mrs. Newhouse," Ryan said sympathetically. "That's why we wanted to see you early to get the ball rolling today. We were hoping to go over your timeline on Thursday, the day you arrived. It's possible that some event or interaction your husband had played a role in what happened to him. Something that might seem small to you could prove important. Are you up for that?"

"Sure," she replied, though it was apparent that she wasn't. She sat down heavily on the couch and they took chairs opposite her.

"Okay," Ryan launched in, pretending not to notice her exhaustion. "You arrived on Thursday, afternoon, correct?"

"Yes, but we got an early check-in around 1 p.m.," she said, 'we wanted to maximize our time."

"So what did you do after you checked in?" Jessie asked.

Bridget thought about it for a second.

"First we grabbed some drinks from one of the pool bars. Then we took a walk on the beach for a while, maybe an hour?"

"What about after that?"

"We came back here to change," she answered. "We had a couple's counseling session that afternoon."

"Oh," Ryan said as if this was news to him. "Was there anything unusual about the session?"

She shook her head.

"No," she answered firmly. "I know it sounds weird: come to an exclusive resort and almost immediately dive into therapy. But like I said before, that was kind of the point of this retreat for us and our friends—to reconnect with our loved ones."

"What can you tell us about the session?" Jessie asked, trying not to sound too intrusive.

"I'd prefer to keep the details private," Bridget replied, though not defensively, "but I assure you that there was nothing discussed that we hadn't addressed before. There were no shocking revelations or massive breakthroughs. We didn't walk out of there on the verge of a divorce or run back here to hop into bed. It was just an opportunity to improve our communication with each other."

Jessie had to clench her jaw to keep from visually reacting to that last statement. She didn't want Ryan to see any response from her and take it personally.

"What did you do next?" she asked quickly.

"We hung out here for a while. I watched some TV. Scott made work calls. Then we got dressed for dinner and headed out."

"Where to?" Ryan wondered.

"A place called The Captain's Quarters up near the main building," Bridget replied. "It's fine dining and dancing. They have a live, old-style, big band and a huge dance floor. When the band ended their set, it turned into a modern nightclub. We were there all night."

"Do you remember Scott getting into any conflicts during the evening?" Jessie asked, "Maybe a dispute with a waiter or some disagreement with someone on the dance floor? It could be as simple as him stepping on someone's toe and them calling him a jerk."

Bridget thought about it before shaking her head.

"I wasn't with him every second once dinner ended," she told them. "There were times that I was hanging at the table while he was dancing and vice versa. But I feel like I would have remembered anything like that. I've been wracking my brain trying to come up with some explanation for how this could have happened. I fixate on little details all the time, hoping to have some breakthrough that will help it all make sense. But I always come up empty. And as far as that evening goes, honestly, it was a pretty normal night out."

Ryan looked over at Jessie and she could tell what he was thinking. Bridget Newhouse wasn't going to add anything new at this point. It was time to go.

"Thanks for your time," she said. "We'll keep you posted. I know you're anxious to leave here and we'll try to make that possible as soon as we can."

They left her casita and headed toward the main building in lockstep.

"I assume we're going to The Captain's Quarters?" Jessie asked.

"It's the only new lead we have," Ryan said. "Maybe something happened there when Bridget wasn't looking, something he didn't tell her about. We can review the restaurant camera footage. Maybe we can have Jamil and Beth run facial recognition to isolate Scott's movements over the course of the evening. Who knows what might pop?"

Jessie kept her skepticism to herself. It seemed like a long shot but they were running out of time and options. There was no point in being negative. She tried to think of something supportive to say and was saved by the ringing phone. Ryan held it up. It was Laird.

"This should be fun," he muttered before answering it and in a much more chipper voice, saying, "Good morning, Chief."

"How good it is depends on what you have for me, Hernandez," he warned. "I've got the press demanding answers about what happened to one of the most prominent public figures in this city. They know you two are on this thing, which has them in a frenzy. After all, HSS doesn't handle deaths by natural causes. And I still don't know if it's safe to call Bridget Newhouse. Is it?"

"Chief," Ryan said, keeping that positive tone, despite everything he'd just heard, "I know you want to reach out to Mrs. Newhouse, but I think that would be inadvisable at this time. We just came from speaking with her and she didn't seem put out by not having heard from you. She's focused on getting back to her kids, but she hasn't made any demands to leave. I think contacting her would only exacerbate the situation. She might make a request that could put you in an uncomfortable situation. And technically, we haven't cleared her yet. Until we do, contacting her might look bad if the press found out."

Jessie nodded approvingly. Anything that made Laird look bad in the media was something he would avoid. Appealing to his narcissism was never a bad move.

"The question is," Laird pressed, "how much longer are you going to be investigating? Do you have anything substantial or are you just spinning your wheels?"

"We're actually following up on a brand new lead right now, Chief," Ryan said as they crested the hill and the main building came into sight. "I think it might be very promising."

"When will you know for sure?" Laird demanded.

"Um," Ryan hesitated, "maybe by lunchtime?"

"So you're telling me I can schedule a news conference for early afternoon then," the chief said emphatically.

"I don't think I'd be so definite—."

"Excellent," Laird interrupted, "I'll tell my girl to set it for 2 p.m. That should give you enough time to prep me. I look forward to the satisfactory resolution of this mess."

He hung up without waiting for a response.

"Why did you tell him lunchtime?" Jessie asked, alarmed.

"I was just stalling for time," Ryan said defensively. "I figured that would give us a few hours at least and if we came up empty, then we could have Decker call him and take the hit for us."

Jessie wanted to ream him out for taking a risk that could backfire badly. But with their personal situation currently so delicate, she worried that any attack from her might seem like more than just professional frustration. So she held her tongue on that point.

"I guess we better get moving," she finally said.

Ryan didn't reply though he did start walking up the hill a little faster.

CHAPTER TWENTY FOUR

Jessie felt like there was stopwatch ticking in her chest.

She sat in the security office with Ryan and Hugo Cosgrove. They were all on speakerphone with Jamil and Beth, who were working furiously to track Scott Newhouse's movements at The Captain's Quarters using facial recognition.

For a while, Jessie and the others had tried to do the same using just their bare eyes, but with the shadows in the club, it was mostly guesswork. Kat had ambled in casually after they'd been there for over a half hour, looking relaxed and happy.

"I thought you'd have it solved by now," she joked, then quieted down when she saw that no one was amused.

As they waited, mostly silent with occasional terse exchanges, Jessie saw her friend pick up on the tense vibe, seeming to sense that the strain between her and Ryan was about more than just the case. Kat raised her eyebrows at her questioningly, but Jessie shook her head ever so slightly to indicate that this wasn't the time. Kat nodded back, though with a worried look on her face.

"We've got it," Jamil shouted over the phone, breaking the uncomfortable quiet.

"What?" Ryan asked with a hint of hope.

"I'm sending you a video that tracks Newhouse's movement's throughout the night. We have ninety-five percent of his time accounted for, except when he goes to the bathroom."

"How long is the video?" Jessie asked.

"They were there for four hours," Beth said.

"That will take way too long to go through," Ryan protested. "We're going to get a call from Chief Laird demanding answers in two hours. I can't tell him we're still scrolling through video."

"You can speed it up, Detective," Jamil said calmly. "And from my first pass, about half his time is spent sitting at their dinner table. I'm assuming that anything worthwhile will jump out on screen."

"Okay, sorry," Ryan said. "That sounds great."

"Hey guys," Jessie said, jumping in to give Ryan a moment to regroup, "Let's expedite this by skipping his time at the table and whenever he was with his wife. If we take her word for now, nothing odd happened when she was with him, so let's focus on when he wasn't. If that's a bust, we can always go back and expand the search parameters."

There was no answer.

"Jamil?" Jessie said.

"He's just rendering that now," Beth answered. "It'll be ready in a minute."

As usual, Jamil beat expectations. Fifty-one seconds later, the revised footage appeared in their inbox. They scrolled though the video, looking for anything out of the ordinary. But there were no fights, no fingers pointed in anyone's chest, no sign of any conflict to speak of. Jessie felt any optimism leaking out of her like a deflated balloon. She was about to glance over at Ryan to see if he was feeling the same when she saw it.

"Hold on," she said, "Jamil, can you back the footage up about thirty seconds and play it at regular speed?"

The researcher did and they all watched the screen. Jessie squeezed her fists in anticipation, waiting to see if she'd really seen what she thought she had. On the screen were Scott and Bridget Newhouse, along with Abby Andrews. The big band was done for the night and they were all dancing to techno music in a tight circle. The other three people in the group—Malcolm Andrews and Matt and Ellie Darcy, were taking a break at the table.

After a moment, Bridget tapped Scott on the shoulder and yelled something in his ear. He nodded and continued dancing with Abby as his wife returned to the table and plopped down.

"What are we looking for?" Kat asked.

"Here," Jessie answered, pointing at the two remaining dancers. "Would anyone else consider that 'unusual?'"

They all stared at the screen, some with open mouths. After several seconds of ordinary dancing, Scott moved behind Abby and seemed to get quite close. What looked pretty innocuous at double speed now appeared much more like a scene out of *Dirty Dancing*. Scott had his hands on Abby's hips and looked to be grinding into her. She didn't look put out. In fact, she seemed to be leaning back into him, with a big grin on her face, her red hair flying everywhere, and her arms in the air, happily matching the beat. They only stopped after Malcolm joined them about a minute later.

"That was extremely friendly," Hugo said, expressing their collective opinion.

Jessie turned to Ryan.

"What do you say we go have a chat with Abby Andrews?"

*

Jessie only unclenched her teeth once she was out of the golf cart.

With time running short before Chief Laird's deadline, Hugo had offered to drive them to the Andrews' casita. But he'd taken the deadline a little too seriously and nearly tipped over on several sharp turns.

"I'll wait out here," he said, once they pulled up.

"Thanks," Ryan said, as if they'd have even considered letting him join them for this.

When he knocked on the door, Abby opened it within seconds. Jessie noticed that she was as effervescent as ever, with a wide, vibrant smile that matched her yellow skirt and floral halter top.

"Hey guys," she said, welcoming them in. "How are you? Are you feeling okay after last night, Detective Hernandez? Matt's a pretty big guy. I'd be sore for weeks after something like that, not that I could have ever done what you did."

"I'll be okay, thanks," he told her before cutting to the chase. "Ms. Hunt and I actually have a few questions for you."

"Oh, okay," she said, surprised at his abruptness. "I'll get Malcolm. He's up working in the bedroom."

"We were hoping to talk to you privately, Abby," Jessie said, hoping that going with first names might make her more receptive to what was to come.

Abby looked perplexed but didn't object.

"Okay, where do you want to talk?"

"How about the back porch?" Jessie suggested, thinking a more relaxed setting would keep things light until they weren't.

"Sure. You guys want anything to drink?"

They declined so Abby led the way to the back. As they passed through the kitchen, Jessie noted that there were two small suitcases resting near the door. Though she didn't comment on it, the sight was unsettling. Clearly the Andrews assumed they were leaving today. She had to imagine the Darcys felt the same way. Unless she and Ryan could find a way to justify preventing their departures, their only credible suspects would all leave the resort, making continued questioning without lawyers all but impossible.

She realized that she was going to have to push harder than she preferred. Once outside, they all sat on patio chairs around a table shaded with an umbrella. When they were settled in, Jessie took the lead.

"So how long have you and Malcolm been married now?" she asked.

"Four years in May," Abby said, beaming.

"You know," Jessie said quietly, conspiratorially, "a lot of people say that the infamous seven year itch everyone talks about is really more of a four year itch. What do you think of that?"

Abby looked at her in confusion.

"What do you mean, itch?"

Even though they were roughly the same age, Jessie suddenly felt old. Had this girl never seen a Marilyn Monroe movie?

"The seven year itch is a term for when a married person begins to feel restless and starts looking at other people," she explained.

Abby looked confused and then, annoyed.

"I've never heard of that," she said. "But I can promise you that neither Malcolm nor I have any itches, except for each other."

"Of course," Jessie said with a dismissive wave of her hand. "It's just that we've been following up on some loose ends and we came across this. Can you explain it?"

She pulled out her phone and played the snippet of video that had piqued everyone's interest earlier. Once it was done, Abby looked up at her questioningly, as if she didn't understand the problem.

"I don't get it," she said.

"Well, Abby," Ryan said quietly, "that's not typically the kind of dancing one sees between two folks who are married to other people."

Only then did Abby's confusion fade. But instead of looking angry, she giggled. Jessie couldn't hide her surprise at the reaction.

"I'm sorry," the woman said. "I don't mean to sound thoughtless but what you're suggesting is ridiculous."

"Really?" Ryan wondered. "Do you think your husband would feel the same way?"

"Actually, yes," Abby said, standing up, opening the patio door, and calling out before they could stop her. "Malcolm, can you come out to the patio for a minute? I need you."

He was down a few moments later and took a seat next to his wife. He looked guardedly puzzled.

"Show him the video," Abby said.

"Are you sure?" Jessie asked.

She nodded so Jessie held out her phone for Malcolm to see, watching his expression closely the whole time. To her astonishment, he broke into a grin, one of the only times she'd seen him do it since they met. When it was over, he looked over at his wife.

"What's the deal?" he asked her.

"They think this is evidence that I was having an affair with Scott," she told him.

Malcolm laughed out loud at the suggestion.

"See, I told you," Abby said, trying not to chuckle herself.

"Can you explain why you both find this so laughable?" Jessie asked.

Abby managed to get control first and answered.

"First of all," she explained. "I love my husband and have no interest in anyone else, certainly not Scott. He was just being a goofball, playing up the lecherous older guy for effect. It was funny. He was acting a part."

"How do you know he wasn't serious?" Ryan asked, "That he wasn't really into you and just hiding it by overdoing it?"

"Listen," Malcolm said, leaning in, "Scott was a relentless flirt but it was all in good fun. He didn't mean anything by it. I was never worried about him."

"But you haven't told us why not," Jessie pointed out. "Just you saying so doesn't prove it's true. This is potentially incriminating video that could suggest a motive for murder, either by you Mr. Andrews, or by Bridget Newhouse. Jealousy is a powerful thing."

Malcolm stopped smiling, sighed, and looked at his wife. When she saw that, her grin faded as well. She shook her head.

"It's not our place to say anything," she protested.

"But if we don't," Malcolm replied, "they're going to keep up with this line. I know it's a violation of sorts, but I don't see that we have any other choice. Do you?"

Jessie fought the urge to butt in and say that they didn't.

"But we don't even know for sure if it's true," Abby objected. "It'd be spreading rumors."

"Come on, sweetie," Malcolm said softly, "It's the perfect rumor because we both know it's true."

"Excuse me," Ryan finally interrupted, "what's true?"

Abby looked at the floor. Clearly she wasn't going to be the one to come clean. Reluctantly, Malcolm did.

"Scott had erectile dysfunction. It was a side effect of his antidepressants. He made a veiled reference to it once when we were on a fishing trip. I never pressed because he seemed pretty embarrassed by it. Later, I heard that Bridget had mentioned something about it to Ellie as well. It was kind of an open secret."

"Okay," Jessie said. "But that doesn't preclude a spouse from being jealous when he's grinding up on someone other than his wife."

"Maybe technically not," Abby said, finally looking up. "But he suspected that we all knew the truth. So when he did stuff like that dirty dancing, it was his way of puncturing the gravity of the situation. It's kind of like someone who's a bad singer doing karaoke and choosing a Whitney Houston song with lots of high notes so they can really butcher it. That way no one can accuse them of being bad and not knowing it. They're leaning into it to undercut any legitimate criticism. He was letting us know he was in on the joke, if you can even call it a joke."

"Anyway," Malcolm added. "The point is that no one thought he was hitting on anyone when he did that stuff because we knew it couldn't go anywhere physically. He was a little like Jake Barnes in *The Sun Also Rises*, minus the bullfighting and the expat, post-war disillusionment. He couldn't cheat, at least not in that way."

"And he *wouldn't* cheat," Abby said, "not even an emotional affair. He was deeply in love with Bridget. Yes, he was a workaholic, always doing something to help the city, and it took time away from them. They had problems like everyone else. But he doted on his wife. When he talked about her, he still sounded like a little kid with a crush."

"Here's the bottom line," Malcolm said emphatically. "Scott Newhouse wasn't having an affair. And the idea that any one of us could have killed him because we thought he was is absurd. Ask the others and they'll tell you the same thing. I'm sorry but you're barking up the wrong tree."

CHAPTER TWENTY FIVE

Jessie didn't speak.

As Hugo drove the golf cart back to the Grand Hall (more slowly this time), she was lost in thought. Malcolm and Abby Andrews' word alone wasn't enough to eliminate the jealous spouse theory. But unless all five people in their group were involved in an elaborate conspiracy to kill Scott and hide it, it was on life support.

She would never dismiss that possibility out of hand, but nothing they'd come across in interviews, financial records, or personal communications even hinted at the prospect. And if that hypothesis was a bust, that meant they were at a dead end, no better off than they had been when the day started.

To make matters worse, Ryan had gone quiet. She could tell that he was frustrated with the case too. But there was something more going on. He looked like he wanted to say something to her but couldn't.

Even after Hugo dropped them off and they walked to the restaurant buffet to grab a bite, he kept silent. She decided not to press. Whatever he was working through, and she assumed it was related to their clash last night, it wouldn't help for her to ask him about it if he wasn't ready. All she could do was keep her fingers crossed that when he was ready to say his peace, it would be something worth hearing.

"I'm going back to the security office," he finally said.

"What for?" she asked.

"It's almost 11 a.m.," he replied. "I'm going to go through everyone's financials again to see if there's any chance that these people have some financial incentive to take down Newhouse. I figured I'd also call Captain Decker to see if he can run interference with Laird. At this point, I doubt we're going to have much to share at lunchtime and I don't want the Chief scheduling a press conference and then having to cancel. That'll only get him hotter than he already is."

"Okay," Jessie said. "Mind if I still go get that bite?"

"Nope," he said. "I'll catch up later to update you."

They went their separate ways without as much as a kiss goodbye. Jessie headed for the restaurant when she ran into Kat, who was dressed in jeans and casual shirt. Her hair was back in its usual ponytail.

"Uh-oh," Jessie said. "Back to your standard uniform, huh? I guess that means you're leaving soon."

"Checking out at noon," Kat confirmed. "The complimentary casita ends then, Besides, my work is done here."

"So what's next?" Jessie asked.

"Mitch is driving down from Lake Arrowhead," she said, referencing her long-distance boyfriend, "He gets in late this afternoon, so I'll spend the rest of the weekend with him before he has to go back tomorrow night. Then I have another case lined up starting Monday. No fancy clothes or jewels unfortunately. Just another rich dude who thinks his trophy wife is cheating on him. I'll probably be sitting in my car for hours. But before that, I was thinking of sitting at the bar for a drink. You in?"

"I'm on duty," Jessie said. "Then again, at this point it doesn't seem like my total and complete alertness is required. If Chief Laird is going to yell at us for failing, I might want to take the edge off a little."

"That's the spirit," Kat said as they walked into a mostly empty pub-style bar just off the restaurant. "Maybe then you can tell me what's going on with you and the lovely Detective Hernandez?"

"What do you think is going on?" Jessie asked, torn between spilling her guts and keeping her romantic travails private.

Kat paused as the bartender took their orders. Once he stepped away, she leaned in and whispered.

"Usually you two are on the same frequency," she said. "Even if you disagree on a case, there's this tether holding you together. This morning that tether looked loose."

Jessie hadn't realized it was that obvious. As she tried to find the right words to discreetly convey what was happening, Kat's phone rang. She answered it, and then listened for several seconds without speaking. Jessie watched the color drain from her face.

"Let me check around," she said urgently. "I'll get back to you."

"What's wrong?" Jessie asked.

"One of the pieces of jewelry they lent me wasn't in the case I returned earlier," she said, sliding off her barstool. "They asked if I might have left it in my casita. I'm going to go look."

"Didn't you tag all the pieces?" Jessie asked.

"I removed them all last night so I wouldn't forget when I returned them."

"Oh. You want some help?" Jessie offered.

"That's okay. You have your drink. You seem like you need it," Kat said. "Also, I prefer to panic alone."

She darted out of the bar just as the bartender brought over their drinks.

"Usually people wait until *after* they've had their drink to make a run for it," he noted drily.

Jessie smiled apologetically.

"She just had something she had to take care of," she explained, grabbing her drink. "Hopefully she'll be back soon."

"Not a problem," he said as his cheeks turned pink. "That actually gives me a chance to ask: are you Jessie Hunt?"

Jessie looked at the guy closer, trying to determine if she should be wary of him. He was tall and good looking with an open smile, sun-bleached blond hair, and a deep tan. His nametag read River and he clearly spent much of his non-bartending time surfing the local waves.

"I am," she said carefully, putting her drink back down on the bar. "Why do you ask, River?"

"Don't worry, I'm not hitting on you," he said, though his eyes suggested that might not be entirely true. "It's just that I thought I recognized you from being on the news. And when I heard that you were investigating the death of Bridget Newhouse's husband, I was almost positive."

"Oh, do you know the Newhouses?" she asked, steering the conversation away from herself as best she could as she picked up her drink again.

"Not him," River said. "But I know Bridget. She's a semi-regular around here."

Jessie had the glass to her lips, about to take her first sip, when she fully processed his words. She put it back down again.

"What do you mean, she's a semi-regular?" she pressed.

River shrugged.

"Just that she's around a fair bit, enough that I know her by face and name."

"But you didn't see her husband around as much?" she wanted to know.

"I don't remember ever seeing her with anyone," River said. "I knew she was married because of the ring and all, but she always came in alone."

"How often?"

"I don't know, maybe a couple of times a month, give or take. It's not like she's in here every weekend," he told her, before adding, "Have I said something wrong?"

"No, of course not," she said quickly so he didn't pick up on her excitement. "I'm just happy to fill in some background. I've actually got to run. Can we settle up?"

River shook his head.

"You didn't even have a taste," he said. "Consider it on the house. Maybe you'll come back later for a fresh one."

"Thanks," she said, hopping off the barstool, "maybe I will."

"At least have one sip before you go," he insisted, "otherwise I'll feel insulted."

"Are you sure you're not hitting on me, River?" she asked.

His cheeks turned bright red. Jessie imagined how Ryan might feel watching this moment and kind of wished he was. Maybe then he'd know how she felt every time Susannah Valentine got overly friendly with him. Though she doubted she'd be back here, she decided to throw River a bone. After all, the kid was sweet and he may have given her a clue to work with.

"One sip," she allowed, "at least for now."

*

Jessie waited at the front desk for the manager to continue his search, doing her best not to appear anxious.

As the older man in the three-piece suit with gelled black hair and a painstakingly trimmed mustache took his time typing her request into his terminal, she again debated whether to call Ryan, and again decided against it. He was busy checking financials and she didn't want to interrupt him unless she had something worth sharing. Right now, all she had was a hunch.

The front desk manager, whose name was Miles David, printed out several sheets of paper and handed them over to her. Other than dates and charges, most of the other information on the pages was gibberish.

"Can you explain what these codes mean?" she asked.

He looked annoyed at the request but answered anyway.

"They represent services that Mrs. Newhouse was charged for on her various visits," he said, pointing at different alphanumeric codes. "These are for massages. These are for yoga practice. These are for personal training. And these are for facials, mani-pedis, and the hair salon."

"And all of these resort visits were solo?" Jessie wanted to know.

"All except the first one a year and a half ago and this weekend," David explained.

"Okay," Jessie said urgently. "I need you or one of your clerks to create a key for me on the first page of this list, showing what each code represents. I'll be back to get it in a few."

"Ma'am," the manager replied officiously. "We are quite busy this morning. I can't promise that we'll—."

"This is directly related to the death of a guest on resort property," she said, cutting him off. "I recommend that you make this a priority, Mr. David. Got it?"

He nodded meekly at the censure. Jessie left without another word. With no golf cart available, she jogged down to Bridget Newhouse's casita. As she got closer, she tried to decide how best to handle this.

The woman had been a widow for barely twenty-four hours so she needed to tread carefully. After all, Newhouse's multiple solo trips to a fancy resort could simply be an attempt to get away from the harried life of a busy wife and mother of three young kids. But they also had the definite earmarks of someone who might be having an affair and using the resort as cover. The fact that she never mentioned anything about her frequent trips without her husband wasn't inherently suspicious. But it was curious.

The first thing she noticed when she got to the front door was that there was no Geordy, Lewis, or Spike. In fact, there was no security guard at all. She didn't think that Hugo would have ended the guard watch without informing her or Ryan.

She knocked on the door. When she didn't get any response to that or her repeated louder, attempts, she tried the door. It was locked. She walked around the exterior of the house until she saw that the sliding door on the enclosed patio was open slightly.

Jessie stood there for a moment, debating how to proceed. Bridget might just be asleep upstairs in her bedroom. She could be listening to music on her ear buds like the first time they came here. Climbing over the patio walls and entering unannounced, as she was considering doing, seemed like a precipitous move. She could just call Hugo and ask him to have the front door unlocked.

But that would take time. What if something had gone terribly wrong? What if Bridget *was* having an affair and her lover, possibly someone who worked at the resort, had gotten envious at seeing her with her husband? What if that person had killed Scott in a fit of jealous rage? What if that killer had come back to shut up the one person who could prove a connection to Scott: Bridget? What if the killer had taken out her security guard and right now, the woman was lying injured or dead inside the casita?

Jessie determined that it was worth the risk. After a quick glance around to see if anyone was watching, she hoisted herself up and over the wall.

Her gun was out of its holster before she opened the sliding glass door. Once she stepped inside, she stood there quietly for a moment, listening for the sound of voices, music, any sign of life inside.

The casita was quiet. She searched the first floor, found nothing, and moved up to the second. There was no one there either. She was about to leave the primary bedroom when she caught sight of something half-hidden under the sheets on the bed. Jessie lifted up the sheet to discover Bridget's phone.

Her phone was here but she wasn't. Something felt very wrong.

CHAPTER TWENTY SIX

Ryan wasn't answering his phone.

Every time Jessie called, it went straight to voicemail.

She decided to try Hugo, who might be with him in the security office. Just as she was about to hit "send," her phone rang. It was the number for police headquarters. She checked the time. It was 12:04 p.m.—lunchtime. She had a sneaking suspicion it was Chief Laird and sent the call straight to voicemail. There was no way she was opening that can of worms right now. She called Hugo.

"Is Detective Hernandez with you?" she asked the second he answered. "I can't get hold of him."

"No," he told her. "He hit a wall looking at all those financial documents and took a walk. I think he said he was going to the cliffs to clear out the cobwebs. Reception is pretty bad out there. That's probably why you can't get him. Is something wrong?"

"I'm not sure," she said. "Why did you pull the security guard off the Newhouse casita?"

"I meant to tell you about that," Hugo said apologetically. "I got calls a short while ago from every member of that group, including Mrs. Newhouse, all complaining that they felt like prisoners and threatening to take legal action against the resort. Since the guards were mostly there to keep them safe from potential threats and they were requesting the removal, I didn't think I had much choice."

"Well, Hugo, that really sucks," Jessie said, frustrated, "Because Bridget Newhouse isn't in her casita and her phone is. I don't want to jump to conclusions here. But since the place wasn't being watched, I have no idea if she went for a stroll or was abducted by the person who killed her husband."

"So you're sure he was murdered?" he asked, dismayed. Apparently he'd been hoping for suicide.

"We have to operate as if he was."

"Oh my God," he said. "I'll have my people scour the area looking for her."

"Fine," she said. "I'm coming back to the Grand Hall. I'll meet you at the front desk."

*

Ryan still wasn't reachable.

Jessie tried not to think about that as she talked on the phone with Jamil and Beth. It helped that Hugo had a guard take a golf cart to the cliffs to see if he was there. With that out of her control, she returned her attention to the task at hand.

"So your theory," Beth said, making sure she understood what Jessie had just explained, "is that Bridget Newhouse was going to Peninsula to have an ongoing affair out of sight of her husband, likely with someone who worked there, possibly a staffer she got regular services from so she could use that to hide what was happening. Is that right?"

"That's exactly it," Jessie confirmed. "And I'm worried that if the staffer saw Bridget here with her husband and killed him in some kind of crime of passion, that person might have realized that she would eventually reveal the affair and provide a new suspect for us."

"Okay," Jamil said, "Based on the pages you sent us with all Bridget Newhouse's services over the last year and a half, there are only two that she got from the same people on every visit. Both are male. One was a masseur named Cal King. The other is a yoga instructor named Jude Austen."

"I met Austen yesterday," Jessie said. "But I haven't talked to Cal King yet. Maybe I should start with him."

"I don't think he's your guy," Hugo said, almost apologetically.

"Why not?" she demanded.

"For one thing, there's no way he's having an affair with Bridget Newhouse," he said. "Cal is gay."

"Are you sure?" Jessie pressed.

"Pretty damn sure," Hugo assured her. "He's actually engaged to Spike, that huge guard who accompanied us to Ronnie Nance's quarters yesterday. Also, Cal is off today. He's not even on campus to abduct or harm anyone."

"Okay," Jessie said, deflated. "What about Jude Austen?"

"I don't know about being a killer, but I'm pretty sure he's straight," Hugo told her.

"Where is he now?"

Hugo hit a few key keystrokes.

"He's supposed to be at the yoga pavilion," he said. "He should be in the middle of a lesson. Should we go check?"

"Yes, please," she said before addressing Jamil and Beth. "I'm hanging up now guys, but please call if you have any updates."

They headed out to the back of the Grand Hall building where Geordy the security guard was just pulling up in a cart with Ryan seated beside him.

"Sorry," he said, hopping out. "I was just at the cliffs clearing my head. I forgot that cell reception is bad there. What's going on?"

"You may as well get back in," Jessie told him. "We're hitching another ride with these guys. A lot has happened in the last half hour."

They got in the backseat and Hugo hopped in the front with Geordy.

"Take us to the yoga pavilion," he instructed.

Jessie was about to fill Ryan in when his phone rang. He pulled it out. It was Laird.

"I wouldn't answer that just yet," she warned. "Not until you have the full story."

"Okay," he said, sending it to voicemail. "I'm glad my calls to him didn't go through when I tried on the way back up here. I saw that he called three times, just like you did. Did the world turn upside down while I was staring at the ocean?"

"Maybe," she said and proceeded to fill him on Bridget Newhouse's solo trips to Peninsula over the last eighteen months, her possible affair with a resort employee, her apparent disappearance, and Jessie's concern that the killer might be cleaning up their dirty work. She was just concluding with Jude Austen's potential as a suspect when the cart rolled over the final hill and the yoga pavilion came into view.

There was a class in session. An older couple was trying to master downward dog. Jessie recognized the person putting them through the paces. With his tall, elegant body and brown, ponytailed hair bobbing up and down, Austen was hard to miss.

The sight of him caused a mixed emotions in Jessie. If he was here, doing his job, that likely meant one of two things: either he was uninvolved in Bridget's disappearance and had just been doing his job, or he'd already done something to her and gone back to work to make everything look normal.

"When did this class start?" Jessie asked Hugo.

"Noon."

"And when did you pull security off the Newhouse casita?' she wanted to know.

"I was on duty there today," Geordy said from the driver's seat. "I got the call at 11:30, told Mrs. Newhouse that I was going, and left right after."

"And she seemed okay at that time?" Ryan asked.

"Totally normal," he answered. "I mean normal under the circumstances. She looked wiped out and like she'd been crying, but nothing more than that."

"And I got to the casita a few minutes before noon," Jessie said. "So that gave Austen a window of about twenty minutes to get in and out of her place and still make his class, assuming he didn't have one during that stretch of time."

"He didn't," Hugo said. "He wasn't booked from 11 to 12 today. And I checked his schedule for yesterday. He wasn't booked for a class during the time of Newhouse's death either."

"That's interesting, "Ryan said. "But how would he have known when security had been pulled off Bridget?"

Hugo had an answer for that one too.

"Every employee is assigned a two-way radio so they can be reached on short notice. With the cell issues you know well, we can't depend on phones. He could have been monitoring the security personnel channel."

They arrived at the pavilion and everyone got out. Austen and the couple looked over, surprised to see the large group converge on them.

"If you guys don't mind," Hugo said quietly, "I think I can make this a little less awkward."

Jessie and Ryan exchanged shrugs.

"Go for it," she said.

Hugo turned on a high-wattage smile and walked over to the confused threesome.

"Sorry to interrupt your practice, folks," he said remorsefully. "But we just got word that there may be a risk of unexpected erosion on this cliff. It's probably nothing. The Beaches and Harbors Department tends to be a little overcautious. But until we get the all clear, we're going to have all guests leave this immediate area. I apologize for the hassle. We can either refund you for the time, or depending on your schedule, rebook you for after we get approval to resume. In the meantime, Geordy is here to escort you wherever you'd like to go."

"I'm at your service, folks," Geordy said enthusiastically.

"Bring a jumbo cart back out here once you drop them off," Hugo whispered to him so that only Jessie and Ryan could hear. "We may need it to transport someone."

Geordy nodded. As the couple shuffled into the cart, Jude gave Hugo a perplexed look. But he knew better than to say anything until the cart pulled away and the couple was out of earshot.

"What's going on Hugo?" he asked. "This cliff was refortified just last fall."

"Mr. Austen," Ryan said, stepping forward, "we need to talk."

Jessie watched Jude Austen's face sink at the words.

"I already talked to your partner there yesterday," he said, nodding at Jessie.

"Only in passing," Jessie reminded him. "We'd like to have a longer chat."

"Okay," he replied cautiously, "about what?"

She fixed her eyes on him closely as she readied to drop her first bomb.

"About your affair with Bridget Newhouse," she said simply.

CHAPTER TWENTY SEVEN

Jessie didn't have to be a criminal profiler to see what was going on in the man's head.

His eyes were wide and his jaw dropped open. It took him several seconds to muster any kind of response.

"I wasn't...," he stammered, "I didn't have...that with her."

"Come on Jude," she said sharply, "We're well past the denials. You have bigger concerns than that at this moment anyway. Where is Bridget right now?"

"What?' he asked. His expression was still one of shock but she couldn't tell whether it was due to being called out for the affair or being asked about Bridget's whereabouts.

"We can't find her, Jude," Ryan said. "It's time for you come clean. What did you do with her?"

"I didn't do anything!" he shouted, his head darting back and forth between them.

And then, with no warning at all, he started running toward the cliff. Ryan, who was the closest to him, was briefly startled but managed to regroup and take off after him.

Jessie grabbed one of the yoga support pillows on the floor of the pavilion and flung it at the man's legs, causing him to stumble briefly. That was enough for Ryan to make up some distance. Austen was about ten paces from the cliff's edge when Ryan threw himself at him, tackling him from behind.

He was up on his knees immediately, pinning down the taller, thinner man as he tried to wriggle away. At one point, he grabbed Austen's ponytail and yanked hard. That appeared to stun the man and, as his hair came loose and fell around his face, he seemed to lose some of his fight.

By the time Jessie and Hugo got to them, he was already handcuffed. Ryan pulled him to his feet. Jude Austen, barefoot and hiding his face behind a wall of hair, looked pathetic. Jessie glanced down and saw his hair tie start to blow away from the ocean breeze.

It only took her a second to process that it wasn't actually a hair tie. It was a thick, navy blue and white ribbon, one that looked exactly like the one that had been used to strangle Scott Newhouse in the steam room. She rushed over, picked it up, and held it out for Ryan to see. She could tell he knew exactly what he was looking at too. He turned to Austen.

"Jude Austen," he began, "You have the right to remain silent."

*

They held him in the same security office interview room where they'd questioned Ronnie Nance yesterday.

A squad car was on the way there to take him to the local sheriff's station, but with Bridget Newhouse still nowhere to be found, Jessie and Ryan had agreed that time was of the essence and they should try to get as much out of Austen as they could now.

He hadn't asked for a lawyer after Ryan read him his rights but he had gone silent. As Ryan question him, he just sat in his chair sullenly, all the color drained from his face. He wouldn't even say whether his panicked run for the cliff was an attempt to escape or kill himself. After several minutes of non-responsiveness, Ryan looked over at Jessie, frustrated.

She knew what he was thinking. Every second was precious now. Chief Laird had called twice more in the last few minutes. Captain Decker must have gotten a tongue lashing from his boss because he was calling both of them now too. Jessie had sent him a brief text saying they were doing an interrogation and would call with details after. Then she put both her phone and Ryan's on silent.

She looked back at Ryan and pointed to herself. He nodded, indicating he was cool with her trying a different tack. If pummeling the guy with questions wasn't working, maybe a softer touch would have more success. She sat down opposite Austen and smiled.

"Jude, I get it if you're afraid to talk," she said softly, "so let me tell you what I think happened and you let me know how close I am. You met Bridget when she and her husband visited a year and a half ago. The two of you made a connection during your lesson together. One thing led to another and she ended up coming out here regularly, using your yoga classes as a cover for…more personal body contortions. How am I doing so far?"

Austen stared straight ahead at the wall, but his previously slack jaw has started to clench.

"Anyway," she continued, "when she came out this time as part of a couple, you didn't like it. It was one thing to know she was married but to see her walking around with her husband was something else. It wasn't just an abstraction anymore. You couldn't take it so you snuck into the steam room at the spa and choked him with the ribbon you tie your hair with."

Austen glanced over at that comment and looked like he was about to say something before stopping himself. Jessie wasn't sure what to make of that, but when it was clear he wasn't going to speak, she went on.

"But then you realized the mess you made and how all it would take was one word from Bridget Newhouse about your affair to make you suspect number one. So you had to take her out too, but because she was always with her friends or in her casita, with security outside, you never got a chance until this morning. That's when you went over. She would have let you in. You're no stranger. And then you did whatever you did."

"That's not true," he said suddenly, still looking straight ahead.

Jessie waited for him to expound on that but he didn't, so she kept going.

"Okay, so what do I have wrong?" she asked. "Maybe you were in this together. Maybe you planned out his death so that you could be together and she'd get all his money. But something went wrong. Did she back out at the last second out of guilt? Did you go ahead with it anyway, thinking she'd go along once it was over? And then start to worry that she'd confess everything and you'd be screwed?"

She let him sit with all that for a bit. It was clear from the way his eyes were bouncing around that something was eating at him. Maybe she was on the verge of getting a confession. Finally he looked over at her.

"You're wrong," he said flatly. "I didn't kill him and I didn't kill her. And I'd like a lawyer now."

CHAPTER TWENTY EIGHT

Jessie sat in Hugo's office, listening quietly as Ryan spoke on speakerphone to Chief Laird and Captain Decker, explaining everything they'd learned. Jude Austen was in the Peninsula security office interview room, waiting for his lawyer to arrive. They could have had a squad car take him to the station, but Jessie was still holding out hope that the guy might have a spasm of conscience and reveal everything so they'd kept him here at the resort for now.

Through the window she could see Hugo, who had graciously offered his office and stepped out so they could have privacy, talking to Kat, filling her in on all he knew. Her friend was holding her travel bag. She'd likely intended to just stop by to say goodbye and walked into this whirlwind.

"Yes, sir," Ryan said the chief, "I think a 4 p.m. press conference is okay. But please hold off until then. That way we still have a few hours. Maybe Austen will crack before then. Maybe his lawyer will convince him he'll get a lighter sentence if he tells us where Bridget Newhouse is."

"Also," Jessie added. "That will allow Bridget's sister to arrive in town. If this woman has been killed, there will be a media feeding frenzy. The family is going to be overwhelmed. The more people those kids have to support them when they learn that they lost both their parents, the less horrific it will be for them, at least I hope."

"That's fine. I want to be sensitive to the family, of course," Laird said before his voice took on a much sharper tone. "But once this is all done, the two of you are going to come by my office with your captain. We need to have a conversation about communication, chain of command, and the consequences for ignoring them. Understood?"

"Yes, Chief," they said in unison.

"Good, in the meantime, there's still a problem."

"What's that, Chief?" Ryan asked, even though they were both wary of the response.

"When I talk to the press, they're going to want some things we don't have. First, they're going to ask where Bridget Newhouse is. I need to have an answer to that question. That means you two need to get it for me by 4 p.m. And I want that confession from Austen."

"But we have him dead to rights," Ryan protested.

"That's all well and good, Hernandez," Laird shot back irritably. "And in a court of law, you're probably right that we're in good shape. The man had motive. He had opportunity. He had easy access to the scene of the crime. And one of his frickin' hair ribbons was the murder weapon. This should be a slam dunk if it goes to trial. But in the court of public opinion, it's not. And as long as we can't locate Bridget, that's all those media jackals are going to care about, which is why I need to get to work on my press conference statement now. I expect good news soon."

As usual, he hung up without another word, leaving the two of them on with Captain Decker.

"Captain," Jessie pleaded, "can't you talk some sense into him? This investigation can't run according to the chief's media schedule."

"Maybe it shouldn't," Decker said with less sympathy than she would have hoped for, "But it does. And that impacts HSS's resources going forward. So rather than complain about it, I need you to get this done. Get a confession from Austen if you can. But whatever you do, find Bridget Newhouse, not just for her sake but for ours as well. Please keep me updated."

Then he hung up as well. Jessie and Ryan sat quietly for a moment. Once again, like earlier, Jessie noticed that Ryan seemed to be on the verge of saying something that was clearly not case-related. She was about to ask him what it was when something she said in passing earlier popped into her head, only this time more fully formed.

"Hey," she said standing up, "something just occurred to me."

Ryan seemed relieved that he didn't have to say whatever was in his head.

"What?" he asked.

"What if we have this wrong?"

"What do you mean?" he asked, clearly not enthused to hear that.

"What if my theory was only half-right?"

"What theory?" he asked, confused.

"When I accused Jude Austen of killing Scott Newhouse in a jealous rage and then murdering Bridget to hide their affair, he said it wasn't true. So I spun another theory that they were in on it together, but then she backed out and he went ahead with the plan anyway. What if I had it backwards?"

"Explain," he said, leaning forward, interested.

"Hold on," Jessie replied as she stood up and motioned for him to follow as she walked out to the waiting area where Kat and Hugo Cosgrove were sitting.

"Hugo, you sent all your staff location data to our researchers yesterday, right?

"Yes," he answered perplexed.

"So it will have all the nametag geo-tags and card swipes for everyone who worked yesterday, correct?"

"It should," he confirmed. "But why? You don't think Austen would be dumb enough to leave his nametag on when he did this, do you?"

"Give me a second," she said, texting Jamil furiously before looking up to see Kat staring at her with a Cheshire cat grin.

"What?" she asked.

"I see the wheels in your head spinning like crazy," her friend replied. "Care to fill us in?"

Jessie sighed. She didn't yet have any evidence to back up her theory but that hadn't stopped her in the past. So she dove in.

"I'm just wondering if Bridget Newhouse is really a victim here. When we were questioning Jude Austen, I suggested that maybe the two of them had planned Scott Newhouse's murder together but then she backed out, so he had to kill her to cover it up. But what if she was the mastermind behind all this?"

"Why do you think that?" Hugo asked.

"Bridget was the one who knew when Scott would be in the spa," she reminded him, "because she was there with him. She could have tipped Jude off so he could sneak in. Then later, she might have insisted that security leave her casita unguarded so she could finally meet up with him to compare notes. Remember, since her husband's death, she's been constantly surrounded by cops, security, or her friends. This would be the first chance for her to sneak off and make sure they were still on the same page."

"That might explain why she left her phone at the casita," Ryan offered. "That way, if anyone ever checked, there would be no geo-location evidence that she'd gone anywhere."

"Right," Jessie agreed.

"But if she's not dead or tied up somewhere, why can't we find her?" Kat asked.

"That is an excellent question," Jessie replied. But before she could say anything else, her phone rang. She answered immediately.

"Hey Jamil," she said. "You're on speaker. What have you got?"

"I did the search you requested," he answered. "I looked at Jude Austen's nametag geo-location and key card swipes for the windows of time you mentioned. And according to the data, he wasn't near the spa yesterday near the time of the murder."

Ryan's brow furrowed at that answer.

"So if this is intended to prove that Austen didn't kill either of the Newhouses," he said, "don't we have the same issue that Hugo just mentioned and that concerned us with Ronnie Nance yesterday? What if he left his nametag and his key card behind and found some other way into the spa?"

"The card info indicates that he was using it during that window of time," Jamil explained, "specifically to get some coffee at one of the restaurants in the Grand Hall and then to enter his quarters. His nametag data matches up with that. I suppose someone else could have used both to cover for him, but wouldn't that be introducing a third person into a murder conspiracy? That seems risky."

"It's definitely a stretch," Ryan conceded.

"So if Jude didn't kill Scott Newhouse," Jessie said, continuing with her theory, "then that leaves one person who clearly had the motive and the opportunity to do it: Bridget Newhouse. She was having an affair with the hot, younger yoga instructor and she was in the spa at the time of death."

"But wasn't she always on the women's side of the spa?" Ryan countered. "How could she have even gotten to him?"

"I don't know," Jessie admitted before turning to Hugo. "Can you look into that? Detective Hernandez and I have to prioritize finding Bridget. I did a cursory search of the spa yesterday and didn't find anything. But maybe you could talk to the staff there to see if there's some access point that only employees know about. Bridget got thirty-six massages there in the last year and a half. Perhaps someone mentioned something or she uncovered a way over on her own."

"I'll go over there myself and start asking questions," Hugo promised.

"But what I wondered before is still bothering me," Kat said. "If Bridget's not dead or missing, where is she? Did she just leave?"

"Why would she do that?" Ryan asked. "Up until this point, we had no reason to suspect her more than anyone else. In fact, it was finding her unattended phone at her casita that partly sent us on this path in the first place."

"I'm not sure," Jessie answered, though she had a guess. "Maybe when she met up with Jude, she got worried that he would crack under additional questioning. Maybe she figured that it was only a matter of time so she should make a run for it while she still could, before anyone was really looking for her. Maybe she never went back for her phone because she knows it can be traced and she doesn't want to be found."

"That's a lot of 'maybes,'" Ryan observed.

"True," Jessie allowed, before the logical conclusion tumbled out of her, "but Bridget knows Jude a whole lot better than any of us. And if she was worried that Jude might crack, maybe she was on to something. Maybe he will."

Without even waiting for the others, she dashed back to the interrogation room where Jude was still sitting forlornly, his wrist cuffed to the table, while a bored security guard stood in the corner. The others followed.

"Jessie," Ryan warned, "you can't question him anymore. He's asked for a lawyer."

"No," she reminded him. "*You* can't question him anymore. You're the cop. I'm still just a consultant. So if I go in alone, we should be safe. Besides, I don't plan to question him. I just have something I have to get off my chest."

Before he could protest any further, she had walked in and closed the door behind her. Jude looked up at her with mild curiosity. She flashed him a smile before saying anything.

"Hey, Jude."

"I already asked for my lawyer," he said petulantly. "You shouldn't be here."

"You don't sound very centered for a yoga instructor," she said calmly. "Anyway, I'm done with the questions. It's just that I worked something out for myself a little while ago and wanted to run it by you. I think you'll find it interesting. No need to say anything."

Jude didn't speak. Instead he deliberately fixed his gaze on the wall behind her.

"I get that you're skeptical but let's see if I can 'wow' you," she said, then went for it. "I've changed my theory of what happened to Scott Newhouse. I think you two were in on it together, but now I'm guessing it was Bridget's idea, kind of a *Double Indemnity* situation. She tells you that she's not in love with him anymore. He's battling depression. Maybe she even tells you about some of his...performance issues and how he can't satisfy her like you do. She says that she's fallen for you. But then she talks about how she can't divorce him because his lawyers would crush her."

She watched Austen's face as she spoke and could tell she was hitting pay dirt. He was struggling not to look at her and his whole body had tensed up. She kept the pressure on.

"But if he died, she'd get everything," she went on, "So she hatched a plan to kill him while they were here on a couple's retreat. And you went along with it because you really have fallen in love with her. But when it came down to it, you couldn't go through with it. You backed out at the last second and she had to kill him herself."

He was looking at her with wide eyes now, as if she'd been reading his diary. But he said nothing. That was okay. She wasn't done.

"But after she did it, you two couldn't connect because she was constantly surrounded by people. You didn't know what to do. And when she finally managed to get to you this morning, whatever you said or did made her seriously doubt your resolve. First you chicken out on the murder. And now you sound shaky when she tries to lock things down. She realizes it's only a matter of time before you crack and decided to bail before you spill everything."

Jude Austen was shaking slightly in his chair and the handcuff attached to his wrist and the table was rattling softly. He looked like he might be sick. She pressed on.

"But even then, when we confronted you and you finally grasped that she was gone and you were in trouble, you said nothing because you still love her and couldn't bear the thought of turning on her. I don't think you were trying to escape us when you ran toward that cliff, Jude. I think you were trying to escape the truth of how the woman you love abandoned you. You were willing to jump off that cliff to the rocks below rather than face what she'd done to you. And she *had* abandoned you, Jude. You know how I know?"

Involuntarily, he shook his head "no."

"Because she used one of your distinctive hair ribbons to choke him to death," she said simply. "Maybe she was trying to frame you in case things went south. Or maybe she was pissed at you for leaving her in the lurch and this was payback. Whatever the reason, a piece of clothing particular to you was the murder weapon. And now she's gone to who knows where, leaving you holding the bag, facing life in prison. Does that sound about right?"

She didn't really expect him to answer and she didn't need him to. His expression told her everything she needed to know. But after a hard gulp, he did.

"Yes," he said.

Jessie walked out of the room, where Ryan was waiting for her.

"It looks like we still have a killer to catch," she said.

CHAPTER TWENTY NINE

Jessie wished it was her idea but it was Kat who suggested they talk to the doormen.

"If she was desperate to get away from the resort," she said as they all ran down the hall from the security office to the lobby, "she couldn't have used a ride share without her phone. That means taking a cab and the cabs would pull up to the main entrance."

By the time they got out the front doors, Ryan had pulled out his phone with a photo of Bridget Newhouse on the screen and was already showing to the doormen.

"Have you seen this woman in the last hour or so?" he asked. "She might have left in a taxi."

All three doormen shook their heads no but one of them pointed to a valet just walking back from parking a car.

"Eddie was working the door too until he switched over to valet at the top of the hour," he said.

"Eddie," Ryan called out as he ran over to the startled teenager. "Do you recognize this woman?"

The kid glanced at the photo and nodded immediately.

"Sure, that's Mrs. Newhouse," he replied. "She comes here all the time."

"Did you see her recently?" Ryan pressed, trying to keep his voice level.

"Yep, I hailed her a cab a little while ago," Eddie answered happily, pleased that he could be of help.

"Did she say where she was going?" Jessie asked.

"No, but I know anyway," he told her.

"Where?"

"I heard the cabbie mention the extra one dollar transportation fee. They only add that for airport trips."

Jessie looked at Ryan with satisfaction, but he wasn't smiling.

"What's wrong?" she asked.

"There are multiple airports in the area," he said. "Both LAX and Long Beach are close, but she might have gone to Burbank or even all the way to John Wayne Airport because she thinks we'd start closer."

"But she's going to LAX," Eddie said confidently.

"How do you know?" Ryan asked.

"It's the only one that charges that fee."

Ryan's concerned look was briefly replaced by a smile, before it hardened again.

"Eddie," he said with renewed urgency, "can you get my car—fast?"

*

Jessie could barely contain her frustration.

She, Ryan, and Kat were approaching the airport and still had no idea where they would go once they arrived. On the drive there, as Ryan sped through traffic with his siren and lights on, Jessie called Captain Decker to ask him to have officers sent to both the Newhouse and Darcy homes.

"There's always the chance that this airport thing is a ruse," she had said, "and that once she got to LAX, she took another cab to her house to gather essentials or went to the Darcys to get her kids."

"I thought her sister was arriving in town today," Decker had replied. "Isn't it more likely that she just leaves them in her care, rather than try to run for it with three small children?"

"Probably," Jessie conceded, "but you never know what a mother will do when her back is against the wall. And one last thing, Captain: I'd definitely make sure that Chief Laird delays that press conference."

Once she hung up, she tried to check in with Hugo, hoping he might have gleaned some information from the spa employees about how Bridget could have accessed the men's side. But the call went straight to voicemail, which could have meant he was busy questioning someone or that the infamous Peninsula cell service was rearing its head.

She had just hung up when Jamil called. She put him on speaker.

"Beth tracked down the cab company," he said. "They said one of their drivers left Peninsula with a woman matching Bridget's description and dropped her off at Terminal 7 just over an hour ago."

"What airline is that?" Kat asked from the backseat.

"United," Beth told them.

"An hour is a big head start," Ryan said, "So assuming she's not playing us by leaving the airport again right away or going to another terminal after having been dropped off, we need to determine which United flight she's most likely to take. Any suggestions?"

There were several seconds of silence, punctuated by the car's siren. Beth finally broke it.

"She's from Springfield, Missouri," she offered. "Maybe she'd try to catch a flight there and get help from folks back home."

"Right," Kat agreed, "or pick a neighboring city. She wouldn't want to rent a car because that would pop in the system but she might call an old friend or relative and ask them to come get her."

"Or," Jessie said, though she hoped she was wrong on this, "she could be booking a flight to a non-extradition country."

Ryan's face sagged at the suggestion, though he nodded that it was a good one.

"We're just pulling up, guys," he said to the research crew. "Can you get us a list of any flights leaving in the next hour from this terminal headed to Springfield, Missouri, or any other airport within two hundred miles of it, as well as flights headed to non-extradition countries?"

"Will do," Jamil said without hesitation.

Ryan pulled up to the arrivals section of the terminal and hopped out, waving for the attention of the nearest airport officer to explain their situation.

"You know," Kat said to Jessie as they got out of the car, "I've dealt with several cases where people have tried to disappear and this may be more complicated than we think. If she planned this scheme well in advance, she's probably gotten a fake ID with fake papers, maybe even credit cards. I wouldn't expect that her name is going to pop up on the manifest for any of these flights."

"Okay," Jessie said, refusing to be daunted. "That just means we'll have to go at this old school. Ryan can head to airport security and look at video footage from the last hour. You can go to the ticket counters and show agents her photo to see if anyone recognizes her. I'll head into the terminal and start checking each gate's waiting area, bathrooms, bars—anywhere she might be hiding out."

Ryan joined them.

"I told the airport cop what's going on and he's squaring everything away. They're processing temporary security badges so we can go anywhere we need."

"That's great," Jessie said, "Because we're going to need to go lots of places."

She filled him in on her idea as they entered the terminal.

"Sounds good," he replied. "I guess this is where we split up."

"Just be careful," Jessie reminded them. "This is a woman who choked her own husband to death with a hair ribbon. If she feels trapped and sees one of us before we see her, who knows what she's capable of?"

With that in mind, they all headed off in different directions, each in search of a murderer.

CHAPTER THIRTY

The woman leaving the restroom looked familiar, at least from the back. She was petite and buxom with blonde hair that draped her shoulders. Jessie ran over to her and grabbed her by the arm.

The woman turned around, startled. It wasn't Bridget. This person was a decade younger than her and bore no resemblance.

"Sorry," Jessie muttered and backed away.

She looked down the long concourse, where hundreds of people were scurrying about in every direction, and processed fully just how unlikely she was to find Bridget Newhouse by simply wandering around. But without a choice, she plowed ahead. Still, she needed to be on high alert now. Bridget could be anywhere.

Jessie's confidence from just minutes earlier seemed foolish now. With the special badge that she was given when she arrived at the security area, getting through the line had been a breeze. She only wished she could keep the thing for personal flights.

Once she moved past the crowd of people getting searched by TSA agents and putting their shoes back, she had darted up the stairs to the main concourse, where she saw the blonde. But after that screw up, Jessie stopped for a moment, allowing her brain to catch up to her body.

After her head cleared, she proceeded to the bathroom that the blonde woman had just left. Two stalls were occupied and she banged on both. "Bridget, come out. There's nowhere to go."

The angry responses she got from both occupants allowed her to judge their voices and determine that neither was Bridget either. Undeterred, Jessie followed the same pattern as she made her way down the concourse: scanning the people at the gates, scouring shops, bars, and restaurants, and accosting unsuspecting women trying to use the bathroom. She came up empty every time.

Sensing time slipping away from her, she messaged Ryan and Kat on a group text: *I'm not having any success so far. What about you guys?*

The response from Ryan came almost immediately: *nothing yet. The airport security camera system is antiquated. Everything takes forever.*

Moments later Kat offered her input: *No one recognizes her yet, but I'm only halfway through the ticket agents.*

Jessie pressed on, scanning passengers at gates, though she also doubted that Bridget would simply sit casually at her gate, waiting for her group to be called up to board. She would likely stay out of sight until the last possible moment.

Jessie was almost to the end of the concourse, trying to fight off the sinking feeling that they were way too late, when Jamil called on a group line with her, Ryan, and Kat.

"What have you got?" Ryan asked.

"I decided to look into Bridget's background," he said, "I was hoping to figure out who she might call back home in Missouri if she was desperate and I found something interesting: Her birth name is Blanca Rivera. She was born in Ecuador. Her family moved here when she was four."

"That *is* interesting," Jessie agreed. "Does the U.S. have an extradition treaty with them?"

"Yes," Beth said, jumping in, "but it's more complicated than that. Ecuador is known for prioritizing political asylum claims over extradition requests. Remember when Edward Snowden was on the run? Everyone thought he might go to Ecuador for that very reason. And Julian Assange spent years holed up in the Ecuadorian Embassy in London while courts fought over whether his asylum claims were credible. And neither of those two are native-born Ecuadorians. If Bridget Newhouse gets there and makes an asylum claim, it might be hard to fight it."

"And," Kat added. "I'm guessing that while that's dragging out, it would be a whole lot easier for her to surreptitiously travel to a non-extradition country from there than from here."

"All good points," Jessie noted. "So I assume there's a United flight to Ecuador leaving soon, Jamil?"

"Yes," he told her. "One leaves for the capitol city, Quito, in ten minutes. It departs from gate 5."

Jessie looked up. She was at gate 29. Gate 5 was back near security. She started running in that direction.

"I'm headed back that way now," she huffed. "Kat, can you check to see if any agents who checked in that flight recognize her?"

"Will do," Kat said. "I'll also see if I can get them to hold the flight completely."

"I'm meeting you there, Jessie," Ryan added in a winded voice that suggested that he was already on his way.

She pumped her legs hard, as if she was making the final sprint in a race. As she passed gate 13, Kat spoke up again.

"I'm being told that eleven people bought tickets for this flight today and that five of them are women," she said, "But not surprisingly, none of the names match. Multiple agents checked these people in so I'm having trouble getting a visual identification. I wouldn't put much stock in that anyway. I'd be stunned if she's not wearing a disguise."

Jessie agreed with that but was too short of breath to reply.

"Also," Ryan added, wheezing, "She could still have bought the ticket to throw us off and caught a different flight or left LAX altogether."

Jessie didn't try to respond to that either as the last few gates whizzed by. People stared at her open-mouthed as she passed them but she didn't care.

"I'm trying to get them to hold the flight," Kat announced. "But tickets agents don't have authorization to do that on their own. One of them is trying to get approval from her supervisor."

Finally, Jessie arrived at the gate and ran up to the agent near the jetway door, which was closed. The gate agent, a fragile-looking young man with a nametag that read "Manny" gaped at her, unsure what to make of the woman in front of him who was desperately sucking in air as she sweated profusely.

"Need you...to hold flight," she gasped.

"I'm sorry ma'am," he said apologetically. "But boarding is closed and the flight is full. It's about to pull away from the gate."

"Not...a passenger," she panted, holding up her temporary security badge. "May be a fugitive...on flight. Don't let it leave. Need to board."

The gate agent appeared at a loss. Clearly, he'd never encountered a situation like this and had no idea how to handle it. As he fumbled for what to say, Jessie allowed herself to take several long deep breaths. As she did, she heard Ryan's voice over the phone.

"At security now," he said, breathing heavily. "Will be there ASAP."

But ASAP wasn't soon enough. Jessie worried that once the plane was delayed, Bridget would realize something was wrong and do something rash—maybe even put another passenger at risk.

"Listen, Manny, my name is Jessie Hunt," she said, now able to complete full sentences. "I'm a profiler with the Los Angeles Police Department. And there's a suspected murderer on that plane trying to escape justice. Passengers may be in danger. First, I need you to open those doors so I can stop her, and then make sure the pilot doesn't leave the gate. Got it?"

Manny looked utterly terrified.

"Listen to her," ordered an older woman in a wide-brimmed, church-style hat and a lavender cardigan who was sitting nearby. "Don't you know who that is? Jessie Hunt catches serial killers, young fellow. There are a lot of people alive today who wouldn't be if not for her. If she says someone's dangerous, you should pay attention."

Between the security badge, Jessie's forceful demeanor and the older lady's vote of confidence, it was too much for Manny. He nodded and opened the jetway door.

Jessie was about to head down when she had an idea and turned back to the older lady.

"Thanks for what you said, ma'am," she cooed. "How would you like to help me catch this person?"

"How can I do that?" the woman asked, stunned and excited.

"May I borrow your hat and cardigan?" she wondered. "This fugitive might recognize me and your outfit could help disguise me a bit."

"It would be my honor," the woman said, taking off the cardigan before Jessie had even completed the request.

Jessie put in on as she walked down the jetway and was just adjusting the hat to hide her face when Ryan piped in.

"Hold on," he yelled. "I'm through security. Don't board the plane without me!"

She stepped onboard and gave the flight attendant a big smile as she muttered a reply.

"Too late."

CHAPTER THIRTY ONE

"I'm with the LAPD," she whispered to the attendant, a tall, redhead in her thirties named Larraine. "Have you been informed of the delay?"

The woman nervously shook her head yes.

"Good," Jessie said, making sure that the large hat was blocking any passengers' ability to see what she was saying. "Just announce that there's a minor mechanical issue that should be resolved soon. Otherwise act normally. My partner will be arriving any minute. Do you know if there's an air marshal on this flight?"

"There isn't," Laraine said quietly.

"That's okay," Jessie said reassuringly. "Just do what I said and it will all work out."

Laraine nodded as Ryan's voice bellowed in her ear.

"Jessie," he shouted, "Just wait. I'm almost there."

"Shh!" she hissed. "I'm already on board. Let me concentrate."

She scrutinized the first class passengers, focusing less on hair or eye color, which were malleable, and more on facial structure, body type, and demeanor. Just as Jessie couldn't hide her lean five foot ten inch frame, it would be hard for Bridget to mask her fundamental features on such short notice.

No one looked overtly suspicious. A few people glanced up, mildly amused by the tall woman in the giant hat, before going back to their phones or books. As she passed the divider from first class to economy, she heard Larraine make the announcement she recommended. The economy section was split into two aisles with groups of three seats on either side and a middle section with four seats.

She was scanning the right side of the plane when she felt a light tap on her shoulder.

"No need to turn around," Ryan's familiar voice said. "See anything so far?"

"Not in first class," she told him without looking behind her. "I was just starting back here. What are the chances that we're just wasting our time and she's on another flight or simply got out of one taxi and into another one right away after she arrived at the airport. How do we know she didn't ask a cabbie to drive her all the way to the Mexican border?"

"I asked airport police to send their footage from the last two hours to Jamil and Beth so they can use facial recognition to try to identify where she went," he replied. "Unfortunately their system is so slow that it's going to take hours just to collect and send it, much less go through it. So we better hope this is the right flight. If not, we may never see her again. Should I take the left aisle and you keep to the right?"

"Sure," Jessie agreed.

"Nice hat, by the way," he whispered with a sly grin. Even when they were having their issues, he was still roguishly charming.

She was about to start down the aisle when she saw Larraine waving at her from the front. Ryan was already well down the left aisle of economy, so she went back on her own.

"What's wrong?" she asked.

"Someone's in the lavatory, even though we asked everyone to return to their seats. It could be nothing but I just thought you should know."

Jessie nodded and moved to the door. Adrenaline was pumping through her and it was all she could do to remind herself to knock softly.

"We're about leave the gate," she said firmly. "It's time to return to your seat."

There was no answer. She tried a different approach.

"Bridget," she said quietly. "You can come out now or we can bust through this door. Either way, the jig is up."

There was still no verbal response but she did hear a flush. She took a step back and undid the holster guard for her gun. A few seconds later, the door opened to reveal a sweaty, heavyset guy in his forties.

"What the hell?" he demanded. "Obviously I'm not Bridget. The plane isn't leaving yet so why don't you and your ridiculous hat leave me alone?"

Jessie took note of the dusting of white powder around both his nostrils and understood why he'd been so slow to reply. He'd been busy. But she wasn't in the mood for any backtalk. She got up close to him and growled.

"Why don't you take your seat right now before I inform the pilot that you were snorting coke in the bathroom and you get hauled out of here for a federal crime? Or would you rather make another crack about my hat?"

Despite his chemically altered state, he seemed to get that he was out of his depth and quickly slithered past her back to his seat. Jessie watched him struggle to clamber past his first class seatmate, despite ample room. As he got settled, her eyes fell on an older woman seated in the row behind him. It wasn't Bridget. This lady was hunched and frail. Still, something Jessie couldn't quite place felt off about her.

After a moment, it clicked and she was briefly ashamed. The woman's shoes were worn and scratched. Her purse was equally shabby, with a broken handle and several frayed areas. She had a wide smile plastered across her face as she giddily sipped a glass of white wine and gawked at her surroundings. It occurred to Jessie that this woman didn't look like a passenger who would normally be in first class. She walked over and smiled down at the elderly lady.

"You excited for the trip?" she asked politely.

"I am," the woman said excitedly. "It's already starting wonderfully. A sweet young woman even switched seats with me. I've never been in first class before."

"That is sweet," Jessie agreed. "Where were you originally sitting?"

"All the way back in 34H."

"Wow, I'm headed back that way myself," Jessie said. "What does this woman look like so I can tell her what a sweetheart she is?"

"That's nice," the older woman said. "She's a little thing with curly black hair and glasses. Please tell her again how much I appreciate it."

"I'm going to do that right now," Jessie promised.

She stepped into the economy section again and looked toward the back. Ryan was already far along, nearing the rear of the plane.

"Ryan, did you hear that?" she asked. "Check 34H. She might have glasses and a curly, black wig. Ryan?"

When he didn't answer, she pulled out her phone. The battery was low but it seemed fine. Maybe the call had just dropped.

"Can you hear me, Kat?" she asked.

"Loud and clear. I don't know what's up with him," Kat answered. "What can I do to help?"

"Give that description to the airport police so they know what to look for," Jessie told her. "Other than that, I'm not there's much you *can* do."

Jessie looked at the seat assignment and saw that "H" seats were on the aisle on the side that Ryan was currently checking.

She tried to count back to row 34 but it was just too far away to get a clear look. She guessed it was near where a large man in the middle section was getting something out of the overhead compartment, just a few rows ahead of where Ryan currently stood. The man handed something to the woman seated across the aisle from him and sat back down.

Jessie squinted at the woman. She had dark, curly hair and glasses. It was too far away to accurately determine facial features but Jessie didn't need to. The woman was staring right back at her. In her bones, she knew it was Bridget Newhouse.

In that moment, Bridget seemed to grasp that Jessie had identified her. She looked behind her at Ryan, then to the front of the cabin, as if calculating which direction offered her the better chance of escape.

Then, without any warning, she popped up and turned to the back of the cabin. Jessie saw what she was holding—a laptop. Ryan, whose back was to her, stood just a few rows ahead of her, blocking her path to the back of the plane. He was unaware of her moving quickly toward him as she raised the laptop above her head.

"Ryan," Jessie shouted as she ran toward them," behind you!"

But she was too late. The engine noise and passenger chatter muffled the sound of her voice and it was clear that he hadn't heard her. To her surprise, instead of swinging the laptop down toward his head, Bridget tossed it across the center row of seats and, in a screech that cut through the ambient noise, yelled "Bomb!"

CHAPTER THIRTY TWO

Jessie saw Ryan's eyes open wide.

He clearly *had* heard that. His eyes followed the path of the laptop as it arced through the air and slammed into a seat on the other aisle. Panicked screams filled the cabin as people got up and rushed forward. Jessie saw Bridget push past Ryan, whose back was to her, and head toward the back of the plane.

"She's behind you!" Jessie shouted, waving her arms wildly. But with the screams and the crush of people, there was no way he could either see or hear her. A moment later, Bridget disappeared from sight amid the mass of fast-moving bodies.

People near the middle of the plane had already opened the emergency exit doors and begun leaping onto the evacuation slides. Jessie had a flash of Bridget doing the same thing near the rear, then escaping among the throng of passengers streaming across the tarmac. The only thing that could prevent that at this point were the flight attendants back there, who would likely insist on a more orderly process than what was going on mid-cabin.

Jessie chose to believe that scenario and decided to act accordingly. Because everybody was streaming into the aisles, the middle section of seats was fast emptying out. That was her path to the back.

She dodged one skinny guy barreling toward first class. A much larger man right behind him was shoving people out of the way. Jessie clipped him as he went past, sending him off to the side and tumbling like a human bowling ball to the ground where, at least for now, he was no longer a menace.

"Stay down," she ordered as she flashed her ID, "or I'll have you arrested for assault."

Satisfied that he looked sufficiently cowed, she moved into the middle row and climbed onto the seat, where she had a better vantage point. It was a long way to the back of the plane but she didn't have much choice.

She put her hands on the seatback headrest and used it like a pommel horse to leap one row back. She did the same thing again, and then again, and another time after that. She could hear Kat's voice in her ear but it was too loud in the cabin to understand a word she said. Instead, she focused all of her attention on getting to the rear of the plane.

At one point, her left hand slipped and she lost her balance, almost toppling to the ground. Using the moment to regroup and catch her breath, she saw Ryan a few rows ahead. He was staring at her and yelling something she couldn't make out. She pointed to the back and yelled "Behind you! Glasses! Curly black hair!"

He shook his head to indicate that he couldn't make out what she'd said. Picturing Bridget shooting down the slide, she returned her attention to the seatbacks. After a few more, she noticed that everyone in the aisles was now ahead of or behind her. She got off the seat and moved into the aisle opposite Ryan.

"Be careful of the bomb!" he shouted over the din, now close enough to be heard.

She gasped for breath. No amount of morning running could have prepared her for what she'd just done.

"There's no bomb!" she finally shouted back, "Bridget tossed the laptop as a distraction. She snuck past you. She was wearing glass and a dark, curly wig."

To his credit, Ryan only looked shocked for a second. Then he turned and rushed back, grabbing people to check their faces, and then moving them out of the way. Jessie did the same on her side. But the herd of bunched up passengers was too much for her navigate.

"LAPD!" she bellowed, holding up her ID high in the air and hoping no one noticed that it actually read "Consulting Profiler." It seemed to work a bit, as the crowd parted and she was able to push through several people to see the back of the plane.

She had a burst of hope when she saw that the flight attendants were doing exactly as they should: making sure that people exited the plane in a quick but organized, methodical manner. She scoured the passengers in line, looking for any petite curvy women, either brunette or blonde. She saw none.

With one more push she was at the back galley of the plane, staring at Ryan. His expression told her hadn't had any success either.

"She probably already got off," he said. "I'm going to warn airport police to hold everyone until we get down there. I just hope it's not too late."

He moved into a corner of the galley to try to get some semblance of quiet. Jessie felt her whole body slump. She didn't know the odds of Bridget getting away now but they were definitely better than they had been five minutes ago.

Trapped on the plane with nowhere to go, Jessie decided to take advantage of the situation and use the restroom. One was occupied but the other was vacant. She was about to step into it when a thought occurred to her.

What is someone doing in the bathroom in the middle of a bomb threat on a plane?

She knew the answer before she'd finished asking herself the question. Quickly she moved toward the flight attendant, a tall woman with short brown hair, and whispered in her ear.

"I work for the LAPD," she said, holding up the ID and nodding at Ryan. "That's my partner. The bomb threat is fake. The person who made it is hiding in that lavatory. Are you able to open the door somehow?"

The woman nodded. Jessie motioned for her to move over to the lavatory door. Ryan had seen the interaction and came over too. Jessie pointed silently at the bathroom. He nodded and unholstered his gun. Jessie did the same, then nodded again at the flight attendant, who lifted up the metal "lavatory" sign just above the red, "occupied" display, and slid a latch to the side. Then she stepped quickly to the side. Jessie yanked open the door.

A petite woman with black hair shot out like a cannonball, aiming right for Jessie, who was ready and half-stepped to the side. The woman missed her completely and slammed into the back of the galley, hitting her head before crumpling to the floor. Her wig fell off. Now blonde again, Bridget looked up, dazed.

"That was a bad decision," Ryan said, holstering his weapon and pulling out handcuffs, which he promptly snapped on her limp wrists. "Bridget Newhouse, you're under arrest for the murder of Scott Newhouse."

While he continued to read her rights, Bridget's hazy expression began to fade, as she became fully aware of her situation. She locked eyes with Jessie and for the first time, the mask she'd been wearing all weekend dropped away. Her eyes gleamed furiously and her mouth twisted in rage. Jessie suspected that's a lot like how she looked as she choked the life out of her husband.

*

Bridget didn't confess to anything; not as she was frog-marched off the plane or through the terminal to the airport holding cell, where she was held until she could be taken to Central Station.

She demanded a lawyer immediately and said nothing afterward. She didn't seem bothered by Ryan asking what kind of mother would abandon her own children. She just sat quietly waiting for her white-shoe attorney to show up.

"I hope they throw the book at her," Jessie said, seething, once they had left her. "This is a woman who killed her husband and was ready to discard her own kids, leaving them in the care of a sister who thought she was just showing up to help for a few weeks. Now she's likely their primary caregiver."

Ryan nodded in agreement.

"I know this is petty," he said to the LAPD officers who had arrived to take Bridget downtown. "But I can't help it. Let's wait until her lawyer shows up here. Then you guys can take her to Central. Make the guy drive around a bit."

They left the airport police station and called Decker to update him. Once they filled him in, he shared some good news.

"We may not need a confession from Bridget Newhouse," he said. "Jude Austen offered one already. Detectives Bray and Valentine barely started talking to him when he broke down. He admitted that Newhouse planned the whole thing; that he went along because he loved her and believed they would be together."

"That explains why he stayed quiet for so long," Jessie said. "He thought they were soulmates."

"Right," Decker agreed. "But apparently once he got cold feet, she turned into a different person, went into a rage. She called him a pathetic coward and told him she'd do what he wasn't man enough to. I think being informed that she used one of his hair ribbons to kill her husband was the thing that truly broke him."

"Took him long enough," Ryan muttered.

"I have another update, this one from a Mr. Cosgrove from Peninsula security," Decker said, referring to Hugo.

"What's that?" Ryan asked.

"Apparently there's a hidden door in the resort's spa that leads from the men's lounge cleaning supply closet to the women's quiet room," he said. "Cosgrove says he was unaware of it, that it was built before his time heading security. It seems that years ago, female cleaning crew members were sometimes required to service the men's area. One young woman was sexually assaulted."

"Oh my God," Jessie murmured.

"Cosgrove sounded shocked too," Decker said. "Apparently the club covered it up but as a pathetic make good, they installed this hidden exit, so that if another cleaning woman had to make a quick escape, she could lock herself in the cleaning supply closet and use this hidden door to get to the women's side."

Jessie temporarily set aside her disgust as she thought back to when she'd been in that quiet room. She pictured the last chair in the room, with the large Ficus plant in the corner and the ocean sunset wall covering behind it, and knew that was where the secret door was. Bridget had selected the chair that offered her easy access to the men's side and to her husband. Decker interrupted her thoughts.

"Obviously the resort policy has changed in the intervening years and only men clean the men's lounge now. It seems that very few people even knew about the door anymore, only female employees who'd been working there back when all this happened about a decade ago. Someone must have mentioned it to Bridget Newhouse."

"Great," Ryan said. "It sounds like we're in good shape, even if she never says another word."

"Yes," Decker agreed. "Of course there is the small matter of Chief Laird. He still wants to have a chat with you two."

"Even after we saved his ass?" Jessie demanded angrily. "If not for us, he'd have been offering condolences to a murderer while going on TV to say someone else was guilty."

"A point that I will raise with him," Decker said calmly. "For now, I've told him that I gave you both the rest of the day off. Perhaps by tomorrow, he'll have reconsidered."

"Thanks Captain," Ryan said before Jessie could add anything. "We'll talk to you tomorrow."

Then he hung up.

"I wasn't done," Jessie said.

"I know, but Decker's not the one you should be mad at," Ryan reminded her. "He's on our side. Besides, Kat is waiting outside and we have to drive her all the way back out to Peninsula to get her car. Plus, that'll give us a chance to thank Hugo for all his help."

Jessie nodded. There was no point in getting riled when they still had work to do with their off time.

"Maybe he'll thank us too," she said hopefully. "I could use a free massage."

CHAPTER THIRTY THREE

Hannah left her final therapy session of the day and walked down the hall to find Merry Bartlett.

It was almost dinnertime and, though she was loathe to admit it out loud, the idea of having someone pleasant to sit with was appealing. She'd even make sure to steer clear of Silvio's special table.

Hannah wasn't one for making friends. Sure, she had a circle of girls from school that she'd sometimes hang out with. But none of them were close, mostly out of choice. How was she supposed to really connect with girls who were focused on dates, clothes, and the mall when, for the last two years she'd been dealing with serial killers, kidnappers, murdered parents, unexpected sisters, not to mention a strong desire to do violence just to feel something? It wasn't exactly food court conversation.

But unlike those girls, Merry already understood that she was damaged, even if she didn't know all the details, and she seemed to like her anyway. That was one layer of potential falseness between them that was already stripped away. It was an enormous relief not to have her guard up every second.

Plus, Hannah heard that the reason Dr. Lemmon wasn't at their scheduled therapy session earlier today was due to some unexpected surgical procedure she'd had done. As a longer-term resident of Seasons with her ear to the ground, Merry would probably know what was actually true and what just psychiatric facility rumor-mongering.

Hannah rounded the corner and came to Merry's room. The door was closed so she knocked.

"Hey Merry, it's Hannah. Want to join me for a kosher meal?"

There was no answer and she was tempted to just leave it at that. But then her curiosity got the better of her and she checked the doorknob. It was unlocked. She knocked again as she opened it.

"Sorry to barge in but—," she started before her words got lodged in her throat.

Merry was lying on her bed with her eyes wide open and empty. Even without the blood, Hannah would have known she was dead. She was intimately familiar with that emptiness. She'd even caused it once.

But there *was* blood, so much of it. Her entire neck was a red mess where her throat had not just been slit, but slashed. The dark, viscous liquid covered her upper torso and the sheets underneath. On the bed beside her bloody right hand, was a large shard of glass, which was also stained red. Her already pale skin was now ashen white.

She stared at Merry for a few seconds, partly in silent mourning, partly in confusion. This wasn't right. This couldn't be. The cheerful, buoyant girl she'd spoken to just hours earlier couldn't have then come back to her room and done this to herself. Could she?

And then Hannah heard herself scream.

"Help!" she howled at the top of her voice. "Help! I need help!"

Within seconds the room was full and she was being ushered out by an attendant with a bewildered look on her face.

"What happened?" she asked.

"I came to invite her to dinner and found…this," Hannah said quietly.

She felt unsteady and the woman eased her down to the floor, where she sat, slumped and cross-legged. Through the doorway, she could hear the attendants talking.

"Call the police," one barked.

"This is so sad," another, older attendant said. "She was doing so well. I can't believe she would do this."

"It wouldn't be the first time she tried," a third said, sounding defeated.

"I'm on the line with 911," came the voice of the security guard who'd led Silvio away at lunch earlier.

"I just can't believe it," the older attendant repeated, breaking into tears.

Neither could Hannah. Even amid her horror at what she'd just seen, something was eating at her, nibbling at the corners of her brain. Everything she saw in that room suggested that Merry had killed herself. And yet something about it wasn't right. It felt somehow…off, wrong. Despite the dark cloud that was closing in around her, she made a promise to Merry and to herself: she was going to find out what.

CHAPTER THIRTY FOUR

Jessie knew Kat wanted to say something; she just didn't know what.

Ryan had gone off to find Hugo, and a valet was getting Kat's car, leaving the two women standing alone in the Peninsula's main lobby. Jessie waited patiently. Kat finally broke.

"Are you guys going to work this out?" she asked.

"Work what out?" Jessie replied, though she knew exactly what her friend was referencing.

"Whatever is creating this tension between you and Ryan," Kat answered. "I'm assuming it has to do with the whole issue over the wedding. You don't have to tell me, but whatever it is—it's reached the point where I'm noticing it. And considering that you guys work with a bunch of detectives, they're going to start noticing it soon too. So unless you want to face some really uncomfortable co-worker questions, you might want to deal with this. More importantly, you might want to deal with it for, you know, the sake of your relationship."

"I'm trying Kat," Jessie insisted. "But I just can't seem to get through to him. He's so dug in. It's really upsetting that he doesn't appreciate where I'm coming from."

"I get that," Kat said. "But let me ask you something: have you ever asked yourself the real reason why he's so dug in? Or are you just assuming you know the answer?" Before Jessie could reply, Ryan arrived with Hugo in tow.

"You're not going to believe this," Ryan said with a broad smile on his face, "but when I went to thank good Mr. Cosgrove here, he turned the tables on me."

"That's right," Hugo said. "I insist that you two spend another night with us, only this time, without having to worry about catching a killer. In addition, since it's dinnertime, we've reserved a table for you at The Captain's Quarters, on us."

"That's way too generous, Hugo," Jessie protested.

"Don't be silly," he said. "You caught a murderer who, to our great relief, was not a Peninsula employee. This is the least we can do."

Just then, the valet pulled up with Kat's car.

"Well this is where I get off," she said, giving Hugo and Ryan hugs, before leaning in close to squeeze Jessie. As she did, she whispered, "good luck."

*

Jessie waited patiently.

Finally, after their main dishes had been served, Ryan said what she suspected he'd been holding back the whole day.

"I'm worried that you're going to resent me," he said without explanation.

"What?" she asked, pausing just as she was about to put a forkful of salmon in her mouth.

"I know you think I'm being obstinate about this whole 'big wedding' thing," he told her, "but it's not just about that. I can see history repeating itself."

"What does that mean?"

"Just like you, this isn't my first time down the aisle," he said. "And when Shelly and I were doing our planning, she kept insisting that we keep things from getting too elaborate. She didn't want me to feel pressured to spend more than I could on a cop's salary. But once I relented, everything changed. I didn't realize that what she *really* wanted was for me to insist on going all out, despite what she said. When I didn't, she was disappointed, like I had failed her somehow. It cast a shadow over things going forward. Obviously, our issues were more complicated than that, but it was a terrible way to start a marriage. And now I see the same pattern repeating itself. I worry that as much as you protest, the second I give in and embrace a more modest event, you'll resent me too—even if you don't believe that you will."

Jessie sat with that for a moment, trying to put herself in his shoes and feel his doubt, his fear that no matter how definitive she said she was, that her feelings would change if he caved. She got it. He wasn't just trying to give her the wedding he thought she deserved; he was trying to ensure that their marriage avoided the problems that had helped doom his first one. Kat had been right. By refusing to consider that there might be more to his position than just wanting a big blowout, she'd been her own kind of stubborn. "Thank you for telling me that," she said quietly, gripping his hand and squeezing tight. "I know it was painful to share and it can't have been easy."

He sighed heavily and she could see that a burden had been lifted. She was happy about that. And she empathized with his plight now that she understood it. But it didn't change the bottom line.

"But Ryan," she added, "I'm not Shelly."

"I know, but—," he started to say before she held up her hand. She wasn't done.

"A good marriage depends on trust," she continued. "And that means you need to trust that when I tell you something, I mean it. I'm not some damsel in distress, hoping a knight in shining armor will read my mind, understand that my words don't reflect my true feelings, and save me from myself. I love you, but you should know by now that I'm my own knight in shining armor. When I say something, I don't expect you to discern my secret, coded meaning. I expect you to respect that I mean what I say."

"I do," he maintained. "I'm just worried about getting burned."

She took the bite of the salmon that she'd been holding off on and chewed it slowly, savoring it. Only after she swallowed did she reply.

"My first husband demanded a giant wedding against my wishes. I wasn't confident enough to assert myself, which I regret. As it turned out, the details of the wedding were less significant than the fact that he was a sociopathic, adulterous murderer. But you can see why I don't want my second chance to resemble the first time in any way. I want what I didn't get that first go-round: something intimate, with only people there who we know really care about us. I actively despise the idea of a big affair and I assure you that I won't change my mind once you come around to seeing things my way. I wasn't kidding when I said that I'd even be happy to get married at city hall and take off for Maui right afterward."

Ryan took a bite of his steak as he muddled over her words.

"So you promise you won't change your mind?' he asked, almost pleaded.

"Oh, I reserve the right to change my mind all the time, without notice," she said. "But about this one thing, it's set in stone."

To her surprise, he began to chuckle.

"What is it?' she asked.

"It's just that last night was our first real fight since we got engaged, and now that it's over, I'm more relieved than I thought possible. My insides have been one big ball of stress all day, and not because of the case."

She smiled mischievously.

"Maybe we should book a session with Honey Potter to help you work through that," she teased.

"That's okay," he said with a wily smile. "I think we can figure out a way to relieve that stress all on our own."

"Deal," she agreed, before an unrelated thought popped into her head. "Sorry to mess with the mood, but I just remember that any stress-relieving activities need to end in time for me to visit Hannah. Maybe she'll actually speak to me this time. I'm supposed to see her at 11 a.m."

"Supposed to?" Ryan repeated, sensing her hesitancy.

"Yeah, I called a few minutes ago to reconfirm the visit and no one answered, which is unusual for that place. They must be really busy tonight."

EPILOGUE

Eden Roth watched the news, taking scrupulous notes. She caught the footage of a woman named Bridget Newhouse in handcuffs, being walked from an LAX terminal to a waiting squad car. Then the story cut to video of Jessie Hunt leaving the airport with her partner, Detective Ryan Hernandez. They had caught the woman, who had apparently murdered her husband at that fancy Palos Verdes resort.

That was the final sign. Once Jessie Hunt had successfully solved her next case and was being lauded in the media, it was an official, irreversible 'go.' She knew exactly what she had to do and when to do it. Everything had been meticulously planned. Now it was time to act. It was time for blood to be spilled.

Andy was going to be so proud of her.

NOW AVAILABLE!

THE PERFECT COUPLE
(A Jessie Hunt Psychological Suspense Thriller—Book Twenty)

Couples are found dead in their wealthy homes in suburban Los Angeles, with seemingly nothing to connect them. As Jessie dives deep into this wealthy town, she comes to realize an awful truth: this killer is hiding in plain sight, ready to strike again.

"A masterpiece of thriller and mystery. Blake Pierce did a magnificent job developing characters with a psychological side so well described that we feel inside their minds, follow their fears and cheer for their success. Full of twists, this book will keep you awake until the turn of the last page."
--Books and Movie Reviews, Roberto Mattos (re *Once Gone*)

THE PERFECT COUPLE is book #20 in a new psychological suspense series by bestselling author Blake Pierce, which begins with *The Perfect Wife*, a #1 bestseller (and free download) with over 5,000 five-star ratings and 1,000 five-star reviews.

A seemingly perfect suburban town holds too many secrets, and Jessie knows it is just a façade. Outwardly perfect, wealthy couples seem to have it all—but when they wind up dead, Jessie must look too deep into their pasts. Horrified by what she finds, Jessie must wonder:

What else are they hiding?

A fast-paced psychological suspense thriller with unforgettable characters and heart-pounding suspense, THE JESSIE HUNT series is a riveting new series that will leave you turning pages late into the night.

Book #21 in the series—THE PERFECT MURDER—is now also available.

Blake Pierce

Blake Pierce is the USA Today bestselling author of the RILEY PAGE mystery series, which includes seventeen books. Blake Pierce is also the author of the MACKENZIE WHITE mystery series, comprising fourteen books; of the AVERY BLACK mystery series, comprising six books; of the KERI LOCKE mystery series, comprising five books; of the MAKING OF RILEY PAIGE mystery series, comprising six books; of the KATE WISE mystery series, comprising seven books; of the CHLOE FINE psychological suspense mystery, comprising six books; of the JESSE HUNT psychological suspense thriller series, comprising twenty one books; of the AU PAIR psychological suspense thriller series, comprising three books; of the ZOE PRIME mystery series, comprising six books; of the ADELE SHARP mystery series, comprising fifteen books, of the EUROPEAN VOYAGE cozy mystery series, comprising four books; of the new LAURA FROST FBI suspense thriller, comprising six books (and counting); of the new ELLA DARK FBI suspense thriller, comprising eleven books (and counting); of the A YEAR IN EUROPE cozy mystery series, comprising nine books, of the AVA GOLD mystery series, comprising six books (and counting); and of the RACHEL GIFT mystery series, comprising six books (and counting).

An avid reader and lifelong fan of the mystery and thriller genres, Blake loves to hear from you, so please feel free to visit www.blakepierceauthor.com to learn more and stay in touch.

BOOKS BY BLAKE PIERCE

RACHEL GIFT MYSTERY SERIES
HER LAST WISH (Book #1)
HER LAST CHANCE (Book #2)
HER LAST HOPE (Book #3)
HER LAST FEAR (Book #4)
HER LAST CHOICE (Book #5)
HER LAST BREATH (Book #6)

AVA GOLD MYSTERY SERIES
CITY OF PREY (Book #1)
CITY OF FEAR (Book #2)
CITY OF BONES (Book #3)
CITY OF GHOSTS (Book #4)
CITY OF DEATH (Book #5)
CITY OF VICE (Book #6)

A YEAR IN EUROPE
A MURDER IN PARIS (Book #1)
DEATH IN FLORENCE (Book #2)
VENGEANCE IN VIENNA (Book #3)
A FATALITY IN SPAIN (Book #4)

ELLA DARK FBI SUSPENSE THRILLER
GIRL, ALONE (Book #1)
GIRL, TAKEN (Book #2)
GIRL, HUNTED (Book #3)
GIRL, SILENCED (Book #4)
GIRL, VANISHED (Book 5)
GIRL ERASED (Book #6)
GIRL, FORSAKEN (Book #7)
GIRL, TRAPPED (Book #8)
GIRL, EXPENDABLE (Book #9)
GIRL, ESCAPED (Book #10)
GIRL, HIS (Book #11)

LAURA FROST FBI SUSPENSE THRILLER
ALREADY GONE (Book #1)
ALREADY SEEN (Book #2)
ALREADY TRAPPED (Book #3)
ALREADY MISSING (Book #4)
ALREADY DEAD (Book #5)
ALREADY TAKEN (Book #6)

EUROPEAN VOYAGE COZY MYSTERY SERIES
MURDER (AND BAKLAVA) (Book #1)
DEATH (AND APPLE STRUDEL) (Book #2)
CRIME (AND LAGER) (Book #3)
MISFORTUNE (AND GOUDA) (Book #4)
CALAMITY (AND A DANISH) (Book #5)
MAYHEM (AND HERRING) (Book #6)

ADELE SHARP MYSTERY SERIES
LEFT TO DIE (Book #1)
LEFT TO RUN (Book #2)
LEFT TO HIDE (Book #3)
LEFT TO KILL (Book #4)
LEFT TO MURDER (Book #5)
LEFT TO ENVY (Book #6)
LEFT TO LAPSE (Book #7)
LEFT TO VANISH (Book #8)
LEFT TO HUNT (Book #9)
LEFT TO FEAR (Book #10)
LEFT TO PREY (Book #11)
LEFT TO LURE (Book #12)
LEFT TO CRAVE (Book #13)
LEFT TO LOATHE (Book #14)
LEFT TO HARM (Book #15)

THE AU PAIR SERIES
ALMOST GONE (Book#1)
ALMOST LOST (Book #2)
ALMOST DEAD (Book #3)

ZOE PRIME MYSTERY SERIES
FACE OF DEATH (Book#1)

FACE OF MURDER (Book #2)
FACE OF FEAR (Book #3)
FACE OF MADNESS (Book #4)
FACE OF FURY (Book #5)
FACE OF DARKNESS (Book #6)

A JESSIE HUNT PSYCHOLOGICAL SUSPENSE SERIES
THE PERFECT WIFE (Book #1)
THE PERFECT BLOCK (Book #2)
THE PERFECT HOUSE (Book #3)
THE PERFECT SMILE (Book #4)
THE PERFECT LIE (Book #5)
THE PERFECT LOOK (Book #6)
THE PERFECT AFFAIR (Book #7)
THE PERFECT ALIBI (Book #8)
THE PERFECT NEIGHBOR (Book #9)
THE PERFECT DISGUISE (Book #10)
THE PERFECT SECRET (Book #11)
THE PERFECT FAÇADE (Book #12)
THE PERFECT IMPRESSION (Book #13)
THE PERFECT DECEIT (Book #14)
THE PERFECT MISTRESS (Book #15)
THE PERFECT IMAGE (Book #16)
THE PERFECT VEIL (Book #17)
THE PERFECT INDISCRETION (Book #18)
THE PERFECT RUMOR (Book #19)
THE PERFECT COUPLE (Book #20)
THE PERFECT MURDER (Book #21)

CHLOE FINE PSYCHOLOGICAL SUSPENSE SERIES
NEXT DOOR (Book #1)
A NEIGHBOR'S LIE (Book #2)
CUL DE SAC (Book #3)
SILENT NEIGHBOR (Book #4)
HOMECOMING (Book #5)
TINTED WINDOWS (Book #6)

KATE WISE MYSTERY SERIES
IF SHE KNEW (Book #1)
IF SHE SAW (Book #2)

IF SHE RAN (Book #3)
IF SHE HID (Book #4)
IF SHE FLED (Book #5)
IF SHE FEARED (Book #6)
IF SHE HEARD (Book #7)

THE MAKING OF RILEY PAIGE SERIES
WATCHING (Book #1)
WAITING (Book #2)
LURING (Book #3)
TAKING (Book #4)
STALKING (Book #5)
KILLING (Book #6)

RILEY PAIGE MYSTERY SERIES
ONCE GONE (Book #1)
ONCE TAKEN (Book #2)
ONCE CRAVED (Book #3)
ONCE LURED (Book #4)
ONCE HUNTED (Book #5)
ONCE PINED (Book #6)
ONCE FORSAKEN (Book #7)
ONCE COLD (Book #8)
ONCE STALKED (Book #9)
ONCE LOST (Book #10)
ONCE BURIED (Book #11)
ONCE BOUND (Book #12)
ONCE TRAPPED (Book #13)
ONCE DORMANT (Book #14)
ONCE SHUNNED (Book #15)
ONCE MISSED (Book #16)
ONCE CHOSEN (Book #17)

MACKENZIE WHITE MYSTERY SERIES
BEFORE HE KILLS (Book #1)
BEFORE HE SEES (Book #2)
BEFORE HE COVETS (Book #3)
BEFORE HE TAKES (Book #4)
BEFORE HE NEEDS (Book #5)
BEFORE HE FEELS (Book #6)

BEFORE HE SINS (Book #7)
BEFORE HE HUNTS (Book #8)
BEFORE HE PREYS (Book #9)
BEFORE HE LONGS (Book #10)
BEFORE HE LAPSES (Book #11)
BEFORE HE ENVIES (Book #12)
BEFORE HE STALKS (Book #13)
BEFORE HE HARMS (Book #14)

AVERY BLACK MYSTERY SERIES
CAUSE TO KILL (Book #1)
CAUSE TO RUN (Book #2)
CAUSE TO HIDE (Book #3)
CAUSE TO FEAR (Book #4)
CAUSE TO SAVE (Book #5)
CAUSE TO DREAD (Book #6)

KERI LOCKE MYSTERY SERIES
A TRACE OF DEATH (Book #1)
A TRACE OF MURDER (Book #2)
A TRACE OF VICE (Book #3)
A TRACE OF CRIME (Book #4)
A TRACE OF HOPE (Book #5)

Made in United States
Cleveland, OH
29 June 2025